DEADLY SHORE

Frank Sullivan

Whimsical Publications, LLC

Florida

To purchase the authorized electronic edition of *Deadly Shore*, visit
www.whimsicalpublications.com

Cover art by Janet Durbin
Editing by Brieanna Robertson

ISBN-13: 978-1-940707-28-0

Published by
Whimsical Publications, LLC
Florida

This time, the agony went on longer until, just as he began to pass out, Ernesto broke the circuit and stepped back. Again, even though the electricity stopped, he continued shaking uncontrollably for the longest time. When the pain eventually subsided and his body fell still, Carlos finally stepped closer and ripped the duct tape from his mouth. There was an acrid smell of burnt flesh, and although he couldn't see or feel them, Conor knew it was coming from his toes.

"Donde esta la bolsa?" Carlos said coldly.

"I...I don't know what you're talking about," Conor replied through chattering teeth.

"Where is the bag?"

"What bag? Please, Carlos, I don't know anything about a—"

"Where is the bag?"

"Please. If you'd just tell me—"

Carlos nodded toward Ernesto and it began again. Without the tape covering his mouth, Conor's agonizing cries were so loud they drowned out the crackling sound coming from the sparking battery. He blacked out for what seemed like an eternity, yet when his senses returned and he opened his eyes, Carlos was still in the exact same position before him and he realized with utter dejection that it had only been a few seconds.

"Once more," said the Cuban. "Where is that bag?"

"Please, Carlos," he groaned. "For the love of God, I don't know anything about a bag." He saw him signal to Ernesto once more, but shouted, "No! Stop! Just stop and I promise will tell you everything. I swear to God, I will tell you."

There was a pause as Carlos considered his words. Shaking, Conor prayed with all his might that the Cuban would not signal to his brother again. He knew his body could take no more.

"Alright then," he finally said without emotion. "Start by telling us why you killed our father."

"But it wasn't me!" stammered Conor. "It was Bob Castagna."

"Castagna's dead," Ernesto growled angrily from behind.

"No," Conor cried. "He's alive. He's alive. I swear."

"Castagna, that weasel," Carlos muttered beneath his breath, his eyes opening a little wider at the prospect that Bob might actually not be dead. "I should have known he had *something* to do with this."

Conor felt his spirits raised for a split second. If they believed him, there might at least be a glimmer of hope.

"So, if what you say is true, where is he?" Carlos asked coldly.

Conor swallowed hard. "Look, I don't know where he is right now. He must have gone into hiding. I heard a shot in the cabin and found him standing over your father with the revolver in his hand. When I tried to call for help, he knocked me out. The police think I killed them both because he was gone when they got there. That's why they arrested me. But he *is* alive. I swear to you."

Carlos considered this for a moment, before saying, "Then if you're telling the truth, where is the bag?"

"What bag are you talking about?" Conor caught the look of anger and impatience on the Cuban's face. "Please, Carlos. What bag?"

"The bag of cocaine our father and Castagna carried back from the island."

"Huh?" he moaned. He was struggling to remain conscious, but this revelation jolted him awake. In his mind, he made the connection at long last. It was a piece that finally fit into the jigsaw. If there *had* been drugs in the bag, then that changed everything. He was now certain the black hold-all was not on the yacht anymore, that Bob now had it. Was *that* what this was about? Had Bob killed Hector Suarez and framed him for a lousy bag of drugs?

"Donde esta la bolsa?" Carlos repeated irritably, growing more and more impatient by the minute. "Tell us where it is or you will suffer like you cannot imagine."

"Bob must have it," he replied, stuttering as he caught sight of the alligator's snout coming out of the shadows.

"Very well. If that is so, then tell us where he is," he said again as he raised his hand.

"But I told you, I don't know. Please."

Carlos motioned for Ernesto to begin again, but before he could connect the battery, Conor shouted, "Wait, Carlos! There *is* something else."

The Cuban raised a hand for his brother to hold for a moment.

"I...I think he may have had help."

ACKNOWLEDGEMENTS

I heard the old, old men say,
all that's beautiful drifts away.

W. B. Yeats

CHAPTER ONE

WELCOME TO MIAMI

As evening wore on, darkness descended upon the vast expanse of ocean heaving and rolling about them. Conor Rogan kept a lone, watchful eye on deck while his two passengers grew drunker and louder inside the main cabin. Switching on the running lights against the impending blackness, he disengaged the catamaran's autopilot and once again took the wheel. The sea was relatively calm that night off the northwest coast of the Bahamas, a warm southeasterly blowing from the island of New Providence, filling their sails, making conditions just right for the return voyage to South Florida.

Conor felt a sense of excitement he had not experienced in a very long time. He hadn't realized just how much he'd missed being back at sea, the trade wind blowing hot on his face. For him, being out there in the vastness of the South Atlantic was like nothing else on earth. Out there, he was not just the captain of the *Aphrodite*, but of his own destiny. The sleek white catamaran and all souls onboard were his responsibility. Their lives were in his hands. His alone. But that fact did not daunt him in the slightest. In truth, it was probably the challenge and responsibility that appealed to him most. The reality was that out there in the middle of the ocean, Conor was in his element. He was confident of his own ability; the master, plotting his own course, savoring every ebb and flow, every pitch and roll.

Just before midnight, he went forward to secure the jib before returning to the cockpit and settling in for the night with a cigarette and a cup of coffee. When the clouds finally parted above the Florida Keys, they revealed another clear sky ahead. It was beautiful out there. Tranquil. As usual, the stars appeared visibly brighter out at sea than on land, and he could once again see the Milky Way etched across the heavens. This wondrous sight had its usual effect on him, instilling in his soul a feeling of humility and insignificance. Suddenly, sitting there alone in the darkness, Conor's own earthly troubles seemed petty and fleeting beneath the vast swathe of stars stretching above to infinity.

For him, though, guiding the *Aphrodite* through the swell was as satisfying as it got. The hours passed by without incident, except for the odd raised voice and burst of drunken laughter from inside the well-lit cabin. He was glad they were enjoying themselves, relieved the earlier tension between them had been forgotten. The wind was blowing from the southwest now, and Conor knew if he maintained a steady course and didn't venture too close to the coastline, he should have the *Aphrodite* back in her Palm Beach marina before sunrise.

But then it happened, and his previous feelings of calm and tranquility were thrown into chaos. Shortly after he sighted the glistening lights of Miami, a loud, resonating boom shattered the stillness about him. It startled him to full alertness, forcing him to sit bolt upright as he tried to make sense of what had just occurred. The blood froze in Conor's veins as a strange and terrifying sensation wound its way down his spine. His first thoughts were of disaster, that they had hit some floating debris or had been rammed by a passing whale. But then his mind focused and he quickly realized that the sound had come from inside the cabin. Inside.

He released his grip on the wheel with great urgency, jumped up without tying it down, and grabbed the handle of the cabin door. Flinging it open, he raced inside to find one of his passengers standing before him with a small black revolver in his trembling left hand.

"Jesus!" Conor exclaimed in a broad Irish accent, pushing past him to find the other man's lifeless body slumped face-down on the polished wooden table in the center of the cabin. "What the fuck have you done?"

A bottle of Cuban rum was on its side in the thick, dark pool, slowly spreading from beneath the man's blood-soaked head. Conor pressed his thumb and forefinger to his neck, but could feel no pulse. It was difficult to judge, however, for even as he did, he could hear little else but the sound of his own pounding heart. So he placed his other hand on the man's forehead and lifted it up, only to discover his face frozen in death, eyes wide open, staring lifelessly back at him. There was a large black hole where his left cheekbone should have been, blood and gristle oozing from the wound. And when he looked down, he found the white leather seat behind was covered in fragments of bone and particles of brain matter.

"You…you've killed him," he stuttered disbelievingly.

Standing up from the body, Conor turned to the man with the revolver, put his hand out, and carefully took it from his sweaty grasp. The man appeared to be in deep shock, remaining motionless, not resisting or saying anything. So Conor put the gun in the waistband of his trousers before turning toward the navigation table by the cabin door.

"Don't touch *anything*," he commanded sternly, growing angrier as his own initial shock began to wear off. "I fucking mean it. Just stay there while I call the coastguard."

As he turned his back and bent over, flipping the switches on the small VHF transmitter, something heavy and metallic came down hard on the back of his head. The pain shot though Conor's body like a bolt of lightning, a strange, disorienting sensation that overcame his entire being. As the numbness spread through his neck and shoulders, he suddenly lost the power of his legs and his knees buckled beneath him. He crumpled face-down onto the wooden navigation table, lay there for a few seconds before slowly sliding off toward the floor. Unconsciousness engulfed him like an icy squall. Once again, Conor found himself floating beneath the waves. Once more being dragged down into the abyss.

One Week Earlier

He spotted Bob Castagna waiting in the arrivals terminal of Miami airport and quickly raised a hand to acknowledge him. The baggage reclaim had been crowded and noisy, bustling with brightly dressed holidaymakers pushing trolleys over-laden with bags and cases as they jostled for space around the luggage carousels. It was mayhem in there. But as soon as Conor grabbed his canvas sail bag and walked through the sliding glass doors, he heard a voice calling out and saw Bob waving enthusiastically from behind the greeting barrier.

"Conor Rogan! Hey! Over here!"

Bob looked exactly like the photo Conor had seen on his company website, a genial, overweight man whose short black hair was graying at the temples and whose dark, tanned skin was leathery from sun exposure. In his fifties, he was immaculately dressed in a gray business suit and blue silk shirt. His collar was open at the top, revealing a hint of gold neck chain peeping out from beneath a tuft of dark chest hair. His shoes were black Italian leather and he wore a large gold Rolex. From his manicured appearance and air of self-confidence, Conor's first impression was one of a wealthy, successful businessman. His second—as Bob drew closer and he saw the broad, welcoming smile on his face— was that he liked the look of his new American employer, and that they would probably get on.

In contrast to Bob, however, Conor Rogan was not a wealthy man. Not by any stretch of the imagination. Nor had he been successful in the world of business. In reality, he was probably the polar opposite to Bob in every respect. If he didn't have his health he would have nothing, he'd told the chatty woman sitting next to him on the long flight over from Ireland. Truth be told, he had confided, ever since his business went under, he was so broke he couldn't even afford a return ticket. He wasn't exaggerating. Things had not been going well for Conor and he needed this job to work out more than anything else in the world.

Born and bred on the rugged West Coast of Ireland, he had spent most of his youth sailing and repairing boats. Yachts and boats were not just his passion, they were his life. Over the years he had braved the icy Atlantic Ocean in everything and anything that would float beneath him, and reveled in the challenge and adventure of it all. "Sure there's more brine in those veins than blood," his mother used to joke. In many respects, she was right. From a twelve-foot sailing dinghy his father and he built when he was a lad, to a half-million dollar cruising yacht he tested for a prospective buyer, to an ancient Irish Currach, covered in goat skins and made watertight by tar and spit. Conor had single-handedly guided each and every one through the ferocious Atlantic swell, had pushed them to their limits and even, on more than one occasion, beyond.

Conor Rogan was in his late-twenties, about six feet tall, and used to the outdoors life. His hair was sandy-brown and probably needed a cut to tidy it up. He wore green khaki trousers and a faded-brown t-shirt; his old canvas shoes were a little worse for wear. He didn't own a watch, or many other possessions for that matter. But then he also didn't put on an act or try to impress. Conor prided himself on that. He was who he was and the devil be damned, he'd say. If nothing else, he was honest to your face and did his best no matter what he tried. As far as he was concerned, you either liked him or you didn't, and by that same token, he either liked you or he didn't. But when it came to friendship, Conor always tried to be there when it mattered. In that regard, at least, there were no half-measures with him.

Bob Castagna smiled broadly as they shook hands for the first time that Fourth of July afternoon. They had exchanged emails for a week or two and then spoke a couple of times on the phone. Conor had replied to Bob's advert looking for an experienced sailor with Sea Master Qualifications—one who was willing to travel to South Florida on short notice for an indefinite period of time. The job description was simply to "manage a new charter business out of West Palm Beach." But in reality, Conor suspected Bob was looking for "the right person" more than anything else. Bob really needed an "*all rounder*," as he put it himself. Someone who wasn't afraid to get their hands dirty. He needed someone who didn't bullshit about *how* they were going to do it, but instead just got stuck in and saw the job through to its conclusion. And most important of all, as far as he was concerned, since they were going to be spending a lot of time together, he really needed someone who was easy to get on with.

In fact, it was Bob who spoke first as they shook hands that day, his powerful voice commanding, yet warm and genuinely hospitable. "Welcome to Miami, Conor. How was your flight?"

"Grand, thanks," replied Conor, wondering for a second if Bob was about to hug him, as he was standing so close.

"Outstanding. Well, I have to say it's exciting to finally meet you in person. I have big things planned for us, you know. For the charter business."

"Sure, I'm looking forward to getting started," Conor said in his rough Irish brogue.

"That's the spirit, glad to hear it. I've already got plans for an overnight down to Nassau and... But, hey, let's not talk business just yet. First things first. You must be pretty beat?"

Conor shrugged as Bob released his powerful grip on his hand. "I *am* a little bit tired all right."

The older man slapped him on the back as he ushered him toward the exit to the parking garage. "Well, relax. You're staying with us for a few days until you get settled. Acclimatized to the lifestyle, so to speak. Then you can move onto the yacht like we planned."

"Are you sure that's not too much trouble? I don't mind moving my gear onboard today."

"Nonsense, Conor, you're staying with us for a few days, and that's that," Bob insisted. "My wife, Eva, has prepared the pool house especially for you. You'll have it all to yourself, I promise. Plenty of privacy."

They were on the ground level in the parking garage and Conor could feel the stifling heat hit him full on, like stepping into an oven. Bob motioned toward a brand new silver Mercedes nearby, pointing his key ring to turn off the alarm. The lights flashed and there was a muffled *clunk* as the doors unlocked.

"Besides," he continued. "I figure it's more practical to have you close at hand for a day or two. That way, we get to spend as much time as possible together. You know, getting things up and running."

Conor squinted his eyes and winced as they pulled out of the darkened parking garage with speed into the intense white sunlight of Miami. Reaching into the back to his sail bag, he took out a pair of sunglasses and sat back in the plush, white leather seat, looking out over the city as they found the ramp onto I-95.

"Heck, you're gonna need those here." Bob smiled, pointing to Conor's sunglasses "You know, I'd swear the rays are stronger here than anywhere else I've ever been."

"Is that right?" Conor said with a nod. "Sure, I'd imagine they're even more powerful when they reflect off the water."

"That is a fact!"

"Would you happen to know what the temperature is outside?"

Bob pointed to the onboard computer. "Ninety four," he replied with a whistle. "Man, I'll tell you something. You might think it's cool in here, but turn off the air con and we'd suffocate in less than five minutes. FYI, South Florida's got the best goddamn climate in the US, my friend, but from June through August, it's a *real* bitch. The humidity is so intense, it'll drain your energy in minutes."

"Is that so?"

"I shit you not. Soak your shirt clean through. Even the goddamn grass withers and dies if it's not watered twice a day."

"Yeah?"

"And then, if that's not bad enough, around August we've got hurricane season. Now that, my young friend, is a time you definitely *don't* want to be out on the water—"

As his voice trailed off, Conor turned to look out the window again. His head was back and he began to feel tired. He yawned, but didn't let Bob see in case he thought he was boring him. He couldn't see the speedometer, but they were traveling pretty fast, leaving most of the other cars and pickups behind on the seven-lane highway. There were no roads like this back in Ireland and he was impressed. Bob saw him looking at the exit signs as they passed the ramps for Hollywood, Fort Lauderdale, and then Pompano Beach.

"We're in Broward County," he said, sounding a little bit like a tour guide. "Miami's down in Dade, but we're heading north to West Palm Beach. That's Palm Beach County. Not far now. You're gonna like it there."

Conor nodded his head in appreciation, but the sign for Pompano had reminded him of someone he knew who lived there. His wife, Grainne's older brother, Danny, had moved to the States about four years ago. He'd been involved in the IRA for a while when he was younger and had served a few years in Mountjoy Prison in Dublin for armed robbery. Conor had always liked Danny. He was a likable guy, but there was no denying that trouble had a way of following him wherever he went.

When Grainne died the previous year, Danny wasn't able to return for her funeral due to an outstanding warrant back in Ireland. *Christ*, Conor thought, as the painful memory of that winter's day washed over him. He closed his eyes and was back in the old gray, rain-soaked graveyard overlooking the cliffs and the sea. The entire village had turned out to pay their respects. There was a sense of shock and disbelief, with young and old crying around him, eyes red, faces pale and ashen in the bitter January cold. Grainne's parents and some of her family stared accusingly at him; others simply sought answers he just did not have. That's pretty much when the old spark died in Conor, when everything around him turned to shit.

"We're here!" Bob announced excitedly as they turned off I-95 onto Southern Boulevard.

Conor's mind returned to the present with a start and he rolled down the window a little to wake himself up. He could see the ocean in the distance now and smell salt in the air. He inhaled the warm breeze and held it in his lungs for a few seconds. It felt good.

"Boy, if I didn't know better, I'd say you looked like a guy who'd just smoked his first joint," Bob laughed, glancing over with a broad grin.

Conor exhaled and smiled back. The older man didn't seem to hold in his thoughts or emotions and Conor liked that about him. He raised his eyebrows in appreciation when Bob suddenly glanced at him for approval. They had just entered an affluent neighborhood. Manicured lawns, electric gates, and enormous white houses with marble pillars as far as the eye could see. And palm trees everywhere, lining the roads on both sides, some taller than two-story buildings. But the truth was that Conor had been impressed since the moment they left the airport. Everything he'd seen so far confirmed to him that he had not made the wrong decision in leaving Ireland to come here.

He let himself hope for a while that South Florida could be the place for him to start over. To rebuild his life. The sun, the clear blue sky stretching unbroken from horizon to horizon, and that magnificent shimmering blue ocean he was now looking at off to their right. The beauty of his surroundings stirred something in Conor. There was a sense of anticipation and excitement he hadn't felt in a very long time.

"Well, what do you think?" Bob said as the ornate metal gates of his house opened electronically, revealing a paved driveway lined by tall Cuban Petticoat Palms. It seemed more statement than question, so Conor just nodded his approval without speaking.

Bob pulled his Mercedes to a stop next to a bright red Porsche convertible and a small silver Chevrolet. An elegant marble fountain stood directly in front of the house, spraying water into the air that glistened magically in the sunlight. But for Conor, the word house did not do it justice. In his eyes, it was more than that. It was breathtaking, a two-story masterpiece of white stucco walls and gleaming marble columns. The windows were huge, like giant mirrors in the sunshine, reflecting the magnificent gardens of orange and lemon fruit trees that were surrounded in turn by beds of glorious multi-colored flowers. He was not used to such luxury.

Bob noticed him admiring the gardens and said, "Nice, huh? But this is Eva's territory, not mine. A gardener comes in once a week to do a little maintenance. Old Cuban guy called Manolo. Does a fine job, but just about every tree, bush, and flower was planted by her."

Conor stepped out, took his sail bag from the back, and stretched in the afternoon sunshine. The air was hot as he inhaled, but it felt good to be standing outdoors after his long flight and car journey. Bob motioned for him to follow as he led him around the side of the house.

"I'll give you the full paid tour after you get settled," he said.

They turned the corner onto a patio area with a beautiful shimmering pool and a cluster of dark green sun chairs. He brought him past them and opened the door of the pool house. It was cool inside, tastefully decorated with fresh-cut flowers on a small coffee table below a whirring ceiling fan.

"So, my friend, this is you for the next few days."

Conor nodded gratefully. "This is grand, Bob. Thanks again."

"Naw, no need to thank me. You're part of the team now." Then, after a moment's silence, "You know, the Bob Castagna team?"

Conor didn't really know if he was joking or not. He decided not to laugh, but just smiled politely. Bob dropped the key into his hand and patted him firmly on the back. Not in a condescending way, but with genuine fondness.

"No, man, I really mean that. We're in this thing together now, Conor. One-hundred-and-fifty-percent commitment.

You know? Teamwork and all that?"

"Sure. Of course. I get it."

"They say there's no 'I' in team," Bob continued. "But heck, let me tell you something. When you're playing on mine, there are plenty of dollar signs for everyone. I treat all my employees with respect and reward them accordingly. You'll find that out as we go." He turned for the door. "Look, I know you must be tired after your flight, so I guess I'll leave you alone to get settled in. Dinner's at eight. We'll do the introductions then."

"Grand so."

"You *do* know it's Fourth of July, right? Independence Day? Should be a pretty good fireworks show tonight." He stopped for a moment and pointed back past the sofa and coffee table to the small open kitchen that was framed by a wide redbrick arch. "I think Eva has stocked you up in there with everything you'll need. Should be plenty of food and snacks. Drinks in the fridge if you're thirsty."

"Thanks," Conor replied, suppressing a yawn. "I *am* fierce thirsty from the heat."

"You drink American beer?"

"Sure."

"Heck, what am I saying?" Bob laughed as he shook his head. "If that isn't the dumbest question ever. Asking an Irish guy if he drinks beer."

Conor smiled back. There really wasn't much he could say to that. He supposed it was true, so he just shrugged his shoulders and nodded.

"Well anyhow," Bob continued. "I'll leave you to it. Try to get some rest and we'll talk again at dinner."

CHAPTER TWO

WEST PALM BEACH

He had just had that same dream again. He was floating in purgatory, in limbo beneath the frozen water, sinking slowly down toward the dark seabed below. Then, from those icy depths, a mysterious shrouded figure began rising upwards. Toward him. He couldn't make it out clearly in the darkness, but it was gaining speed as it approached, drawing nearer and heading straight for him. He panicked. Trying to swim up toward the light, he opened his mouth to scream, but gasped as the frozen salt water rushed into his throat and lungs. It drew closer.

Conor woke in a cold sweat at about six-thirty in the evening, and for a second or two, didn't know where or even who he was. The curtains were drawn and the small bedroom was in darkness but for a thin shaft of white sunlight peeping through the shutter, dancing off a painting on the opposite wall. Horses were grazing by a stream in a field of long grass. It reminded him of home, and for a brief moment, his mind reflected on the past. He felt that same knot tighten in his stomach, a sense of overwhelming sadness and grief. No, he reminded himself. He had made a promise he would not go there.

Sitting up, he rubbed his eyes, and then coughing, walked naked into the bathroom to shower. Before he came out, he dressed, putting on a clean black shirt. He washed his dirty t-shirt and socks in the sink with a bar of soap before hanging them over the shower rail to dry. He lit a cigarette, sighing wearily as he blew an arc of blue smoke toward the whirring ceiling fan overhead. He was hunched down get-

ting himself a beer out of the fridge when he suddenly heard
a loud splash from the patio.

The young girl in the pool outside was an excellent swimmer. She wore a pink one-piece bathing suit and white swim
hat. Each time she reached an end, she would flip expertly
over and begin her next lap. Each stroke was as strong and
precise as the previous one and there was no sign of her slowing down or tiring. She didn't notice him watching from the
open doorway of the pool house, leaning against the doorframe with a cigarette in one hand and his beer in the other.

"Having fun?" a voice asked from out of nowhere.

Startled, Conor stood upright looking left to right, feeling
a little bit embarrassed. "Hello?"

A woman rose from one of the nearby loungers facing
away from him. Wearing a silver bikini and a light, see-
through sarong, she was quite a bit older than he, but still
incredibly beautiful. Her long blonde hair framed her light
suntanned face, reminding him of a painting he'd once seen
in a Dublin gallery of a Greek or Roman goddess. Oozing
sensuality, she walked slowly toward him with a glass of red
wine in one hand, her long, glistening legs moving purposefully and elegantly as she approached with the confident gait
of a model on a catwalk.

There was a moment's silence that seemed to last an age
as she stood facing him, studying him, her dark green eyes
staring deep into his. Her gaze penetrated Conor and made
him shift a little uncomfortably. It felt as if she wasn't just
looking at him, but was in fact sizing him up, reading his
mind.

"Got a light?" she finally said nonchalantly, moving closer.
So close he could smell her suntan lotion and feel the heat of
her breath on his face. He could also smell alcohol and knew
she'd been drinking quite heavily.

"No problem," he replied, taking a dented lighter from his
pocket and flicking it to life as she raised a cigarette to her
lips. He was definitely feeling uncomfortable now. She was
deliberately too close. He took a half step back.

"I'm Eva," she said in a light Southern accent with a mis-
chievous, seductive smile. "Bob's wife?"

"Nice to meet you," he responded, shaking her outstretched, palm-down hand. "I'm Conor Rogan."

"Oh yes, I know who you are. You're the sailor from Ireland we've been hearing about. Bob's new project."

"Er, yeah, that's right." Conor was surprised by his reaction to her. Maybe it was the heat, or perhaps the jet lag, but he distinctly felt the hairs on the back of his arms stand up, noticed his heart beating a little faster. She was older by about fifteen years, he guessed, probably in her mid-forties. But she still emitted the sexual radiance of a much younger woman. Eva Castagna was definitely *not* how Conor had pictured Bob's wife.

"Thanks for letting me stay," he finally said after an awkward pause, gesturing back through the open doorway into the pool house.

Stepping closer, she looked him straight in the eye, placed a hand on his arm, and whispered, "You think it's big enough?"

"Oh aye, plenty big," he replied, immediately regretting his choice of words. He thought he caught her looking down in the direction of his crotch, but couldn't be certain.

Eva smiled teasingly and took a drag from her cigarette before blowing the smoke skywards. "You know, Bob seems very excited about this new business venture of his."

Just then, Conor noticed the young girl had stopped swimming laps. She was moving slowly toward the ladder on the far side of the pool. Eva caught his distraction and glanced back to see her climb out and slip her swim cap off. In one elegant movement, she bent forward so her long blonde hair completely covered her face, and then whipped her head back with an expert motion that sent it flowing perfectly behind her. Conor couldn't help notice her resemblance to her mother. A younger version, perhaps—she only looked about eighteen or nineteen—but just as beautiful.

"Does it make you feel excited?" Eva whispered softly as he watched the young girl with fascination.

He couldn't remember the last time he blushed, but he was sure, if he had seen himself in a mirror, he would be have been blushing then. "I'm sorry?"

"This new charter business," she continued nonchalantly. "I was wondering if it excited you as much as Bob?"

"Oh aye, of course, the charter business. It's very er...exciting."

She smiled wickedly and rubbed a hand suggestively on his chest. "Well don't get *too* excited. It's not good for you in this heat."

Conor smiled uncomfortably. She was teasing him, toying with him. Maybe it was just her way, or perhaps it was simply because she'd been drinking. Either way, he was getting a little bit tired of it.

Eva turned toward the girl who was wrapping a towel around her waist and beckoned her to approach. "Abi! Come meet Daddy's new friend."

There was something about her raised voice that surprised Conor, maybe even hinted a little about her relationship with the young girl. She had been speaking so softly and seductively to him, yet now to her daughter, her tone became a lot harsher and more commanding. She had obviously downed a few glasses of wine, but he imagined it was more than that. He sensed she flirted with the male species in general, that it was in her nature to play these games.

Abi was on their side of the pool now, walking slowly toward them. She looked even better up close. Not as tanned as her mother, even paler than one would expect for someone living in such a sunny climate. Standing next to Eva, though, she seemed fresher to him, and somehow, even though he couldn't quiet put his finger on it, there was a sense of goodness and innocence radiating from her.

"Abi, this is Conor."

The young girl smiled shyly at him, showing her braces, and leaned forward to shake his hand. "Hi."

"Hello," he said politely.

"How was your flight?"

"Grand, thanks."

"Conor is from Ireland," said Eva.

"Is it really true that it rains most of the time in Ireland?" Abi asked inquisitively.

He just smiled and said, "Yeah, I suppose it does. That's probably why everything is so green."

"I believe it's very beautiful, though."

"Now that *is* true," Conor replied.

"You know, I'm a big fan of William Butler Yeats' poetry. He was from Ireland, wasn't he?"

Conor nodded and smiled politely.

"I find it so moving," Abi continued before pausing thoughtfully for a moment. She looked him directly in the eye, causing the hairs on the back of his neck to stand up as she softly whispered, "'I heard the old, old men say, all that's beautiful drifts away.' You know it?"

Conor was a little taken aback by her passion. She was young, yet he sensed wisdom. Not what he had expected. "Can't say as I know that one," he replied. "But they *do* say Yeats is one of the best."

"And James Joyce," she added. "I think *he* was a genius."

"You've read Joyce? That's *really* impressive. I wouldn't have thought someone so young—"

"Abi is our very own little Wikipedia," Eva interrupted. "She has more books in her bedroom than the Palm Beach library. Don't you, honey?"

Abi nodded shyly, smiling a little, but he could tell she was clearly feeling embarrassed.

"She was reading at the age of four, you know. A regular little bookworm. Isn't that right, honey?"

"What part of Ireland do you come from?" Abi asked Conor, trying to change the subject away from herself.

"I was born in Connemara. I don't know if you've ever heard of it?"

"Oh yes," she said knowingly. "That's above Galway on the West Coast, isn't it? Close to where Yeats was born."

"That's right. But it's very wild there. Damp. Full of bogs and forests. Not at all like here."

She smiled. "Did you know that here in Florida, there is more rainfall in summer than the entire UK all year round?"

"Honey, don't you have study?" interrupted Eva. "I'm sure you said you did."

Conor wondered for a moment if she resented Abi getting attention from the opposite sex. Perhaps she felt her daughter was stealing the limelight?

Abi appeared a little flustered as she said, "Oh yes, yes I do." She turned to Conor, smiled politely again, and said, "I hope you'll excuse me, but I *do* have to go. I'll see you at dinner, though."

"Right so." He tried not to watch as she walked away for fear her mother might get the wrong idea. But then again, Conor mused, what was he thinking? Maybe she would get the *right* idea. He couldn't help but admit to himself that he was even more attracted to Abi than her mother. Granted, she was a lot younger than he, but there was something about her, something that was so irresistibly sweet. Of course, he reminded himself, he had no intention of pursuing his attraction toward her. That would be crazy. And by the same token, he had no designs on her mother either. But he did have to concede, Bob was a lucky man. Both the Castagna women were stunners.

Turning to Eva, he said, "She's a lovely young girl, Missus Castagna. Very bright. You and Bob must be very proud of her."

"Call me Eva," she said, knocking back the last of her wine. "Missus Castagna sounds so formal. Makes me feel old."

"Okay," he said apologetically. "Eva."

"Actually, she *is* very bright," she confided matter-of-factly. "She gets it from me, I think. Because as it happens, Abi is not actually Bob's *real* daughter. She's only his step-daughter. He's impotent, you know, can't have children of his own."

"Oh."

"Yes, you see, I had Abi before we were married. Before I met him."

"Oh, right." Conor found himself shuffling his feet a little uneasily.

"Of course I wouldn't mention it to him," she continued in a more serious tone. "He's a little sensitive about it, you see. Abi is still his 'little girl.' He won't let anyone say a thing against her." He sensed a bit of jealousy in her voice now as she continued. "Oh yes, believe me, she is the absolute apple of his eye. Has been since we married."

Conor just nodded without reply. After all, what was he supposed to say? There was an awkward silence before she finally placed a hand gently on his arm again and smiled.

"Go on, go ahead and finish that beer while it's still cold. I've got to go now, but I'll see you for dinner at eight."

"Okay. See you later so," he replied as she instantly turned to follow Abi into the main house.

But Eva didn't look back, just walked slowly away with a quick wave of her hand to acknowledge the remark. Conor watched carefully as she went, hips swinging seductively. He was well aware that it was for his benefit. She knew his eyes were uncontrollably fixed on her ass as she walked away down the invisible catwalk.

Back inside the pool house, Conor grabbed another beer from the fridge, sat at the kitchen counter, and began thumbing through the address book on his phone. He eventually found the number he was looking for, took a deep breath, and then pressed dial.

"'Lo?" said a voice.

His phone was old and not very expensive. The salty sea air probably hadn't done the speaker any favors over the years. The voice on the other end sounded hollow and distant, but he recognized it nonetheless, and felt strangely comforted to hear a familiar voice.

"How are you, Danny? It's Conor."

"Huh?"

"Conor Rogan."

"Con?" Danny McNamara was completely taken by surprise at the sound of his voice. Conor couldn't blame him. After all, they hadn't spoken for at least two years. "Man, it's powerful to hear from ye," Danny said excitedly. "Where the fuck *are* you?"

"I'm here," Conor replied. "In Florida."

"Well, Jaysus Christ, man, that's only brilliant. What's up? Are you here on holiday or what?"

Conor lit another cigarette. "No, not on holiday. I've got a job here now, setting up a charter company in Palm Beach."

"A what?"

"A charter company, Danny. You know, for holidaymakers? They rent a cruiser and a captain, then go sailing around the Caribbean. Maybe down to Jamaica or the Bahamas or what not. There's good money in it, and you know me, anything to keep sailing."

"Jaysus, Con, we've *got* to get together. I haven't seen you for fuckin' ages."

There was a brief pause. Conor sensed what was coming.

"Listen, man, I'm really sorry I couldn't make it home for Grainne's funeral. You *did* understand, didn't you?"

"Yeah, of course," Conor replied. "I understood." He felt uncomfortable talking about it.

"It's just that those fuckin' cops back in the old country still want to talk to me."

"Yeah, yeah," Conor interrupted, a slight hint of irritation in his voice. "Look, it's fine, Danny. I understand."

"So, man, what's the story?" Danny said after a pause, cheerfully raising his tone. "What are we gonna do now that you're here? Hey, you *do* know I'm only down in Pompano, don't you? It may not be as up-market as your Palm Beach, but it's still only a few minutes down the road from ye."

"Yeah, I know. Look, I'll tell you what, Danny, I only landed here this morning. Was just calling to let you know I'm nearby. I need a little time to sort a few things out first, but how's about I give you a call in a day or two and we'll meet up somewhere?"

"Yeah, yeah, that would be deadly," agreed Danny. "You know, I think I still owe you a few beers."

"Alright so."

"Jaysus, I still can't get over hearin' your voice."

"Talk to you soon, Danny."

"Okay, Con. See you later, man."

Dinner was at eight sharp. For some reason, Conor had half-expected servants and a cook. But instead, Eva and Abi prepared the food themselves and brought it out into the dining room from the adjoining kitchen as Bob poured everyone a glass of wine. The table seated ten, but they all stayed together at one end. Bob at the head, Eva and Abi to his right, and Conor on the other side facing them. It was actually quite pleasant and normal, and he felt a bit foolish now for having expected some type of banquet.

To his relief, they were dressed casually. Bob wore Jeans and a white polo shirt that clung a little too tightly to his belly. Abi was in a pretty green summer dress with a cute green hair band, the color of which he suspected was chosen in his honor, while Eva wore a short black skirt and white silk blouse. Her hair was tied back, revealing a pair of simple gold earrings. She didn't wear much makeup, yet still managed to look better than most of the women he knew half her age.

Before them in the center of the table was a display of white orchids and lilies. Each place was set with sterling silver cutlery, crystal wine glasses, and gold-leafed china plates. The dining room itself was impressive, like the property in general, with gray marble floor tiles, white Romanesque pillars, and elegant gold picture frames lining the walls. Conor complimented Bob on the decor, the house, and gardens, but his new employer took none of the credit, citing Eva as the one with all the taste and know-how. As the women came in with the last of the food and took their places, he explained how his wife ran the household like clockwork, and how a Cuban housekeeper only came twice a week to do general cleaning and laundry. And then of course there was Manolo, whom he'd already told Conor about. He came on Tuesday afternoons to maintain the gardens. His son Fernando cleaned the pool, a very polite young boy who had to translate for his father since he spoke almost no American.

"So, Conor, what about you?" Eva asked.

"Me?"

"Yes, you. Why don't you tell us a little bit about yourself. You said you grew up in Ireland? You must find our way of life here in the United States quite different from what you're used to?"

"Oh sure. For a start, it's a lot warmer here."

"What about the other things? I mean, the people, the standard of living, the bigger highways and houses? That sort of thing."

Bob laughed. "Hey, hon, you don't think they all go around in horses and carts, do you?" Then, smiling at Conor, he said, "You'll have to excuse my wife, Conor. I think she still believes Ireland is full of leprechauns and fairies."

Eva scowled back at him, but he didn't seem to notice. Conor couldn't decide if it was a playful glance or not, deciding it best to turn his attention to the food. It looked wonderful, having been placed in the center of the table for them to help themselves. So, taking Bob's lead, he leaned across to fill his plate with pasta and salad.

"Well, as it happens," he said, looking across at Eva. "I actually did grow up in the countryside. We lived on the edge of a village near the sea, in a small thatched-cottage."

"Now that's what I was talking about," Eva exclaimed, smiling and casting a triumphant glance toward Bob. "I'm picturing something small and quaint, like one of those little white houses in the picture postcards?"

"Yeah, exactly like the postcards," said Conor. "Only a lot colder. It didn't have central heating, just an open turf fire. Believe me, you talk about the heat being hard to take here, but in the depths of winter, you'd barely venture away from it. Stick your frozen feet right into it if you could. Anyway, when I was seventeen, I moved up to Dublin. Shared a flat with three other lads while I served my apprenticeship as a mechanic."

"Oh, what kind?" Abi asked with interest.

"A diesel-fitter," he replied as he cut into his steak. He chewed for a second, looked at Eva, and said, "Mmmm, this is really delicious. Very tasty."

She was sprinkling cheese on her pasta, but smiled politely back to acknowledge the compliment. She seemed a lot better behaved than earlier that evening by the pool.

"So, my young Irish friend," said Bob. "What about sailing? When did you get into that?"

"Well, to be honest, I've been sailing since I was a young lad. But while I trained as a mechanic, I spent evenings and weekends getting my Sea Master Certificate."

"Yeah? That sounds interesting," said Bob. "Tell us more."

"Yes, fascinating," Eva added with a yawn.

Conor caught a hint of sarcasm in her voice and knew she was getting a bit bored. Sailing and all things nautical was clearly not her thing.

"Well, first off, I taught part-time at a sailing school on the east coast. You know, to help pay the bills and save for my own boat. Then, when the recession hit Ireland, I got laid off. So, I decided to throw caution to the wind. I took out a loan, bought a small twenty-five footer, and went ahead and opened my own business."

"Good for you," Bob exclaimed as he knocked back his drink.

"To begin, I started teaching young children and older couples to sail. That was grand. Really enjoyable. But then, because of my mechanical experience, I sort of drifted out of that and ended up doing more marine repair work." He finished his glass of wine and nodded a thank you as Bob refilled it without asking.

"Yeah, we repaired and refitted motorboats and sailing cruisers. Engines, water heaters, wind generators, that sort of thing. Bought and sold a twenty-foot day cruiser."

"Did you still teach sailing?" asked Abi. He could tell she was genuinely interested in his story.

"Well, to be honest, not really," he replied. "I suppose I wanted to. But the thing of it is, running a business in Ireland is mighty expensive, so our overheads were pretty high. We found the *real* money was in repairs. Especially running repairs. You see, the truth of it is, if you're out on the ocean and your engine packs in or your generator goes bang, you'll pretty much pay anything to get it up and running again. And that's where we came in. We could sail out and do most of the repairs on the spot. Usually have you back up and running in no time."

As he spoke, he felt a strange, unexpected sensation in his crotch. Under the table, a foot began nudging against his testicles, toes exploring the bulge in his trousers. He shifted uncomfortably and almost choked on his food as he pushed his chair back and began coughing.

"Wooo, are you okay?" Bob exclaimed with concern.

The foot was withdrawn as Conor glanced accusingly toward Eva. To his surprise, however, she acted as if nothing had happened, didn't even look up from her plate. He drank a full glass of water to clear his throat, glancing over at Abi, whom he found smiling politely back at him.

"Fine, thanks. Something just went down the wrong way," he said, looking confused.

"Drink some of your wine," Bob advised, not realizing what had just happened.

Conor knocked back his glass.

"That better?"

"Aye," he replied. "Thanks."

"Anyway," Bob continued as he topped him up again. "What you were just saying about the client willing to pay anything? I think that's *damned* good capitalism. I have always found that if you want to be successful in business, you've got to know your market. And when you do, you have got to corner it. Like, for example, buying food in Disney World. Sure, once inside, the tourists know they're paying over the odds, but hell, what are they going to do? They've got no choice."

After clearing the table, Eva returned with four plates of dessert. Some sort of fruit and meringue mixture covered in strawberries and cream. Conor didn't know what it was called, but it was delicious. He offered to help, but she and Abi wouldn't let him, saying he was a guest and should relax. Abi brought in four coffees as Bob opened another bottle of wine and refilled their glasses. Conor said he couldn't remember the last time he had eaten so well. It was true. He wasn't lying.

With that, Bob raised his glass and said, "Okay, guys, here's a toast to the Fourth of July. Independence Day!"

They all took a drink in response.

"You said *we*," Abi commented as Conor put his glass down. He noticed she hadn't drunk more than a small mouthful of wine all night.

"We?" he asked.

"Yes, when you were talking about your business just now, you said 'we' repaired boats. Did you have a partner or someone working for you?"

There was a moment's pause as Conor gathered his thoughts. "Well actually. I mean. Well, you see, my wife, Grainne, and I ran it together."

"Oh, I didn't even know you were married," Bob remarked, looking up from his dessert with a puzzled expression. "Guess I didn't think to ask."

"Will she be joining you?" asked Eva.

Conor took a deep breath, exhaled slowly, and said, "No, I'm afraid not. You see, she died last year."

"Oh, I'm sorry," exclaimed Abi.

"Yes, that's terrible. How did it happen?" Eva asked, appearing interested again.

"Well, it's still a bit difficult to talk about," he replied quietly after another pause, turning his eyes down to the table and flicking at his fork with his forefinger. He was hurting inside, finding the memory too painful to recall.

"Heck, we don't have to discuss it if you don't want to," Bob offered sympathetically. "After all, this *is* supposed to be a happy occasion, not an interrogation."

Conor managed a thin smile and nodded his appreciation.

"So what happened to your business?" Eva asked after a few seconds.

"Well, after Grainne... Well, I mean, I suppose I kind of lost interest after that. Didn't seem to have the same enthusiasm anymore."

"That's really sad," Abi offered sympathetically.

"Anyway, look, that's why I'm here," he continued, raising his tone, putting on a brave face, and trying desperately to change the subject away from himself. "I would like to thank you all for your very kind and generous hospitality.

And you, Bob. Thanks to you, I now have a chance to make a new start of it again. In a new country."

"A *great* country," Bob corrected him, nodding his head enthusiastically.

"A different environment and a fresh start is probably what you need," agreed Abi, seeming to understand instinctively what Conor meant.

"Aye, I think that's it exactly," he replied.

"Well, here's to new beginnings and the new charter business," Bob said cheerfully, raising his glass again. "And of course, to new friends."

"New friends," Abi repeated, looking to Conor as she held up her glass with a smile.

Eva raised hers to her lips without speaking.

"To new friends," Conor agreed. "Slainte!" Then, when he saw the puzzled look on their faces, said, "That's Irish for good health."

He put his wine down as Bob leaned forward with a more serious expression. "Now, my new young friend, speaking of the charter business..."

After dinner, Conor and Bob found themselves exiled to the patio at the rear of the house. Smoking a couple of fat Cuban cigars Bob had produced from his office, they continued finishing off the remains of the fourth bottle of wine. As they watched the fireworks display overhead, they sat back on two of the loungers overlooking the pool, side-by-side like a pair of old friends who had known each other for years. The water was magnificently lit by underwater fluorescents, luminous blue, shimmering in the darkness about them. Overhead, multi-colored bursts shot up into the blackness, followed each time a split-second later by a loud boom and a distant crackling as the sparks faded and died. With the rockets exploding above, the sky was transformed into a canvas of dancing lights, becoming for the briefest moment a place of wonderment and awe.

Bob continued discussing the new venture as they watched the unfolding show. It was a little cooler now, but still quite hot. Conor noticed small beads of sweat glistening on the older man's forehead as he spoke, his polo shirt wet in patches where it squeezed too tight around his belly. He liked Bob and his seemingly unending enthusiasm. The excitement showed on his face as he started explaining how he actually owned four companies, making a nice little profit from each. He was a businessman through and through. Making money excited him.

"My first venture here in Palm Beach was a web design company, which I started ten years ago with a young guy called Scott Harper. Scott's a bit of an oddball. A computer geek, but he knows his stuff. We still run it from a small suite downtown." He paused as another particularly loud burst erupted overhead. "My second was a digital printing company, which operates from the same office. I employ two married ladies who work part-time, Toni and Alison, to run it for me. Now, my third business is all about selling and maintaining vending machines, but heck, Conor, I won't bore you with the details."

He knocked back a gulp of wine and continued. "But now here's where it gets interesting. My latest and most profitable business is a property company called Gold Coast Developments. We've pulled off some pretty big deals this past year, made some serious bucks. Oh right, before I forget, I run that with a business partner called Hector Suarez. You've probably never heard of him, not being from around these parts, but he's a pretty powerful, well-known guy here in South Florida. Well connected. Owns a couple of nightclubs in Miami and Fort Lauderdale. And, as it happens, is actually opening a new one tomorrow night in Boca Raton and has invited us all to be his guests."

"Is that right?"

"Cuban, you know. Yes sir, he's got great contacts down there in Miami. Heck, I guess even I have to admit, without those, we wouldn't be doing half as well as we are."

Bob gave Conor the distinct impression that Hector Suarez was the dominant partner in the development business, even though he never actually said the words. He explained how their company had bought and sold various properties and parcels in South Florida over the past year, and how they were now in negotiations to buy a small hotel near the town of Nassau in the Bahamas. He told him he was thinking they could take Suarez on a trip down there in the next couple of days to view the development firsthand, and maybe also test the new yacht in the process.

"Kill two birds with one stone, as they say."

"I will, of course, have to check her out first," advised Conor.

"Of course you will," agreed Bob. "Heck, after all, you *are* the captain. But I mean, if everything checks out tomorrow, it would be a great first trip." He downed the last of the wine. "Anyway, look, if this Nassau deal comes off, it will be worth a hell of a lot of bucks to us. Could be the end to all my troubles."

"Trouble?"

"Huh? Oh right. Heck, you know, nothing to worry about. Just your usual everyday cash flow problems. An occupational hazard of being an entrepreneur, I'm afraid."

He was drunk now and slurring his words, so Conor decided not to ask him to elaborate on what he meant. Besides, he was simply an employee and didn't really want to get into anything too detailed about Bob's business *or* personal life. He was, after all, only there to sail a boat. Plain and simple. Anything more could cause complications he didn't need.

"Well, I have to say, from where I'm sitting, you look like you're doing pretty good," he observed, waving his hand to encompass the beautiful surroundings. "You certainly have a fine home and a lovely family."

Bob smiled broadly, showing his teeth. "I do, don't I? Heck, I am a lucky man, no doubt." He leaned in close to Conor, burped, breath now smelling strongly of alcohol. "You know, family is *the* most important thing in the world. Yes, sir. Cars, houses, all that bullshit—it wouldn't mean squat if I didn't have my beautiful Eva and, of course, my sweet Abi too. God damn it, Conor, they mean everything to me. You know?" Then, totally out of the blue, he said, "Hey, by the way, I've been meaning to ask you something."

"Huh? What's that?"

"Did you ever do any hunting back there in Ireland?"

There was silence for a moment while Conor digested the question. He supposed his brain wasn't working as fast as it usually did as he had drunk a little too much himself. "Sorry, Bob? What was that?"

"Hunting," the older man repeated slowly, as if talking to someone who didn't speak the language. "You gotta keep up, Conor. You know, life moves at a faster pace here in the US.

I asked if you hunt?"

"Nope," Conor finally replied with a shrug. "Never even shot a gun."

"Well, boy, you are in America now. National pastime. You'll love it." Bob smiled broadly as he sat up, clapped his hands together, and began rubbing his palms in a circular motion. "When this charter business of ours is up and running, I'll take you out hunting in the Everglades. You familiar with them?"

"Eh, not really."

"You're kidding? The Florida Everglades? Only one of *the* most isolated places in the state. Probably in the country. And only about forty minutes' drive from here."

"Hunting for what?" Conor asked inquisitively.

"Heck, I don't know. Anything that moves, I guess. Deer, snakes, alligators, varmints. You name it, I've shot it." Bob stood up awkwardly and staggered for a few seconds before finally steadying himself using Conor's right shoulder for support. It was time for bed. "Yes, my friend. Trust me. There's a real sense of freedom when you're out there in them Glades. You can really get back to nature, leave all this bullshit behind. You know? One of the last great wildernesses left on this overpopulated planet of ours."

"Oh aye, sounds great," Conor said. "But to be honest, Bob, I'm not sure I'd want to actually kill anything. It does sound like a grand place to visit though."

"We'll make an American of you yet." Bob laughed heartily as he left him and started back toward the house. "Heck, I guarantee, when you get a twelve-gauge in those hands, you'll see things differently. You'll be shooting at anything that moves."

"I don't know about that," Conor called after him as he walked away, his steps too precise, like a man stopped for drunk driving trying desperately to walk a straight line.

"Mañana, amigo," Bob cried from the other side of the patio, raising a hand to say goodnight. "Get some rest because you are in for a treat in the morning. After breakfast we'll take a drive down to the marina to see my baby, and then you can tell me what you think of her. Hundred bucks says you'll fall for her at first sight."

When he was gone, Conor lay back on the lounger, staring skywards. Alone now on the patio, he watched the impressive climax to the Fourth of July fireworks display. With one hand behind his head and the other clutching the glass balanced on his stomach, he stared up in fascination at the bright, luminous bursts of red, white, and blue overhead. He had seen fireworks before, of course, but never from such an exotic, luxurious location. It was a beautiful, balmy South Florida night. His belly was full, and he felt a nice, warm sensation from the alcohol.

On the southern edge of Boca Raton, a young Cuban man stood in a darkened basement, watching the lightshow through a narrow dust-covered window high up on the gray un-plastered wall. With one hand in his pocket and the other holding a cigarette, he stood in silence as the fireworks display reached its noisy conclusion. Giant sparkling flowers of light burst forth in the blackness, their fiery petals spreading outwards to become one with the night. When the final rocket exploded overhead, the sky fell back into darkness and silence once again descended upon the sprawling neighborhoods and business districts of Broward and Palm Beach County.

Carlos Suarez didn't seem to be in any hurry. He slowly dropped his cigarette butt to the dirty concrete floor and squashed it meticulously beneath his brown leather shoe as he exhaled downwards a cloud of bluish-grey smoke. In his late-twenties, he was a short and stocky man with dark skin, square jaw, and hard, chiseled features. At first glance, he resembled a businessman, immaculately dressed in a white satin shirt and black trousers. But a closer inspection revealed the eyes of a killer, cold and dark, shark-like, without the faintest hint of kindness or empathy.

Turning from the narrow window, his attention was drawn to the other side of the basement where a vicious-looking alligator shifted angrily on a bed of dirty straw. It was held firmly in the corner of the room by a short metal chain fixed around its neck. But its calculating eyes followed Carlos' movement with interest, its tail slamming hard into the floor as it watched, sending clouds of dust toward the ceiling.

The Cuban smiled to himself as he turned away, looking back across the blackness to the center of the room where, beneath a bare, flickering light bulb, a young woman was tied to an old wooden chair with silver duct tape. Her wrists were fixed tightly to the armrests, her ankles taped to each of its two front legs. The chair was leaning backwards on its rear legs, an unnatural position that left her helplessly lying back facing the ceiling. Behind her, a second man was holding a plastic Wynn Dixie shopping bag over her head, gripping it firmly about her throat as she thrashed and writhed in agony. Following a signal from Carlos, the man loosened his grip and pulled the bag off with a snap. There was a glint in his eye as he did so, a thin smile. He was clearly enjoying himself.

The woman gasped and lurched forward, coughing uncontrollably as oxygen filled her aching lungs once more. She started crying, a pitiful wailing that filled the room. Her hair was soaked from perspiration, her face ashen and full of terror.

"Maria, Maria," Carlos said calmly, almost as if scolding a young child. "Why oh why are you putting yourself through all this?" He hunched down beside her and gently brushed a lock of hair behind her right ear. "The choice is yours, of course. But if you continue to lie to us, you must know this will not end well for you."

She emitted a low, gut-wrenching groan and said something that was inaudible amidst the sobbing. Carlos stood up again and stepped away with his arms folded in front of him.

"Please, Maria, you know it doesn't *have* to be this way. On the contrary, if you will just admit that you have spoken to the police, I promise there will be no more pain. We simply need to know *who* you have spoken to. That is all. A name. Just one name. That is the quick way to end all of this...this unpleasantness."

He fell silent for a moment as the young woman continued sobbing, muttering something beneath her breath.

"But if, however, you continue to lie, to deny what we both already know, I assure you, Maria, it will be slow and more painful than you can possibly imagine. I am truly pained to see you like this. Believe me, I take no pleasure in it. But you know my brother, Ernesto here." He gestured to the older man standing behind her who now had a broad grin on his face. "You *know* how much he enjoys inflicting pain."

"I...I...Please, Carlos. I know I made a mistake," the

young woman sobbed, pleading for mercy with swollen, tear-filled eyes. "But I had no choice, I swear. You've got to believe me. I'm so sorry. So sorry."

"Shhh, Maria. Shhh, that's better. Now, *who* exactly did you speak to?"

"I...I don't know."

"A name, Maria? Think for a moment. What was the detective's name?"

"Shoemaker," she groaned. "I think his name was Shoemaker."

Carlos nodded to himself, a look of satisfaction on his face. He knew this particular detective's name quite well and was not in the least bit surprised that it had been him. So, at last she had admitted it, he mused, had finally told him what he already suspected. But he had really only just wanted to hear her say it. He needed her to admit it to his face.

"Please, Carlos, I have told you the truth. If you let me go, I will do anything you say."

"Shhh, I know," he whispered with a rueful smile. "You are a good girl, Maria."

The young woman caught a look in his cold eyes that sent a shiver down her spine. "Please, Carlos. Please, I beg you."

Carlos ignored her, looked calmly toward his brother standing behind her, and blinked slowly. That was all he had to do. Ernesto knew what was expected and immediately slipped the bag back over her head, clutching it about her throat as before, forcing her to squeal as she lurched violently from side to side. But in the end, it was no use. She was incapacitated in the chair and could do nothing but gasp and groan in agony as her throat burned and her lungs felt like they would explode from the lack of oxygen.

Finally, after three or four long minutes, she stopped struggling and her head dropped lifelessly to her breast. Ernesto left the bag over her and stepped back to brush the dust from his trousers. The basement was silent now, except for a thin trickle of urine that seeped from beneath her buttocks and dripped to the concrete floor below. It was over. Carlos Suarez had kept his word. There was no more pain. In some respects, Maria had actually been lucky. In comparison to what they were capable of doing to her, it really had been the quick way.

Detective Bradley Shoemaker sat alone at the counter of an all-night diner on Sunrise Boulevard, staring thoughtfully into his half-empty coffee cup with the Metro section of the *Sun Sentinel* open in front of him. It was late and the place was deserted except for him and a middle-aged woman polishing her nails behind the counter. Shoemaker was tired, miles away, lost in his own thoughts. He had just finished a slice of fruit pie and was now preparing to head home alone after another long, exhausting shift.

He had worked two homicides in Miami that afternoon. In an electrical shop in North Beach, a guy had shot a co-worker simply because he changed the radio station, and elsewhere in Hialeah, an elderly man didn't like the fact that his neighbor's dog had crapped on his lawn. *Both deaths could probably have been avoided if the perpetrators didn't have such easy access to firearms*, Shoemaker mused thoughtfully. But then, the Constitution *did* state that everyone had the right to bear arms. He wondered if the founding fathers ever imagined the long-term consequences of that declaration. If they had ever envisaged a day when an innocent guy could be shot three times in the chest because his wife's Chihuahua took a dump on their neighbor's grass.

"Ready for a refill, hon?" asked the woman behind the counter. She looked bored, chewing gum as she leaned on the polished formica top and stared directly at him.

"Naw, thanks, I'm good," he replied, glancing up from his coffee with a polite smile.

Shoemaker estimated she wasn't much older than thirty-five. She was a good-looking woman, but he noticed her face was lined and wrinkled way beyond its years. He wondered for a moment if this was from over exposure to the sun, which was not uncommon in South Florida, or due to a more sinister reason. Heavy drinking perhaps, or maybe just the telltale signs of a life of stress and hardship? He was no stranger to stress, had known his fair share during a lifelong career in law enforcement.

Shoemaker was an African American in his late forties who had served on the Miami Dade police force for almost twenty-three years now, fifteen of those as a lieutenant in homicide. Tall and slim, with broad shoulders and a strong jaw, he saw the evil people did firsthand on a daily basis and lived with those gruesome memories every day of his life. While most folks went about their day in a reasonably safe cocoon, he knew from bitter experience the evil and brutality some of them were capable of.

"Quiet night, huh?" the waitress suddenly said, breaking his thoughts, still looking at him in the hope of striking up a conversation to alleviate the boredom.

"Pretty quiet in here, I see," he replied.

"Guess everyone's home with their family for the Fourth of July," she continued. "Only volunteered to come in myself 'cause I'm on my own. Ain't got no family, you see. Got two cats, though, but I guess they don't really count."

"Uh huh." Shoemaker nodded.

"What did you think of those fireworks?"

"Not bad," he replied, not really wanting to engage, but having little choice, as she was so persistent.

"You on your own too?" she asked.

"Yep," he said, shrugging his shoulders and nodding. "I guess so."

"I'm off at midnight if you feel like getting a drink."

"Thanks, but maybe some other time," he replied with another polite smile. "Afraid I've got an early start in the morning."

"Oh yeah? What line of work you in?"

"I'm a cop," he replied. "Miami Metro."

Standing up, he reached into his pocket to pay the check. It was going to be a long day tomorrow, so he decided that now was as good a time as any to head home and get some sleep.

CHAPTER THREE

THE APHRODITE

Conor breathed in the warm salt air as they stepped from Bob's Mercedes in the parking lot beside the marina. It was barely nine-thirty in the morning, yet the sun was already beating mercilessly down. He stared out across the rows of gleaming white yachts and speedboats, letting the sea breeze cool his face. The light was intense, so much so that without his sunglasses, he would surely be blind. But this was heaven to him. The kind of environment where he felt most at home. The smell of the ocean in his nostrils, the sounds of sea birds gliding above the marina. Gulls, terns, and skimmers all hovering low above the fishing boats, vying noisily for air space as they greedily watched for any discarded scraps or crumbs.

This was Conor's world where, for the moment at least, the heartbreak of his past was a faded memory. This was where he wanted to be, not stuck behind a desk or chained to a factory bench. The outdoor life was his domain, where he needed to be if he was ever to find peace or any kind of happiness again. His thoughts drifted back for a moment, but he quickly dismissed the sadness and concentrated once again on the sounds and smells of the marina around him. He had really missed it badly this past year. After all, he realized, the ocean was where he felt most alive.

As Bob led him down one of the numerous wooden piers toward the yacht, he explained enthusiastically how he had acquired her as a re-possession through a contact of Hector Suarez at the bank. How, if all went well, he might actually have the opportunity to acquire another so he could expand the business.

Conor felt a surge of excitement he hadn't experienced for a while. The sounds and smells of the sea and the marina vitalized him. The squawks of the gulls, the *tink-tink-tink* of loose metal ties banging against swaying masts. He knew by the rattle of a distant diesel engine sputtering across the harbor that it needed a service. He could tell by the rhythm alone how its plugs were worn and in need of replacement. The tide was coming in. He felt the wind speed and direction on his face as they walked and knew instinctively what kind of sailing conditions could be expected.

"So, here she is," Bob said, breaking his thoughts as he stopped and began pointing toward his new acquisition. "She's called the *Aphrodite*."

Conor remained silent for the longest time.

"Well, what do you think of her? Was I right or not? Is she or is she not a real beauty?"

The *Aphrodite* was a forty-five foot long ocean going cat-amaran. She had two magnificent white hulls that stood side-by-side in the water with a flat deck and large cabin joining them together. She was sloop-rigged, which referred to her single mast, as opposed to a ketch that had two. Onboard, she boasted a two hundred horsepower diesel engine, an echo sounder, and a wind generator, as well as a row of solar panels fixed just above her main cabin. And at her stern was a low, wooden bathing deck, above which hung a large rubber dinghy with a small outboard engine.

Conor was rendered speechless by her beauty. So much so that he said nothing, just hopped onboard and set about inspecting every inch of her. As Bob looked on in silent expectation, Conor felt the pride and excitement of a father whose wife had just given birth. The new arrival would be his to guide and care for. A special bond.

But he also experienced a little trepidation, inspecting every joint and seal like a midwife examining the newborn baby, checking there was nothing wrong, no unforeseen birth defects. Bob needed a sign from Conor to confirm that everything was okay, so he held his breath when the young Irishman suddenly swung himself down from the cabin roof into the cockpit. He must have thought Conor was about to speak, as he raised his eyebrows in anticipation, but Conor said nothing, did not even make eye contact. Instead, he just slid back the cabin door and disappeared inside.

The temperature within the main cabin was a lot cooler. With tinted glass windows reducing the intensity of the light, he was able to slip off his sunglasses and hook them onto his t-shirt. Before him was a polished mahogany table surround-ed by white leather seating, and to his right, a navigation desk complete with VHF radio. Below him, the dark blue car-pet felt luxuriously plush beneath his thin canvas shoes. He took a few steps forward and turned left to view a set of steps leading down to the port hull. On this side of the *Aph-rodite* lay a good-sized galley, a small shower room, and two double berths. The steps to his right led down to her star-board hull. Again, another two double berths with lots of storage space, and an even larger shower room.

When Conor eventually reappeared on deck, he looked directly at his new employer and beamed. "She's amazing, Bob. Truly. A rare beauty. Everything you said she was and more."

"I told you!" the older man shouted with jubilation. "I may not know a hell of a lot about boats, but heck, I *do* know a lady when I see one."

"Well you've got yourself a grand one here," Conor told him.

Bob smiled with deep satisfaction, clapped his hands, and started rubbing them together with excitement. He was clearly delighted with the verdict. "Heck, I think that calls for a cold drink."

They sat either side of the table in the main cabin, drink-ing longnecks from a small picnic cooler they had brought onboard. They had filled the galley's fridge freezer with its contents—beer, bottles of wine, rum, sodas, steaks, and packs of processed meat. Bob had also brought a canvas hold-all, from which he filled the overhead cabinets with packets of pasta and rice, tins of beans, and soup. Conor checked the oil and started the diesel engine to let it idle for a half hour or so as they spoke.

He told Bob the *Aphrodite* only needed a light engine overhaul and also a bit of general service and maintenance. But apart from that, and a few minor repair jobs like replacing a section of the fuel line, she was in excellent condition. He estimated the work would only take a couple of days at most, but in the meantime, said she was still perfectly seaworthy.

"Well, while I was waiting for you to arrive, I had Scott set up a new website for the charters, as well as advertising in the local papers and radio," Bob told him when he was finished. "Toni has designed a nice little flyer, which I'm planning to put in every hotel and motel from here to Naples."

He produced a leaflet from his pocket and placed it on the table in front of them. The front was a full color photograph of the *Aphrodite,* which had been Photoshoped to give the impression it was out at sea. The main heading read, *Luxury Catamaran—day trips, overnights and full week charters available*.

"The website and marketing, accounts, orders...all of that will be taken care of on my end," Bob said. "Your job, Conor, is simply to keep this beauty maintained and ready to set sail at a moment's notice." He took another sip of beer. "As the orders start coming in, you will have to meet and greet the customers. You know, give them some of the old 'Irish Blarney.' That sort of thing. Take them out, show them a good time, and hopefully, they'll come back again, or at the very least, recommend us to their friends and associates."

"That's fine," Conor said. "Not a bother."

"Of course, I don't want to tell you your business," Bob continued. "But heck, I'd imagine most are just looking for a smooth night's sailing and maybe a day's sightseeing and shopping ashore."

Conor nodded in agreement. "Don't worry, Bob. I've taken day-trippers out before. I'll make sure they go home happy."

Bob sat back with a satisfied smile and sipped at his beer, looking extremely pleased. "She is a beauty though, isn't she?"

"One of the best," agreed Conor. "I'm really looking forward to taking her out. But just one thing."

"Huh?"

"What made you call her the *Aphrodite*?"

Bob smiled with great enthusiasm, obviously delighted for the opportunity to explain why he had chosen the name. "Simple fact is, I've always been fascinated with Greek mythology," he said. "So when I saw this beauty, I kind of knew what to call her right away. You know anything about Greek mythology?"

"Can't say as I do," replied Conor.

"Well, back in the day, Aphrodite was the daughter of Zeus and Dione. She was the most beautiful woman anyone had ever laid eyes on. But when Zeus saw how the other gods were fighting over her, he got fed up and married her off to an ugly, deformed guy called Hephaestus. But that didn't stop her. No sir." He smirked, winking knowingly. "Heck, I think she was a bit of a party girl. Know what I mean? Took herself lots of lovers."

Bob was about to elaborate further when his phone suddenly rang. He greeted a man named Hector, who Conor assumed was the Cuban business associate he had talked about the previous night. He didn't speak for two or three minutes, just listened, during which time Conor got the distinct impression he was being told off, or at the very least was getting bad news. After a few minutes, Bob slipped the phone back into his pocket and stood up, looking a bit distant, even troubled.

"Everything okay?" asked Conor.

"Heck! I'm really sorry to have to do this to you. Really sorry. But I've got to go to an urgent meeting down in Coral Gables."

"But I thought we were going out on the first sea trial together," Conor said with surprise.

"We were, we were, but I've got to take this meeting or it will set me right back. Can't be avoided, I'm afraid." Then, after a few seconds, he said, "You will be okay on your own, won't you?"

"Aye, of course, that's not a problem," Conor replied, trying not to show his disappointment too much. He had really been looking forward to taking Bob out, to showing him what he and the *Aphrodite* could do. "I'll be fine on my own. I'll do a few more checks, then maybe take her out a couple of miles beyond the point to see how she handles. Probably won't get back until late afternoon, though."

"Do you want me to come back about six?" Bob asked. "Or hey, if you like, I could get Eva to swing by."

"No thanks, Bob, there's no need. I'll be grand. I'll just get a taxi back to the house when I'm done."

"Fine," said the older man. "I'm really sorry, but that's what happens when you have your fingers in so many pots."

"Not to worry." Conor shrugged. "I understand."

"So, look, I'll see you back at the house this evening then. You can give me a full report on how you get on." He slid open the door and stepped out into the cockpit. Taking careful hold of the handrail, he stepped awkwardly down on-to the wooden dock as Conor came out to see him off from the stern.

"Oh, by the way," he said as an afterthought. "Don't tire yourself out *too* much. We're planning to go out celebrating tonight. Remember? Hector has invited us all to the opening of his new club in Boca Raton."

"Oh aye. That's right. I'll take it easy so," replied Conor.

Bob began walking away, but stopped after a few feet, turned, and took a step back toward the stern. It seemed to Conor as if he had just remembered to say something. Something clearly too discreet to shout out loud. Intrigued, Conor leaned forward on one knee with a look of curiosity on his face.

"Everything alright?"

"Er, this is a bit awkward," Bob said quietly. "But heck, it needs to be said." He paused for a second. "Look, I know my Eva can be a bit...how do I put it? Well, damn it, she likes to tease a bit. You know, flirt?"

Conor kept his mouth shut and tried not to express any emotion.

"But she doesn't mean anything by it. It's just her way, you understand?"

"Bob, you don't have to—"

"No, no," the older man interrupted, waving a hand. "Look, I really don't want you to feel uncomfortable in any way. You and I have a good relationship and it's important you don't feel uncomfortable. But, you see, she's just, heck, I don't know. I guess she just gets bored. I guess she's just Eva being Eva."

Before Conor could respond, Bob turned around and was gone, heading off back down the dock toward the parking lot. Conor took a deep breath, whistling awkwardly to himself as he watched him go. After a moment's contemplation, he got back to the business at hand, stepped up onto the roof of the cabin, and headed forward to check the jib and anchor. He mulled over what Bob had said as he commenced the usual checks in preparation for the *Aphrodite's* first sea trial.

As he had decided the previous night watching the fire-works, he was just an employee. And if he was to remain in his job, which was, after all, so important to him, the last thing he could afford to do was get involved in any of Bob's personal shit. If he *was* to succeed in creating a new life, he had to distance himself from Eva's flirting and any of Bob's other dealings, to concentrate solely on his own work. To do this, he realized he would have to get the hell out of that pool house and move onboard the *Aphrodite* as soon as possible.

About fifteen minutes later, as he swung himself down into the cockpit to go below, Conor thought he spotted Bob still in the parking lot by the entrance. It struck him as odd because the older man had said he was in a hurry and should have been long gone by then. But since it was too far to be certain, he grabbed a set of binoculars from their shelf by the wheel and stood up on the roof of the cabin for a better view. Sure enough, as he brought the lens into focus, Conor got a clear sight of Bob talking to a small, red-haired man in a brightly-colored Hawaiian shirt. Embroiled in conversation, they were standing by a dark green vehicle that resembled an old World War II Jeep. He saw the red-haired man take a small manila envelope from Bob before they shook hands and parted. Conor lowered the binoculars and shrugged to himself. Bob was a busy man, he mused, with so many contacts and deals going on at the same time, it was hard to keep track. He just shrugged again, thought nothing more of it, and returned to work.

While on deck shortly after, preparing to finally get underway, he noticed a young dark-skinned boy standing on the pier beside the *Aphrodite*, watching his every move with intense curiosity. He couldn't have been more than eight or nine years old, his short black hair shaved at the sides, dark brown eyes full of wonderment and curiosity.

Conor smiled down and he smiled back politely, but they didn't speak. He noticed when he went forward to unhook the cable joining the catamaran to the electricity box on the dock, the boy walked along parallel so he wouldn't miss a thing. Eventually, after a few minutes of this, Conor stopped what he was doing, looked down, and said, "Hi there. How's it goin'?"

There was no response. The youngster looked, on but still said nothing. So Conor just smiled to himself and began whistling as he bent down to close an open hatch.

"Are you a pirate?" the boy suddenly asked.

Laughing, Conor turned around. "Now why would you ask that? Do I look like one?"

The boy shrugged nonchalantly and said nothing.

"You *do* know that pirates are not the good guys," Conor told him with a mock serious expression. "They attack ships out at sea and make their prisoners walk the plank."

"Yes, but I still like them," replied the boy.

So Conor changed tack, telling him that when he was older he could be a good pirate. The boy seemed to like that idea and warmed to Conor a bit more. He began to open up to him, becoming more talkative as the conversation progressed and they got to know each other. They chatted for a while about pirates, boats, and school, before a young Latina woman suddenly came hurrying down the dock looking extremely flustered.

"Emilio," she chastised him. "I thought I told you to wait in the office?"

The young boy just looked at her innocently, saying nothing.

"I'm so sorry. I hope he wasn't bothering you," she said to Conor.

"He was no bother at all," he replied. "We were just talking about pirates and stuff."

"I'm Rita Morales. I manage the marina." The young woman reached up to shake Conor's hand as he leaned over the rail. "And this is my son, Emilio, who, as you can see, doesn't always do as he's told."

After Conor introduced himself and assured her again that the boy had been no trouble, she seemed to relax. He studied her as they spoke, noticing that Emilio had his mother's good looks. She was in her early thirties, olive-skinned with gorgeous brown eyes and black hair tied back in a ponytail. She wore a simple gold chain with a tiny crucifix around her neck and small gold earrings. There was a pencil behind her ear, and he also noticed she was not wearing a wedding ring.

"You talk funny," Emilio said to him, interrupting them at one point.

Conor laughed. "That's because I'm from a country called Ireland."

"Ireland?" he repeated to make sure he said it correctly.

"It's an island," Conor told him, pointing out to sea. "That way. About four-thousand miles in that direction."

"Is it true that it rains a lot of the time there?" Rita asked with a genuinely serious look on her face.

He smiled and said, "Yeah, most of the time. That's why everything's so green."

"I like your boat," Emilio exclaimed enthusiastically. "Does it go fast?"

"Oh sure," he told him. "It's probably the fastest boat *you've* ever been on."

"He's never been on a boat before," Rita said, smiling.

"You're kidding?" Looking mystified, Conor waved a hand at the scores of yachts and motor cruisers scattered about them in the marina. "How come he's never been on a boat?"

"Because I just work here," she replied. "Most owners don't like people going near their boats when they're not around."

"Well," he said, looking very seriously toward the boy. "If it's alright with your mom, you can jump up here and take a look for yourself. See if you have the sea legs to make a good pirate."

"Are you sure?" Rita asked with a hint of surprise.

"Sure I'm sure. It's really no problem. Come onboard yourself for a few minutes and we can sit inside out of the sun. Maybe have a cold drink."

Rita was visibly taken aback by his hospitality and said, "We wouldn't want to impose." But on seeing Emilio's excitement, she agreed and stepped up, holding on tightly to her son as she did. Conor slid open the door for them and she followed him inside, admiring the cabin's décor as she did so.

They spent the next half hour just sitting there, chatting about everything and anything, while Emilio ran about the cabin playfully. First he skipped down the low steps into the starboard hull, ran up and down the narrow hall for a while, then sprinted back up and headed excitedly for the steps leading down into the portside hull. Rita was apologetic, but Conor just laughed, saying it was nice to see him enjoying himself so much.

"So, how do you like South Florida?" she asked after he told her about his arrival and recent employment.

"It's grand so far," he replied. "Very hot, though. Not what I'm used to at all."

"Oh I wouldn't worry about the heat. The longer you're here, you'll find that your blood thins out," she assured him knowingly. "Everyone's the same when they first come here. But you eventually adapt to the climate."

"I hope so, 'cause I really need to make this job work," he said. "My finances are pretty low and I kind of need to start earning a steady pay check as soon as possible."

"Where are you staying?"

"In my boss's pool house for a couple of days. It's not ideal, though. When things are up and running, I'm planning to move my gear onboard and stay here."

"So, what's he like?"

"Who?'"

"The guy who owns the boat?" she asked. "I only met him once when they brought it in a few weeks ago. He signed the papers and paid the marina fees in the office. We didn't talk much, but he seemed okay."

"Bob? Yeah, I like him. I think he's sound."

"What does that mean?"

"Sound?" Conor realized it was not an expression she was familiar with and smiled. "Oh, it just means, like, good. You know? Okay."

"Never heard that one before," she laughed. Then, after a few seconds, said, "So, what about family back in Ireland?"

"I'm afraid there's no one left," he told her. "My father died when I was a lad, my mother about seven years ago. I have a sister, Aishling, who lives in Australia, though. She's married with two girls. What about you? Have you got family here?"

"Family? More like an army."

"Really?"

"You see, my parents came to South Florida from Cuba. At the last count, I guess there were about a hundred of us." She laughed. "Seriously, though, we are talking about a big,

big family, with brothers and sisters and aunts and uncles and even more cousins than I can keep track of. But I have to admit, it's very nice to have them. We are all very close and spend Sundays and holidays together."

"That does sound nice," he agreed.

They looked at each other and smiled without speaking, a short, comfortable pause. There was something about her that Conor found very appealing. There was a glint in her eyes, a smile that was genuinely friendly and warm.

"So, how long have you been working here at the marina?" he asked.

"Oh about four years now," she replied with a shrug. "I do the accounts, run the supply store, and man the small coffee shop by the office."

"Sounds like you're kept busy."

"Oh sure, but I like it that way. One day I might be dressed up giving the guided tour to rich couples thinking of mooring here, the next I could be wearing wellington boots, knee-deep in S-H-I-T, trying to unblock the toilets." She smiled warmly. "But hey, it does keep the job interesting."

Conor let Emilio play with the VHF radio, which kept him amused, while he made coffee and spoke a little more with Rita. He knew he liked her from the start. Not just her good looks and slim, gorgeous figure, but she was very open and didn't seem to hold back or put on airs or graces. He liked that about her. She was funny and down-to-earth, and she made him laugh, which he realized, with a hint of sadness, was something he hadn't done for quite a while.

After he told her about his business closing in Ireland, she proceeded to tell him how Emilio's father had left shortly after he was born. She said it was because he didn't want the commitment and decided to pursue his "musical career" on the other side of the continent. They were not married and, against her family's protestations, she never went after him for maintenance. She decided that not being in their lives was *his* loss, and that they didn't need him. She would provide everything her son would ever want.

"My sister usually looks after him when I work," she said. "But she had to go to a friend's wedding in Georgia today. She should be back tomorrow, though."

"You live alone with Emilio?"

"Yes, we have a small apartment in Fort Lauderdale. It

could be bigger, of course, but the neighborhood is okay and the location is perfect for us. It's close to his school and only a few minutes' drive to my sister's and my parents'. So we aren't *really* alone. They are always close by if we need them."

As they said their goodbyes, Rita smiled and said, "Hey, Conor, since you're going to be around, and since you don't know too many people here, maybe you would like to meet up for another coffee sometime?"

"Really?" Conor found himself hesitating like an awkward teenager. He had enjoyed her company and, truth be told, had thought of asking her out. But he was surprised that she was the one taking the initiative. He told himself he would have eventually gotten around to doing it, then slowly acknowledged that he probably wouldn't have. But then, realizing she was still waiting for a response, he felt stupid for the hesitation. She had just caught him off guard, thrown him a little. "I mean, yeah. Sure, Rita, I'd love that."

Rita smiled, putting him at ease. He was relieved she wasn't offended by his hesitant reaction and wondered for a second if she liked the fact that there was a little bit of shyness about him, that he hadn't come across as an overbearing, over-confident ladies' man.

Reaching into her pocket, she took out a small marina business card and handed it to him. "Look, here's my number at work, and also my cell. Give me a call sometime when you're free."

"For sure," he said with a warm, enthusiastic grin. "Definitely."

"Maybe, if you like, we could even have lunch. There's a little place near the marina that serves coffee and sandwiches. It's a nice spot to sit outside and watch the world go by."

"That sounds grand," he replied. "I'll give you a call in the next day or so."

"Anytime you want." She smiled as she took Emilio by the hand and stepped off the *Aphrodite*. "I'm free most lunch times. Just call me first, though."

"Bye, Emilio," he said after them.

"Goodbye Conor. Thank you for letting me play on your boat."

As Rita and Emilio walked away hand-in-hand back down the dock toward the marina office, Conor lit a cigarette on deck and watched them go. He suddenly found himself smiling. He was beginning to feel optimistic again for the first time in God knew how long. And why not, he mused? He had found a job he loved and was now living here in paradise. Spending time with Rita would definitely be good for him, he thought. He felt he would like to get to know her a bit better. The boy too. But the realization of how he felt came as a bit of a surprise. True, he was doing exactly what he set out to when he answered Bob's advert. He was beginning again, getting back in the water and venturing out into the world of the living. But the thing of it was, the more time he spent here in these beautiful surroundings, the more he actually wanted to make it all work. Perhaps it was a natural process. Perhaps it had just taken time. Either way, he decided, he now felt he was ready. And regardless of anything else, things *were* looking far better than he could have hoped.

As he moved about the catamaran's deck, untying the mooring lines, making ready to cast off for the first time, he genuinely felt his luck was changing for the better. He pushed the *Aphrodite's* throttle forward and motored slowly away from the berth. Swinging her wheel to port, he took a direct course toward the mouth of the harbor, smiling to himself, face to the wind, telling himself that after such a long time on land, it was a truly glorious day to be setting sail once more.

CHAPTER FOUR

LA AZTECA

The music was deafening, the light show spectacular. The walls, ceiling, and floors of the nightclub shook, vibrating around them with the loud, rhythmic beat. Conor wasn't familiar with Latin American music, but from what he heard, he had to admit he liked it. The powerful beat was addictive, hypnotizing. The pulsating floor was packed to capacity with a gyrating mass of good-looking Latino men and women, their dance moves leaving little to the imagination. Ultraviolet strobes flashed in the darkness above them, a dazzling laser show in time with the beat, giving the illusion they were moving as one in slow motion. And then the smoke machines kicked in at ground level and their lower bodies became lost in a swirling cloud of luminous white gas.

La Azteca was fashioned after a Meso American temple, with square stone pillars full of ornate carvings and plaster wall panels depicting grisly scenes of human sacrifice. The DJ in the booth above the crowd was shirtless, jumping up and down like a man possessed, in a large Aztec headdress of green Quetzal and pink flamingo feathers.

Conor sat with Bob and Eva at a table in the VIP booth on the balcony. He had been introduced to Señor Hector Suarez, Bob's business associate, who sat at the head of the table with a glass of brandy and a large Cuban cigar. Hector was friendly toward him, welcoming him and insisting that all drinks were on the house. He was older than Conor had expected, maybe in his early sixties, but dressed in tight white trousers and a bright pink and green floral shirt that was open halfway down his chest. His dyed black hair was thinning on top, and he tried to hide it with a comb-over that didn't quite work. He wore a large gold medallion that bounced on his graying chest hairs, and so many gold rings they looked like knuckle dusters on his stubby, nicotine-stained fingers.

"So how do you like my new club?" he shouted across the table in a gruff Cuban accent.

Bob placed his Scotch on the illuminated glass tabletop and leaned forward, shouting, "Hector, it's amazing. Truly amazing."

The Cuban looked to Eva and waved both hands in a sweeping movement, gesturing to the surrounding décor. "Everything is new, Eva. Absolutely everything. It cost a small fortune. The leather seating, the glass dance floor, even the bar has been rebuilt. We had a Mexicana artist design and carve all those stone panels."

Eva was sipping champagne at Bob's side and agreed with Hector that the club had indeed been transformed for the better since he'd taken it over. Conor could see from his reaction that he valued her opinion on the matter. He could also sense, however, there was something not quite right between Hector and Bob. He couldn't exactly put his finger on it, but his new employer seemed on edge and was being overly nice and complimentary to the Cuban all night. Eva sat like a mediator between them, her skintight dress showing a lot of cleavage and barely covering the cheeks of her ass. She was in her own world, her head moving back and forth in time to the beat, her shoulders swaying from side to side as if she was dancing where she sat. He noticed she was also drinking a hell of a lot of champagne.

"Bob tells me you're going to take us down to Nassau," Hector shouted loudly toward Conor, struggling to be heard above the now almost deafening *boom boom* beat. "What do you think of his new boat?"

"She's a fine craft," replied Conor.

"But are you sure it can make the voyage safely down to the Bahamas?"

Bob leaned over and shouted, "Relax, Hector, I told you, she's in perfect sailing condition."

Hector cast an unconvinced glance toward him, then looking back at Conor, saying, "Well, I hope you know what you're doing. I wouldn't want us to sink out there."

Before Conor could reply, however, two extremely tough-looking men approached the table looking very serious and businesslike. The older and heavier-set one stood back with hands folded in front of him, appearing alert and dangerous, with pockmarked skin and a deep scar above his left eye, standing like a bouncer just waiting for a fight to break out around him. The younger of the two, leaned down over the back of the red leather sofa and whispered something into Hector's ear. Hector listened intently as he spoke, nodding his approval every few seconds. When the younger man finished and stood upright, Hector leaned back a little and looked up at him.

"Gracias, Carlito. Very good, hijo. I'll leave it in your hands." He then turned to the table where everyone had been watching with interest, and looking at Bob and Eva, said, "Of course, you remember my son, Carlos, don't you?" He motioned to the other man nearby. "And this is my eldest son, Ernesto."

They both acknowledged Hector's sons with a polite smile, yet Conor couldn't help but notice how neither of the two Cubans smiled back. There was definitely tension there. In fact, he caught a distinct look of disdain as Carlos glanced over at Bob. The Suarez brothers appeared to be very serious guys. Ones you would do well to stay clear of. He had known individuals like that back in Ireland and knew what they were capable of. Hard, dangerous men who were all about respect and reputation, who could be friendly to you one minute, then stick a knife in you the next. The only sure way to handle them, he felt, was to give them a wide berth.

The mood picked back up a little when Carlos and Ernesto left. Hector called for another bottle of champagne and there were a few toasts. The conversation covered everything from the state of Florida's economy to what was happening in baseball. Hector was interested in a big Jai Alai tournament taking place down in Miami that week.

"What's that?" Conor asked to their amazement. "I've never heard of it before."

"Jai Alai? It's a game popular among the local Hispanic population," Hector told him with great enthusiasm. Conor could tell he was a big fan. "The players carry weaved baskets called 'cestas' attached to their arms. And with these, they throw and catch a hard, rubber pelota against a wall."

"It's a very quick game," Bob added. "Heck, some say the fastest in the world."

"Sounds interesting," Conor remarked. "I wouldn't mind going to see one sometime."

"Really? Then I will organize it for you," Hector insisted eagerly. "You will be my guest."

"Thanks. I'll look forward to that."

"Tell me," said the Cuban. "Has Bob here shown you his famous gun collection yet?"

"No, he hasn't," Conor replied. "I didn't even know he had one. But he did say he is going to take me out hunting next week."

"Well, if I were you, I would also get him to show you the gun cabinet in his office," he advised, taking a long drag from his cigar before blowing the smoke low across the tabletop. "He has a very fine collection."

They both looked to Bob, who simply shrugged off the compliment, saying, "Heck, let's just say it's a work in progress. I do have a small collection of modern weapons, alright, but also some very special antique pieces, which I am in the process of adding to."

"Oh, like what?" Conor asked with genuine interest.

"Let's see, well, I have a pair of dueling pistols from the seventeenth century. And also a Brown Bess from the War of Independence." Then, on seeing the puzzled look on his face, he said, "That's a flint lock musket. British. Extremely rare to find one in such good condition."

"They can also be quite valuable, no?" said the Cuban.

"That's true. But then, you know me, Hector. Heck, the only hobbies worth pursuing are the ones that make money."

Bored with the conversation when the two men started talking business again, Eva nudged Conor in the ribs and asked him to dance with her.

She clung a little too close to Conor as they moved together among the sea of gyrating, writhing bodies, her eyes never leaving his for a second. Her hips moved against him invitingly, and every now and then her right leg came up and hooked itself around his lower back. She was drunk now and very, very horny, and it took almost every ounce of energy he possessed to discretely resist her advances without actually throwing her to the floor.

At one point, she put her lips to his ear and whispered something, but he couldn't make it out above the deafening music. Then she ran her tongue down his cheek and stopped just short of his lips. He nudged her away a couple of times, glancing up, hoping Bob was not watching. But she just laughed at his discomfort and pulled herself back even closer.

She was at it again. He was in no doubt she was not simply flirting, as Bob had advised him that morning. And as her left hand slowly slid down his stomach into his trousers, he knew Eva was not just playing either. She grabbed hold of him and started squeezing.

Flinching, Conor pulled back so unexpectedly that she hurt her wrist as it came out of his trousers. He'd had enough. Grabbing her by the shoulders, he turned her away from him and frog marched her back to the edge of the dance floor. She tried to resist, but he was too strong and in no mood for games. In protest, every now and then, she would stop and wiggle her ass so he would bump into it. Each time he did, she emitted a little groan of pleasure. But he ignored her protestations and kept pushing until they were off the floor.

He guided her up the winding staircase like a scolded child, back toward the VIP table to where her husband was waiting. She stopped fighting him just as they reached the top of the steps and came into Bob and Hector's sight. Both men stood to allow her to sit down between them again and Bob raised his glass to motion Conor back to his seat too. But he'd had enough for the time being and told them he needed to use the bathroom. As he walked away, he glanced back to see Eva sitting between them with arms folded, glaring angrily in his direction. The two men were ignoring her, still discussing business, and by the looks of it, not in agreement.

Conor lit a cigarette in the alley behind La Azteca and inhaled a lung full of smoke before blowing it skywards into the black, starless night. Sighing, he leaned his back against the wall of the club and let his head rest upon its brickwork. He could still hear the low *thump, thump* of music from within, could feel the entire building vibrating behind him.

The maze of alleyways behind the club was noisy and chaotic with various groups of Latino men and women laughing loudly and joking amongst themselves. He watched a young black-haired woman being sick behind a nearby dumpster, while her concerned girlfriends held her hair back from the vomit. A couple appeared to be having sex against a wall in one of the dark recesses at the opposite end of the alley, and it was at this he was looking when a hand slapped down hard on his shoulder. He turned around in surprise to find three young stocky Latinos standing menacingly before him.

"Hey, puta!" snarled the one in the middle. "What the fuck did you say to my old lady back there?"

Taken aback, Conor raised his eyebrows in puzzlement, looking from one to the other for an explanation. The guy talking to him was small and heavy-set, bald with a spider tattoo on the side of his head. He looked tough, and was definitely high, drugged-up, and ready to explode.

"Yeah, man, I'm talking to you," he continued angrily.

"Me?" Conor said. "You've got the wrong guy, friend. I didn't say anything to anybody."

"Are you calling my man a liar?" snapped the taller Latino to his left. His eyes were red, bulging out of their sockets with rage. He looked like he was on something nasty, and Conor could instinctively tell by the way he was standing that he was getting ready to throw a punch. He was balancing his weight on his back leg with his right fist clenched tight in readiness for the blow.

"No, I'm not," Conor answered, realizing with surety that no matter what he said or did, he was about to be set upon in the next few seconds. He was going to take a beating no matter what. And it wasn't going to be pretty. These weren't the type of guys who would leave you be when you went down. "Look, I'm just saying that I didn't—"

"Shut your fuckin' mouth!" the first man roared in his face. His teeth were yellow and his breath smelled of stale tobacco. "You disrespected my woman, you cock-sucking puta. And now we're gonna break your legs and smash your stupid fuckin' head in."

Conor winced, tensed his body, and prepared for the inevitable. His back was to the wall, so there was no escape.

He quickly decided he would try his best to block the first punch and then go for whoever threw it with everything he had. He wasn't stupid. He knew he didn't stand a chance, but realized he didn't have any other choice. He wasn't a fighter by any stretch of the imagination, but he resolved to at least go down trying.

"Oye!" a familiar gruff voice shouted as the man to the left swung his arm back to smash a fist into Conor's face. Someone standing behind him grabbed the man's raised forearm in mid-swing and violently twisted it downwards before he could react. As the Latino's wrist snapped and his body spun sideways, Conor suddenly saw his friend, Danny McNamara, bring his forehead down into the man's face. It hit with such force that even he winced. The young man's nose shattered and he emitted an agonizing scream as blood began bubbling from both nostrils. He crumpled to the ground at Danny's feet like a sack of potatoes.

Danny moved with such speed and savagery that it took everyone by surprise. Without the slightest pause, he turned on the second young Latino in the middle and slammed the base of his palm up into his exposed throat, sending him sprawling backwards with such force that his feet left the ground and he collapsed choking onto the dirty concrete. As he hunched over and began vomiting, Danny quickly turned his attention to the third man.

"Hey, dude. Hey, hey, tranquillo. I swear I don't want no trouble," the man blurted nervously, stepping back and raising his hands in a gesture of submission.

Danny stopped in mid-stride with a genuine look of disappointment on his face, lowered his fists, and said, "Alright then. But you better get your scumbag friends out of here before I get mad and do some *serious* damage."

Conor watched him closely as he spoke, realizing he hadn't even broken a sweat. From the moment Danny intervened, Conor had not moved one inch, had literally been fixed to the spot, watching in awe as the big man took down his attackers in a matter of seconds. It was as if it all came so naturally to Danny. Second nature. The big man was a friendly guy, but he had a dark side, could switch on the violence with the same ease as flicking on a light.

The standing Latino quickly helped his friend with the broken wrist and nose to his feet, hooked an arm around his waist and led him off down the alley, groaning in agony as they went. The young man with the spider tattoo on his head finished spilling the contents of his stomach into the gutter and hurriedly joined them, hunched over, holding his swollen larynx as he scurried away. None of them looked back. Danny watched to make sure of it.

As soon as the show was over, the crowd of young people who had witnessed the sudden violence got bored and moved away to return to their separate noisy conversations. Danny then turned his attention to Conor as if absolutely nothing out of the ordinary had just happened, a warm, almost childlike smile on his face.

"Well, will ye look who finally decided to get a sun tan!"

He was a big, tough-looking man, broad and muscular with a shaved head and a misshaped nose that looked as if it had been broken more than once. He wore a white Miami Heat basketball vest with a round collar and no sleeves that showed off his huge, sunburned biceps. To those he didn't like, he could be the meanest, violent adversary, but to those he did, he was without doubt one of the most genuine friends you could ever have. Thankfully for Conor, unlike the unfortunate pair of Latinos, he fell into the latter category. For as Danny lifted him off the ground and hugged him tightly, he knew the big man had the power to break his back.

"Aww, it's great to see you, Con. How long's it been?"

"Almost two years," Conor gasped. "And believe me when I tell you, it's *really* great to see you too. Thanks for savin' my bacon. Those lads were about to kick the bejaysus out of me."

"What, that wee scuffle? Sure, that was no big deal." He shrugged as though it had been nothing, released his grip, and took a step back. "So, when did *you* start coming to Mambo dives like this?"

Conor sucked in a mouthful of air as soon as he was free. "I'm here with my new boss and his wife," he said, genuinely pleased to see his former brother-in-law so unexpectedly, and not just because he had saved him from a beating. "They know the guy who owns the place."

Danny gestured his surprise with raised eyebrows. "You mean Hector Suarez? That Cuban motherfucker? Here, man, I don't know what you've gotten yourself into, but you had better watch your arse around that guy."

"He's gay?" Conor asked in amazement.

"No, you Muppet. He's not gay. But he is one of *the* most dangerous operators around these parts. Owns a couple of bars and clubs here in Broward and down in Miami. But they're just a front for what he's really into."

"Huh?"

"Yeah, truth be told, he's got some nasty shit going on that you don't want to know about. And as for those two psycho sons of his... Hey, I don't know if you've met them yet, but let's just say, they're no choirboys either. My advice is to stay well away from them all."

Before Conor could reply or even digest the information, Danny stepped to his left. He swung an arm around a young, good-looking black woman who had been standing with another black couple behind him, shielded from his vision by Danny's bulk. "This is my woman, Shawna."

Shawna was chewing gum and seemed miles away, eyes glazed like someone with a few drinks inside them. But she seemed friendly, and smiled warmly at him. Then Danny introduced his tough-looking friend, Shawna's older brother Anton, and his girlfriend Cassandra. The girls were dressed for a night's clubbing in skimpy miniskirts and belly tops. Both wore lots and lots of jewelry, hooped earrings, and heels so high every step taken without toppling over was an absolute miracle. Anton was shaved bald but had a long ponytail hanging from the back of his head, and wore a short, combed goatee on his chin. Danny made friends no matter where he went. He had always been a popular guy, fun to be around.

"Where are you all off to?" Conor asked when the introductions were done.

"Well, we *were* tryin' to get into this kip," Danny replied. "Supposed to be the hottest new club in town. But it seems we're not good enough for the dump. Apparently, there's no entry unless you're either a Latino motherfucker or pals with the owner."

"Do you want me to see if *I* can get you in?" Conor asked, appreciating that the last remark was a dig at him.

"Naw, man, fuck that shit!" Anton growled. "Say, why don't you blow these enchilada-eaters off and come party with us?"

"Yeah, Con, that's a deadly idea," boomed Danny. "There's a place on the waterfront that's buzzin'. The drinks are on me, and Shawna can probably hook you up with one of her girlfriends."

Shawna nodded enthusiastically.

"Sorry, Danny, I can't," Conor said, shaking his head with regret toward them all. "Some other time, okay? I've got to get back to these guys. For my job, you know. But hey, I promise, I'll definitely call you in the next day or so and you can show me around."

Anton and Cassandra were already heading arm-in-arm away down the alley toward the lights of the waterfront. Danny probably would have stayed longer, but Shawna linked her arm around his and started pulling him after them, giggling as she did so.

"Have a good night," Conor shouted. "And Danny...thanks again for what you did."

"Call me, yeah?" Danny yelled as she dragged him away.

Conor smiled and shook his head, wondering in amazement how such a petite-looking woman could have that strength.

Eva was very quiet in the taxi on the drive home to West Palm Beach later that night. She sat in the back between Conor and Bob, the latter having passed out by now with his head resting against the side window. There was a trickle of saliva running down the glass from the corner of his mouth and he was beginning to snore softly. They had to carry him from the door of the club to a waiting taxi. He was singing all the way, but once inside, went quiet. Eva slid in after him, leaving Conor to climb in beside her. When she gave the driver the address, he raised his eyebrows in appreciation of such an affluent neighborhood, but then put the car into drive and took off without delay.

On the way, Conor tried his best to get a conversation going on more than one occasion, but Eva was still angry with him for not accepting her advances on the dance floor. He was being given the cold shoulder. She had been made to look foolish and was not used to such treatment. She was definitely not used to being turned away by the opposite sex. Especially not by a mere employee like him.

"Good night?" the driver asked after a few minutes,

glancing back through the rearview mirror. "Did you guys see the fireworks the other night?"

"We did," Conor replied, happy to break the stony silence in the back seat. "They were pretty good, weren't they?"

"Yes sir, they were." Then, after a short pause, he said, "Hey, man. You wouldn't be from the UK, would you?"

"Ireland," Conor replied. "You know it?"

"Know it? Sure, I know it. You've got U2 and Colin Farrell, right? And I believe it also rains a lot."

"Yeah, it does," Conor said, sighing as he turned his gaze out the window toward the rows of tall yellow lights illuminating the dark gray empty streets.

"You guys play soccer there, ain't that right?"

"Yeah, but we call it football," he replied.

The driver turned the taxi onto Ocean Boulevard, getting close to the house. It was still dark out, but there was an orange glow above the water on the horizon to their right. The sun was getting ready to come up.

"Well, we got football here too, you know, but I guess it's more like your rugby than soccer. Yeah, we got the Dolphins in Miami, but their quarterback's having a bad season so they won't be making the play-offs anytime soon." He swung into the driveway and rolled up to the house. He put on the handbrake before turning back to Conor. "You know basketball? We got the Miami Heat here. Ever heard of them? Now there's a team..." But on seeing the inebriated state Bob was in, he stopped in mid-sentence and said, "Hell, man, you need help getting that guy inside?"

Shaking her head, Eva handed him the fare with a generous tip, then she and Conor guided Bob with great difficulty into the house and upstairs to bed. She slipped off his shoes and removed his pants as Conor quickly headed toward the door. He was halfway down the winding marble staircase when she came out of the bedroom and called after him from the landing above.

"Hey, would you like a nightcap?"

He was taken by surprise at her sudden willingness to talk to him, and considered for a moment how best to phrase his response. "Erm, I don't think that would be a such a good idea."

"You don't find me attractive, is that it?"

He leaned on the stair rail, looking down at his feet for a

moment or two, sighed, and said, "Listen, Eva, I think you are a beautiful woman. I really do. And the truth is, I do find you *very* attractive."

"Then why did you push me away?" she asked. "At the club?"

"Because you're married to Bob, that's why. He is my friend."

"Friend? Ha, that's a joke."

"Look, he's given me the chance to start a new life here, Eva. I can't afford to jeopardize that, you know. The last thing I want to do is screw it up." He turned and continued down the stairs heading toward the door.

"Well fuck you, then!" she suddenly shouted angrily as he opened the door to leave. "You think you're starting a new life here, but you're wrong, mister. Take it from me, because I know."

He said nothing, just kept walking.

"Oh, and by the way, Bob is *not* your friend. He's your fucking boss, and don't you forget it. He's only friendly to you while you can be of use to him. So, whatever shit you're leaving behind, don't think coming here is going to be any better. I promise you, it follows you no matter where you go. You hear me? No matter where you go!"

Conor closed the pool house door behind him and stood with his back to it for a few minutes in the darkness. The silence was welcomed, his ears still ringing from the deafening music earlier and the tirade of abuse he had just endured. He took a steadying breath, staring up at the spinning ceiling fan, wondering how the hell he had gotten himself into such a mess. After a while, he dropped the door key onto the table, and without turning on the light, headed to the kitchen for a drink. As soon as he hunched down and opened the fridge, a beam of yellow light stretched across the tiled floor toward the bedroom. It was only then he noticed a pair of women's white satin underwear on the floor in the doorway.

Clutching a soda can, and without closing the fridge, he walked hesitantly toward the bedroom. The lights were off, but the window was open with the curtains blowing inwards on the warm breeze. He stepped pensively toward the bed to where he could just make out a figure beneath the sheets, and then slowly, carefully switched on the small bedside lamp.

"Hi there," Abi said yawning, leaning on a pillow with her head in one hand. She smiled up at him a little awkwardly, showing her braces. It was not a wicked smile, not even a seductive one. It was simply an innocent curl of her lips that was matter-of-fact, as if the situation they were now in was a perfectly normal one.

"Jesus Christ, Abi, what on earth are you doing here?" he exclaimed. Even as he asked, Conor realized it was a stupid question. He knew full well what she was doing there. And what she wanted.

"Do you want me to leave?" she whispered, showing no indication of feeling insulted or rejected. "Is that it, Conor?"

"Christ, Abi. You're *too* young to be here." Even as he said it, though, he saw the look of hurt on her face and felt bad about his choice of words.

"I'm eighteen. I'm old enough to do what I want."

"I know you are," he said apologetically. "But you have to understand that I work for your father. That puts me in a position of trust. I can't take advantage of that. You understand, don't you? It just wouldn't be right."

"But he wouldn't have to know," she interrupted eagerly, sitting up. She was holding the sheet to her breasts, but the corner fell down, revealing a hint of nipple. "I wouldn't say anything."

"Abi, it's not that I don't like you, or that I don't find you attractive. God knows you are a beautiful young woman. It's just that—"

"What?"

"Well, I can't do this."

"Can't or won't?"

He sighed again. "I need you to go, Abi. I'm really, really sorry."

It took all of his willpower to continue, for as he spoke, she slowly swung out of the bed and stepped naked down onto the tiled floor. Her body was without doubt one of the most perfect he had ever seen. How in God's name, he wondered, had he ever gotten himself into such a predicament?

Abi picked up her panties in the doorway and stepped back into them, then took her t-shirt and pulled it on over her head. Barefoot, she casually turned to him before leaving and said, "Hey, Conor, keep this between us, okay?"

"Sure, Abi. I won't say a word. I promise."

"Okay. But, hey, let me know if you ever change your mind. Because I can come back any time you want."

CHAPTER FIVE

A FIRM HANDSHAKE

Conor and Rita had lunch together two days later, sitting beneath the shade of a large yellow awning outside one of the coffee shops facing the marina. They ate freshly baked ham and cheese rolls and shared a side order of fries. They drank coffee with their food, then ordered two iced teas and sat relaxing in the glorious Florida sunshine. He and Rita got to know each other better while watching the world go by, chatting about this and that, telling each other a little about their lives and their upbringings. They both felt at ease in each other's company, the atmosphere very relaxed between them, as if they had known each other far longer than they actually had.

Conor asked after the boy and Rita explained how her sister, Marisol, had returned from Georgia and was taking care of him for the day. She talked a lot about him and he could see he meant everything to her. It was clear to him that she was a good mother. And it didn't bore him to hear the stories. In fact, he enjoyed them. He had taken a liking to Emilio the other day and told Rita he thought he was a "bit of a rascal," reminding him a little of himself when he was that age.

She told him how he absolutely hated school, yet oddly enough, loved his teacher and had lots of friends there. It was a strange contradiction that she couldn't figure out, she said. She also spoke about the struggle lately to get him to eat "proper food."

"I don't know about Ireland, but there is far too much junk food here," she said, sipping her tea and looking beautiful in a lilac-colored dress flowing just above her knees in the warm midday breeze. Her raven black hair was not tied back today, and swayed majestically about her face as she spoke. "It's so very hard for kids these days, you know? Every time they turn on TV, there are pizzas and burgers and all kinds of fast food."

"Well, he seems a pretty healthy lad to me," observed Conor.

"I suppose so, but he *can* be a handful at times."

"Yeah? In what way?"

"Well, for example, last week he put a clothespin on the tail of our neighbor's cat."

"You're kidding?"

"No, I'm not."

"So what happened?" he asked, suppressing a smile.

"What do you think? The poor thing went berserk. I mean, it was screeching up and down the hallway of our apartment building for about fifteen minutes. It took four of us charging around like lunatics before we finally corned it and removed the clothespin."

They both laughed.

"You know, when I was a kid back in Ireland, I got up to all sorts of mischief like that myself. I once mitched off school with my pals and we spent the day fishing in a small stream that ran behind our village. We forgot, of course, that our teacher's house backed onto the stream. She spotted us as soon as she got home that afternoon. Holy Mary and Joseph, we got into so much trouble. The school principal called us into his office the next day and gave it to us good. You would think we had just committed murder. Hell, even the parish priest was called in to tell us that our souls were surely destined for hell if we ever did anything like that again."

"What's mitched?" asked Rita.

"Oh, it means playing hooky. You know? Like when you don't go to school but hang out with your friends for the day."

"Oh, hooky. Well I never did *anything* like that," Rita said, giggling a little bit.

"Never?"

"No."

"So you're asking me to believe you never played hooky?"

"Yes."

"You must have been a right little angel then."

"Yes," she laughed. "That's what I was. Really. A perfect little angel."

They spoke for another fifteen minutes or so, exchanging stories and anecdotes, until eventually she looked at her watch and sat upright with a bit of a shock, announcing that she had to get back to work. Conor agreed it was getting late and said he also had to get back to the *Aphrodite* to finish replacing a section of fuel line. He told her he had to make a few other minor repairs as well before they set off for Nassau the next day.

Rita linked his arm as they strolled slowly back to the marina, past holidaymakers, sailors, and sightseers. She stopped at the entrance gate and said, "Hey, do you like parties?"

"Sure," he replied curiously. "Who doesn't?"

"Well, it's Emilio's birthday today. We're having a small family celebration at my parents' house this evening. You'd be very welcome to come."

"What age is he?" he asked.

"Eight. But, as you saw, he sometimes acts like he's fifty-eight."

"Well, yeah, of course I'd love to come. What time?"

"Say about six, six-thirty. Here, let me give you the address." She wrote it on the back of one of her business cards and handed it to him, leaning up and kissing him gently on the cheek before leaving to go back into the marina office.

Hector Suarez and his sons were finishing lunch in La Azteca, sitting in one of the small circular booths opposite the bar. It was early afternoon and the club was deserted except for two cleaners and a solitary barman. The cleaners were middle-aged, overweight Latina women who were in the process of mopping the floors. They were chatting quietly amongst themselves as they moved parallel to one another across the dance floor, gossiping about a woman they knew who just discovered her husband was cheating on her with a neighbor while she was at work.

The barman was busy restocking the shelves after another busy night. Their two-for-one cocktail deal had been enormously successful. The Mojitos were by far the most popular, so he was ensuring there would be twice as much vodka behind the bar that coming evening. Last night he had to send one of the younger barmen down to the basement when they ran out. The kid had been AWOL for almost fifteen minutes during one of their busiest times, so he was determined not to let anything like that happen again.

Sitting in the booth between his father and brother, Carlos Suarez was busy totting up last night's takings. Armed with a calculator and a box of bar receipts, he was writing down the various totals in a large hardback notebook on the table. Hector sat opposite, drinking thick black coffee and smoking a cigar, while Ernesto sat quietly on the outside, finishing a spicy chorizo sandwich and a plate of fries with little or no regard for table manners. Each time he took a bite of his sandwich, large pieces of sausage and lettuce fell to the table by his elbows to be casually brushed to the floor. As he did so, a deliveryman entered the club and walked up to them with a carbonated order book in one hand and a cheap pen in the other.

"All done, Señor Suarez," he said respectfully. "I've left five boxes in the hall like you asked."

Without speaking, Hector held the cigar between his teeth, took the book, and signed at the bottom. The deliveryman ripped out the perforated top sheet and left it with him before heading back to his van. The moment he opened the big wooden door to leave, however, a deluge of blinding white daylight came flooding in from outside.

"So, I hear the police are looking for Maria Gomez," Hector said as a plume of blue cigar smoke left his mouth, taking on an eerie quality as the sunlight reflected off its swirling mass. As soon as the spring-loaded door closed, however, it once again became invisible in the darkness.

"So, let them look," Ernesto muttered almost unintelligibly as he stuffed the last piece of sandwich into his mouth and began licking his fingers. "They won't find nothing." He picked up his fork and began stabbing at the remaining fries on his plate.

Hector turned to his other son for reassurance and was greatly relieved when Carlos nodded in agreement.

"Ernesto's new pet has taken care of the evidence," Carlos said without emotion.

It was not that Hector didn't trust his eldest son, Ernesto.

It was just that he was not as reliable as Carlos when it came to matters requiring intelligent thought. Everyone had their own strengths and weaknesses in life, he conceded. Ernesto's strength was that he knew no fear, and would stop at absolutely nothing to carry out his orders. His weakness, unfortunately, was that he was not the brightest son a man could have. Or, as a kid in his school had once joked years earlier, "He was a few fillings short of a burrito." That, of course, was before Ernesto put him in the hospital.

"You *do* know that you can't keep that creature tied up in the basement forever," Hector grumbled matter-of-factly. "It's already beginning to stink down there."

Ernesto simply shrugged indifference as he began chewing another mouthful of fries.

"Not a bad night's takings," Carlos exclaimed as he finished his accounting and closed the notebook. He carefully put it and the calculator into the receipt box and replaced its lid.

"How did we do?" asked Hector.

"Six-thousand at the door and almost fifteen at the bar."

"And our little sideline?" Hector asked with raised eyebrows.

"So far, we've unloaded two-hundred and twenty pills," replied Carlos. "At twenty dollars each, that's another four-thousand four-hundred cash."

"Not bad for a weeknight," Hector said with satisfaction as he gulped down the remains of his coffee and sat back with arms folded. Then, noticing an uneasy look on his son's face, said, "What's wrong, Carlito? You look like you have something on your mind?"

"You know what it is," the younger Cuban grunted distastefully. "I don't like the fact that you are still planning to go ahead with this business with Castagna."

"Look, I know you don't like him, hijo, but there *is* a lot of money to be made," Hector replied. "This new venture of ours could almost double our turnover."

"You're right, Papa, I *don't* like him at all. He drinks too much and he talks too much. But what bothers me most is that I just do not trust him. You may be putting everything we have worked for at risk by getting involved with this man."

"Life *is* risk," said Hector. "Listen to me, if you want to live without it, don't get up in the morning, Carlito. Stay in bed."

"But this is different. The risk we are taking with this man far outweighs any gain there might be."

Hector nodded thoughtfully, sat forward, and stubbed his cigar butt into the ashtray. He put his elbows on the table and locked his fingers together. He valued his younger son's opinion, knew that he was the future of the family and must be taken seriously.

"Okay, so what do *you* suggest we do?"

"Me? Well, first of all, I say we rid ourselves of this Bob Castagna. One way or another," Carlos advised quietly. "I suggest we take that boat of his and continue our new business venture without him. We don't need him anymore. He already has a captain in place, that Irish guy, so we simply get him to work for us."

"Your plan does make sense," agreed his father. "But for me, at this particular moment in time, there are too many unknowns. With Castagna in the picture, we still have a pawn we can sacrifice if anything goes wrong. I say we should let him remain the figurehead of the operation for the time being at least. It is, after all, very important that we see how this trial run to Nassau goes first."

His son sighed wearily without reply.

"But then I promise you, Carlos, once we get everything set in place, once we get things moving smoothly, *then* we can do as you say."

"And Castagna?" asked Carlos with raised eyebrows.

Hector shrugged indifference. "I don't care. Once we complete this first run successfully, we won't need him anymore. Then perhaps Ernesto here can deal with the problem."

As Ernesto grinned his approval, the main door creaked open and, once again, an explosion of light came flooding back in. All three men looked over to see who had entered, but were temporarily blinded by the intensity of the glare. They squinted their eyes, but could only just make out two silhouetted-figures approaching. As soon as the heavy door closed behind them, however, the two figures immediately became clearer in the half-light. Both wore suits, the black man in his late forties, the woman much younger, pale-skinned, and with reddish-brown hair.

"Hey, hope we're not disturbing your lunch," Detective Bradley Shoemaker said with a hint of sarcasm that wasn't lost on them. He took his badge from his breast pocket and flashed it for less than a second. "I'm Detective Shoemaker and this is my partner, Detective Childs."

"We *know* who you are," Hector replied with disdain. "You are the one who has been making false allegations about us. Who has been harassing our workers and suppliers for information, spreading lies about our business."

"Hey, I'm just doing my job, guys. All I did was ask a few harmless questions," Shoemaker replied. "If you've got nothing to hide, you shouldn't have a problem answering them."

"What is it you want?"

Shoemaker stood over them at the end of the table while his partner stayed in the shadows a few feet back. He paused for a moment, looking down at the three Cubans with a visible expression of contempt on his face.

"I asked what you are doing here?" Hector repeated irritably.

"What I'm doing here, Hector, is looking for Miss Maria Gomez."

Hector shrugged his shoulders and shook his head, feigning puzzlement at the question.

"She *does* work for you, doesn't she?"

Carlos took over, speaking in a more composed, businesslike manner. "Yes, detective, she does. But we have not seen her in three or four days."

"So which is it?" Shoemaker snapped accusingly. "Three or four?" "I think four," Carlos replied calmly, not taking the bait.

"And you didn't think that strange? You didn't think to report it to anyone?"

"Officer, we are trying to run a business here. If we reported every employee who took a few days off, we would get nothing done."

"We would also be in trouble for wasting police time," spat Hector. Then, after a short pause, he said, "Look, detective, what *exactly* is your interest in this particular employee?"

"Miss Gomez was in contact with Miami Metro a few days ago. She claimed to have information about certain illegal activities being conducted from this club."

"Nonsense!"

"Not according to her."

"Really? Then let her come forward, because this is certainly news to us," Carlos said with a furrowed brow.

"Officer, this is indeed very upsetting to hear," Hector agreed, joining his younger son in a look of shocked indignation. "But rest assured, we will have our staff questioned on the matter, and if we find *any* of them doing anything illegal, I promise to call you straight away."

"You're a model citizen," Shoemaker muttered distastefully. "A real pillar of the community."

"Watch your tone!" Carlos snapped angrily. "My father *is* a pillar of this community. He sits on many local committees and makes many donations to charities in the area. And by the way, he also knows the mayor, as well as your own Captain Mendoza."

"Yeah, I'm sure he does," grunted Shoemaker. "I've no doubt he knows *lots* of important people." Then, after a moment, he said, "So, what about it? Getting back to the elusive Miss Gomez. You're telling us you know nothing of her whereabouts?"

"She is probably just on vacation," Carlos said, sitting back with a confident, insincere smile. "Her paycheck is upstairs in the office, so I'm sure she will be back soon."

But Shoemaker wasn't letting it go that easy. "What about you, Einstein?" he said, turning to Ernesto, whom had remained silent up until now.

Without reply, Ernesto gave him a vicious glare, hatred burning deep in his dark brown eyes. One word from his father or brother and he was ready to jump up and stab the negrito in the jugular with his fork.

"That go for you too?"

Ernesto still said nothing, just cast a glance to Hector for guidance.

"Hey, I'm talking to you. Do you think she will be back soon?"

"Look, detective, we have answered your questions," Hector grunted irritably, interceding before Ernesto could open his mouth and say the wrong thing. "Now if there is nothing else, we have work to do here. We are, after all, trying to run a business. So please, allow us to get back to it."

Shoemaker dropped a contact card into the middle of Ernesto's plate of fries. "If any of you hear from Miss Gomez, I expect you to call me right away," he said.

"Just out of curiosity," Carlos asked after him as he turned to leave. "Exactly what *illegal activities* are you talking about?"

"Oh, let me see. Importing and distributing drugs, for starters, prostitution, counterfeit cigarettes and alcohol, extortion—"

"Detective, I would be *very* careful if I were you!" snapped Hector. "That sounds very much like more malicious slander to me. You were already warned about that. You know, our lawyer could have your badge for such unsubstantiated remarks."

"You had better not go around repeating these kinds of allegations without proof," added Carlos.

"You're right, we don't have any yet," replied Shoemaker. "Conveniently for you, Miss Gomez up and disappeared before she could come down to the station to talk."

"I think you should leave," Hector said angrily. "And you have my word, detective, I *will* be in touch with Captain Mendoza about these outrageous allegations. Believe me, this is not over."

"You are right," Shoemaker muttered back as he followed his partner toward the exit. "As far as I am concerned, this is not over by a long shot."

Back in their car, Shoemaker slammed both palms onto the steering wheel in frustration. "Shit! Did you see their eyes? Those bastards were laughing at us. They killed her. I'm sure of it now."

"You want to try and get a search warrant for the club?" asked Childs.

"On what grounds?" he muttered beneath his breath. "Naw, there's no point. Maria Gomez is probably out in the bay by now, tied to a concrete block."

"Well, wherever she is, Bradley, you shouldn't start blaming yourself," said Childs. "You offered her protection and she refused. What more could you do?"

Shoemaker sighed deeply. "I guess I could have insisted. I could have made her."

"Time out, partner, you need to ease up on yourself. Maybe this Gomez woman just *did* up and leave, like they said. You of all people know what Florida's like. It's a transient state, partner. People come and go all the time."

"Naw, there's more to it than that. I can feel it."

"You know something, Bradley, it's a wonder to me how you have lasted on the force all these years. You let things like this get far too personal."

"This *is* personal," he grunted angrily. "I swear, I will not rest until every one of those Suarez scum are behind bars. Father *and* sons. They may have everyone else in this town fooled, but I know them. I know what they are like. Hypocrites, prancing around like superstars, acting like they're so fucking interested in helping the community when all the while they're the ones sucking the life out of it, dealing their drugs and prostitution as if they're untouchable."

"You *do* realize there's absolutely no proof to any of that," Childs offered quietly. "And the captain *has* told you she'll have your badge if you don't back down."

"I'll get the proof somehow. You just wait and see. And when I do—"

"Christ, you can't let it get to you like this, Bradley. You'll give yourself an ulcer." Detective Childs opened the lid on a cup of cold coffee and took a tentative sip. She grimaced with distaste, put the lid back on, and then dropped the cup out the open passenger side window into the gutter.

"Funny," Shoemaker said thoughtfully. "My wife always said I took things *too* seriously, that I needed to lighten up. She always said I'd give myself an ulcer working such unsociable hours."

"Well, there you go. Maybe she was right."

"In the end, she divorced me because she said I didn't take our marriage seriously *enough*."

"Yeah? So how long were you married?" Childs asked.

Shoemaker turned the key in the ignition and started the engine. "About nineteen years, eight months. Give or take a day. Been divorced two years this September."

"So, what now?" she said. "Wanna grab some lunch?"

"Sure," he replied, pulling the car away from the curb to join the rest of the traffic heading west on Palmetto Park Road.

"You're not going to let this go, are you?" Childs sighed wearily after a moment's silence.

"You know, I was thinking that maybe over lunch we could put a list together. You know, start calling on anyone who does business with the Suarez family. Who knows, maybe someone out there can shed some light on what happened to Maria Gomez."

"If that's what you want to do, I'd say I have about eight or nine names here already," Childs remarked, thumbing through her notebook that contained, among other things, some of the names and addresses of the Suarez family's known associates. "Who do you want to start with first?"

"Don't care. You choose." Then, after a moment's consideration, he said, "Wait, maybe we should start with the ones closest to here. We can work our way down the list from there."

"Let's see," she muttered as she flicked through the pages, scanning the addresses. "There are a couple here in Boca, three in Fort Lauderdale, and then one up in West Palm Beach."

"Palm Beach? Nice. Who's that?"

"Let's see. Oh yeah, here it is. A Mister Bob Castagna. He's a local businessman and a partner of Hector Suarez in a company called Gold Coast Developments. No record. Seems clean enough."

"Can't be *that* clean if he's involved with Hector," Shoemaker grunted.

Childs just shrugged her shoulders without reply.

"Alright then," he said. "So, it looks like we've got a plan. After lunch, we'll start here, work our way down to Fort Lauderdale, and then, if there's enough time, make our way back up to Palm Beach. Who knows, maybe I'll even get home in time to put my feet up and watch the Dolphins game."

Conor told the taxi driver to pull up outside the house on the corner, the one with the multi-colored balloons tied to the front porch. He paid the fare, then walked through the front gate carrying a gift-wrapped box under his arm. On the way over, he had called into a local shopping mall to buy Emilio a pirate costume complete with cutlass and eye-patch. The female shop assistant wrapped it free of charge, assuring him it was a good choice for a little boy who liked pirates.

Rita's parents' house was nice, a well-maintained bungalow set in a large, tree-filled garden. The gravel drive was packed to capacity with the cars of friends and family, which were also parked all the way down both sides of the narrow street. Even before he stepped up onto the porch, he could hear loud Latino music and voices raised in laughter from inside.

The door opened before he got a chance to knock, and he was immediately welcomed by a woman who looked uncannily like Rita, only a little heavier and about ten years older. She shook his hand and kissed his cheek politely, telling him she was Rita's sister, Marisol. She then led him through a crowd of talkative guests and children playing noisily toward the back of the house. He sensed a few heads turning as he passed, but wasn't quite sure if it was just out of curiosity at a new face, or because he stood out like a sore thumb among so many Cubans.

Rita's mother ambushed him in the kitchen before they made it out onto the patio. She put her arms around him and hugged him close, kissing him lovingly on both cheeks with great affection, as if she'd known him for a very long time. Missus Morales was in her late sixties and overweight, but she was so warm and welcoming he took an immediate liking to her.

Her English was not good, so he began speaking to her in Spanish. It was like turning on a porch light on a dark, moonless night. People were drawn to the conversation like flies, all wanting to know more about him, joking about how they never thought they'd see the day when Rita would invite a man to the house. That's when Rita saw him through the glass patio doors and quickly came in to rescue him.

"You never told me you spoke Spanish." She smiled as she kissed his cheek and led him outside with her arm linking his.

"Well, I don't really know *that* much," he replied above the noise. "I just picked up a few phrases when I was in Spain."

"Oh my God, I've always dreamed about going to Spain," she said. "What part were you in?"

"One summer, when I was in my teens, I taught at a small sailing school near Valencia," he replied. "Maybe I'll take you there someday on Bob's yacht. I know you'd love it."

"Wait there while I go pack my bags," she laughed.

"But yeah, we sailed all around the Spanish east coast that summer. From Valencia up to Barcelona and then from there, across the Mediterranean to the island of Mallorca."

"Where did you like best?"

"I'm not really sure which I preferred. They're all amazing places."

Rita got them a couple of cold beers from an ice bucket on a table by the pool, and they continued their conversation sitting in the shade by the side of the house. As they sipped from their bottles, she started pointing out different guests scattered around the backyard, telling him who each one was and how exactly they were related to her. She seemed to have a bit of funny gossip on each of them. Stories about what they were up to now, or who they were dating, or just silly little anecdotes about things they got up to as children.

Not long after, her father and two older brothers came over to say hello. Conor stood up and politely shook hands with them all as Rita made the introductions. Mister Morales said he liked him just by shaking his hand because, he informed him, you could tell a lot about a man by his handshake. Rita and her brothers groaned in unison, having heard it all before. But he was determined to share his theories with Conor and would not be dissuaded.

"You know, a person forms their first impression of you in less than ten seconds," he told him in a strong Cuban accent as his sons said goodbye and left to get more beer. "Ten seconds. That is why a handshake is so important, you see."

"I'll get Emilio so you can give him his gift," Rita interrupted, rolling her eyes up and smiling, leaving him alone with her father for a few minutes.

"You see, the first thing I noticed when I shook *your* hand was that you stood with shoulders square to me. And very important, you maintained good eye contact."

"That's interesting," Conor said. "So what exactly does that tell you?"

"First, I could tell by the feel of your hand that you are not afraid of hard work. Your skin is not soft like a woman's. That is good. Second, your firm handshake tells me that you are a confident young man. A man who can be trusted."

Conor smiled at the compliment and took a sip of beer. He liked the old man. He was in his seventies, but seemed strong and full of life and energy. He gave the impression that he had spent a lifetime working hard, probably doing manual labor. But he was a deep thinker, and proud of it.

"So, what if my handshake *wasn't* that firm?" Conor inquired.

He knew by the glint in mister Morales' eyes that he had struck pay dirt, that he had just asked the million dollar question.

"Ah ha! It *is* interesting that you ask that. You see, *if* the handshake is too light, it signifies weakness or indifference. Too hard means a person is trying to manipulate you. If it is too quick, it could signify that the person wants to keep you at a distance. And then, worst of all, a palm down handshake means that person wishes to dominate you."

"That's really interesting," Conor muttered, remembering Eva Castagna's palm down handshake by the pool the day he arrived. "Did you study psychology?"

"No, no," the old man said, shaking his head. "I have simply studied people all my life."

Before Conor could reply, however, Rita returned, being dragged along by a very excited Emilio. He released his mother's hand when he saw Conor, running over to give him a hug.

"The boy likes you," Mister Morales commented, raising his eyebrows, even more impressed now that his grandson had given his seal of approval.

"Conor, it's my birthday!" cried the boy. "You should see all the cool presents I got."

"Happy Birthday!" Conor laughed. "Well, here's one from me. I hope you like it."

Before anyone could intervene, Emilio ripped open the package and started dancing with joy. "A pirate sword!" he shouted. He then proceeded to put on the eye-patch and pirate hat before taking off back toward the other children who were in a tree house down the end of the garden, waving his new sword as he ran.

"Hey, what do you say?" Rita shouted after him.

"Thank you!" he cried. Seconds later, he was gone from view.

After sharing a laugh, Mister Morales and Conor chatted for another couple of minutes, but when a nephew arrived with his wife and new baby, the old man apologized and left to greet them. He shook Conor's hand again before he departed, telling him to enjoy the rest of the party, and that he was welcome in his home anytime he felt like dropping by.

Rita fetched two plates from the barbeque, and they sat eating by the pool with one of her brothers and a few cousins who he found to be friendly, but very opinionated. Heated debates broke out over almost every topic they discussed. From sports to movies, the economy to politics, these people were very passionate and loved nothing better than a good argument. He sat back and enjoyed the show, soaking up the warm family atmosphere. As he was only a guest, a new face to them, he decided to sit on the fence a little, not committing too much on any particular subject. Besides, the truth was, he found it far more enjoyable to just sit back and listen.

After a while, Rita and her sister disappeared into the house, only to arrive back on the patio a few minutes later carrying a massive chocolate birthday cake. Everyone sang Cupliaños Feliz to Emilio, whose eyes were wide with excitement as he blew out the candles. The older children began milling about with great enthusiasm, making sure everyone got a piece of cake on a paper plate.

Eventually, as it got late and the party wound down, Rita walked Conor out to the front gate. After saying his good-byes to her family, he had called a taxi to bring him back to the Castagna's house in Palm Beach, but decided it would be better to wait for it outside. It was quite dark now and the street was not well lit, so he was worried the driver might have trouble finding the address.

"Thanks again for coming," Rita said quietly, linking his arm as they walked. "I hope you had a nice time?"

"Yeah, I really did," he replied. "Thanks for inviting me, Rita. It was a grand party. And your family is so friendly. I still can't get over how welcoming they are. It's very easy to feel at home with them."

"You seem to have made a good impression on them also." She smiled. "Especially my parents. I think my papa really likes you." Then, after a short pause, she said, "You know, you have also made a bit of an impression on me too."

"I'm glad to hear you say that." He smiled.

"Look, Conor Rogan, I don't exactly know how to put this. Well, I don't know where this is going between us, but I just want to tell you that I like you."

"I like you too," he replied, feeling the warmth from her body as she snuggled in close beside him.

"Well, I have to tell you up front that I'm not used to dating," she continued. "I mean that. I have only gone on a handful since Emilio's father left. But the truth is, it seems that every man I have met out there is a jerk." She looked up into his eyes with great sincerity. "I was beginning to think it was pointless to even try anymore. Until the other day when I met you, that is."

"Listen, Rita," Conor said in a more serious tone, stopping as soon as they reached the gate. "There *is* something I have to tell you before we go any further. This is awkward for me to talk about, but..." He hesitated for a moment, sighed heavily, and said, "Well, the truth is, Rita, I was married back in Ireland."

Her face dropped, taken completely by surprise at the revelation. "Oh, I see. I get it."

"No, no, you don't," he said, raising a hand gently to her cheek. "I'm not married anymore. You see, my wife died about a year and a half ago."

"Oh my God! I'm so sorry, Conor."

"I've been alone since it happened," he said quietly. He paused for a second or two, thought about it, and said, "Well, I've been kind of lost ever since. That's why my business went to crap. And, I suppose, the rest of my life as well. I just couldn't cope with the loss. I suppose I sort of gave up, you know? I don't think I could see the point in trying anymore."

The taxi pulled up in front of them.

"Well, I'm glad you told me," she whispered.

"It's so long since I've been on a date myself, I'm kind of having trouble remembering how it goes. You see, I really wasn't planning on this happening, Rita. I mean, the last thing I expected when I came here was that I was going to meet someone like you."

"Thank you for that," she said softly.

"But, the real truth is, until I met you the other day, I had no interest in even trying."

"I do understand what that's like," she whispered, nodding and blinking her eyes.

"But I like being around you. And I would really like to spend more time with you, get to know you better. That is, if you still want me to."

She smiled a little, stepped in close, and kissed him softly and slowly on the lips. As she did, she took him by the hand

and, to his surprise, placed a key in it.

"What's this?"

"Take the taxi to my apartment," she whispered quietly in his ear. "I'll ask my parents to keep Emilio overnight and then join you there."

"Are you sure?" he said, feeling his heart beat a little faster.

"Yes, I am sure. Let yourself in and make yourself at home until I get there. I shouldn't be more than a half hour."

She told the driver her address in Fort Lauderdale as Conor opened the back door of the taxi and climbed in. When he closed it, she leaned in the open window and kissed him again on the lips. "See you soon, Conor Rogan."

CHAPTER SIX

BACK AT SEA

The following morning, Conor arrived at the marina to find Bob already waiting for him onboard the *Aphrodite*, looking slightly uneasy and acting a little strange. The gulls were hovering noisily above the dock, keeping vigil over a group of marlin fishermen who had just returned from an overnight trip. There were four of them; middle-aged men in creased t-shirts and baseball caps who appeared to have been drinking far more than fishing. Looking the worse for wear, they were in the process of unloading their motorboat as he passed by and nodded hello, smelling of beer and fish and cigarettes as they formed a noisy human chain to maneuver their heavy gear down from the stern of their boat onto the pier.

Bob was talking on his cell when Conor entered the catamaran's main cabin, pacing up and down, speaking in low, agitated whispers so he could not be overheard. He was wearing a pair of Oakley sunglasses, a loose-fitting polo shirt, and Bermuda shorts that fell below his knees. There was also a small wheelie suitcase resting against the table nearby and a large black hold-all on the floor by his feet.

"Hey there," he said when the call eventually ended. "So, how did you enjoy your party last night? Knocked on the pool house door this morning, but figured you hadn't come home when there was no answer. Heck, I was just hoping you hadn't forgotten about our trip today."

"No, not a bit of it," Conor said, smiling reassuringly. "I hadn't forgotten at all. In fact, I'm really looking forward to it."

"And the party?"

"Oh yeah, thanks, it was a grand party."

"So, what age is the boy?" Bob asked.

"He's eight."

"Eight," the older man repeated thoughtfully. "Heck, that's a good age to be. He's got it all ahead of him, hasn't he?"

"Aye, he's a good kid," Conor said, nodding.

"You seem to like his mom too," Bob teased with a little knowing smile.

"I do," Conor replied with a short intake of breath. "She's really great."

With that, Bob fell strangely silent for a time, and Conor could sense his thoughts were clearly on other things that morning. It wasn't that he was purposefully being rude. He simply seemed to have other, more pressing matters on his mind.

"Everything okay?" Conor eventually inquired.

Bob shook his head as if clearing the cobwebs from his brain. "What? Oh yes, sorry, my friend, I'm fine. Everything's fine." He gestured to the yacht. "I was just wondering, how soon do you think you could you get us underway?"

Taken slightly aback, Conor said, "Well, I suppose right away, if you want. The fuel and water tanks are full, both batteries are charged, and I think I have all the relevant charts and maps below."

"Good."

"But I thought we weren't going 'til this afternoon?"

Bob didn't respond. He still seemed distracted, lost in his own thoughts.

"Are we still going to the Bahamas?" Conor persisted after a pause. "Bob?"

The older man looked through him in a way he had not done before. He had come across as a friendly, lighthearted individual these past few days, full of confidence and on top of everything. But now he seemed a little off to Conor, uncharacteristically serious, and a bit concerned about something. Conor really didn't know him well enough to decide what was going on with him.

"Bob?"

"Hmm?"

"I said, are we still going to Nassau?"

"Sorry? Yes, yes, we're still going. That was Hector on

the phone when you arrived to say he's on his way now. I told him we could set off this morning rather than later on. Heck, I hope that's not a problem, is it?"

"No problem at all. Oh, and by the way, the forecast is pretty good for the next couple of days," Conor told him.

As they waited for Hector, Bob apologized again for drinking so much at the nightclub the other night, and then thanked Conor for helping Eva get him home. He asked him what he thought of the new club, saying personally, *he* believed Hector had a real goldmine on his hands.

"I know it's none of my business," Conor said after a few minutes. "But are you okay, Bob? You seem a bit preoccupied this morning."

"Naw, I'm fine," the older man assured him. "Heck, don't mind me. I'm just having one of those mornings, that's all. And I suppose I am a little nervous about the trip. It is *very* important that this Nassau deal works out. Also, of course, I suppose I have so many irons in the fire that sometimes it's just exhausting trying to keep on top of them all."

To be honest, Conor didn't doubt that this was the case. To him, even trying to keep track of the different businesses Bob ran had been very difficult when the older man had explained them the other day. But he had seemed so enthusiastic at the time. Now he just seemed dejected, preoccupied with other matters. It was all very strange.

"The price of the big house and fancy car," he told Conor with a shrug of his shoulders. "If you want to live the lifestyle, you've got to keep making those big bucks."

As he spoke, a voice called to them from outside, beckoning them to come out. They emerged from the cabin to find Hector and his son Ernesto standing on the pier looking very solemn and businesslike. Hector, dressed in a black shirt and white trousers, stepped on board without waiting to be invited. Ernesto followed close behind, pulling a large wheelie suitcase and carrying a smaller bag on his shoulder. Greeting them with a nod, Conor took the luggage from the big Cuban and proceeded to carry it into the cabin.

"Careful with those," Hector barked gruffly, his tone not as friendly as it had been the other night. "They are genuine alligator leather."

"I'll put them in the starboard cabin," Conor told him. But then, when he caught the look of puzzlement on his face, said, "The one on the right."

He left Bob and Hector talking on deck, went below, and placed the case carefully by the foot of the large double bed in the forward starboard cabin. He set the hand luggage down on a small dressing table by the door before opening the two small cabin windows to allow some fresh air to flow in. A few minutes later, he returned to start the engine and untie the mooring lines. Ernesto had gone ashore at this point, and looking back at his father as the yacht pulled away, waved and shouted, "Buen viaje, Papa. Llamame cuando estas volviendo," which Conor translated to himself as something like, "Have a good trip, Papa. Call me when you're coming back."

Bob and Hector went forward to a cushioned seating area on deck to take in the view and talk business as they chugged out of the busy harbor. Conor kept the diesel running smooth and slow, carefully guiding the large catamaran through a maze of gleaming white vessels bobbing left and right about them in the swell. He returned a wave to a group of day-trippers passing by in a smaller mono-hull Benetau, their faces burnt red from the unforgiving sun. A few minutes later, they cleared the mouth of the inlet and he continued on for about a mile before eventually cutting the engine to silence.

The moment he hoisted the *Aphrodite's* mainsail, the wind caught it and she began moving at speed. He tightened the slack on the sheets until there was no give in the canvas and tied them off on spring cleats in the cockpit before taking the wheel and heading south at six-knots toward the Florida Keys. The wind was blowing just right for the first leg of their course, south-southeast toward the nearby coastline of Miami and South Dade.

It was a glorious day and they almost had the ocean to themselves. He spotted a cruise ship on the distant horizon, heading home to Miami after a weeklong voyage in the Caribbean. He imagined the passengers sitting by a pool or eating lunch in one of the air-conditioned restaurants onboard. During their trip, they had probably been on day tours in Jamaica or the Bahamas or one of the many Mexican holiday ports. To Conor, it was more like a floating hotel than a ship, and while he acknowledged the fact that it was a luxurious way to see the Caribbean, he personally preferred the smaller, more hands-on experience of a sailing yacht.

As the evening wore on, the western sky darkened to a hazy burnt orange, and the wind shifted and began blowing due west from the mainland. He switched on the running lights and adjusted the mainsail, tacking a new course southeast toward the Bahamas and the island of New Providence. He sat alone in the cockpit that night, the breeze on his face, content with a mug of hot coffee and a cigarette. Bob and Hector remained in the well-lit cabin, drinking rum and talking loudly. Every once in a while, one of them would let out a roar and they would both laugh. Bob's mood seemed to improve as the day progressed and Conor was glad. He didn't like seeing his employer so troubled. He had grown fond of him over the past few days and wasn't happy seeing him look so worried.

They had just finished a hot meal of grilled steak and mixed peppers, stir-fried in a small wok Bob produced from one of the galley cabinets. They had drunk coffee and smoked cigars and were now happily getting drunk.

Conor had sat with them earlier for five minutes to get some food, and Hector, a lot friendlier and more relaxed than earlier that day, had asked him about Ireland and how he liked Florida. It amazed him to hear there were no snakes on the island, and that the population of the Republic consisted of less than four-and-a-half-million people, less than a lot of American cities. They engaged for a while in some more polite conversation before he cleaned his plate and returned back to the cockpit.

"Oh, Conor, I hope you don't mind, but there's been a slight change of plans," Bob called after him as he left.

"Oh? How do you mean?"

"Well, instead of sailing directly into Nassau, could you possibly moor on the other side of the island in a place called Clifton Bay?"

"Shouldn't be a problem," Conor replied without questioning the request. "I'll check out the chart and adjust our course when we get there."

"When exactly do you expected to reach land?" Hector asked.

"All going well, should be there by first light," Conor told him.

"First light? When exactly is that?" the Cuban inquired with a puzzled look on his face.

"Say, about five-thirty in the morning."

Hector laughed at this, saying, "Well, captain, don't wake me *that* early. I am not exactly what you would call a morning person."

Bob and he were both still laughing heartily when Conor left them. They were pretty drunk and finding humor in the slightest thing. But it was good to see them enjoying themselves. Getting on. There had been times, at the club the other night and earlier that morning in the marina, when there seemed to be a bit of tension between them. Now it seemed the rum was doing its job and they were both happy in each other's company.

The rest of the night was uneventful. Conor stayed at the wheel as the two men slept. His plan, when they reached New Providence, was to moor just offshore in a small cove he found on the chart near Clifton Bay, the spot Bob now wanted to go to. He intended to catch a few hours sleep while the two went ashore to visit the hotel they were interested in purchasing near Nassau.

He went forward for a quick inspection at about three a.m. and popped into the cabin to pour himself another cup of coffee. Someone was snoring loudly below deck, but he wasn't quite sure which one of them it was. He switched off the main cabin light on the way out, just leaving on a small yellow side lamp to break the darkness. Back in the cockpit, he checked their speed and heading, and then settled himself in for the rest of the voyage. He stared into the darkness as a million stars sparkled overhead, thinking about Rita and the events of the previous night.

He felt a warmth inside when he thought about her. Meeting someone like that was the last thing he had expected to happen when he decided to take the job in South Florida. There had been a painful void in his life since Grainne's death—one, until now, he had no desire to fill. But meeting her and the boy had awoken something inside him. He felt a sense of excitement at the prospect of seeing them again. That was a *good* emotion, he told himself. A healthy state of mind and being. It was worth at least pursuing that type of feeling. God knew, after all that had happened, he needed more of those in his life.

But at the same time, he also felt an overwhelming sense of achievement and fulfillment as he guided the *Aphrodite* onwards toward the Bahamas. After all that had happened, he was at sea again for the first time in over a year. At sea, where he felt most comfortable. To him, being at the helm was the greatest feeling in the world. He knew the ocean, wherever he found her. She may have been cruel and unforgiving to some, but to him she was dependable. She would never leave him. No, with her he could just be himself. All she asked was that he respect her and did not take her for granted. While out there on the ocean, at least, he was the master of his own fate.

Eva Castagna opened the front door in her dressing gown to find detectives Shoemaker and Childs standing before her on the porch. It was dark that evening, moonless, but the sky above was clear and the stars were bright enough to take the edge off. Outside in the garden, the sounds of tropical house crickets filled the hot air, their chirping pulses resonating in the grass and bushes. Tiny geckos darted across the asphalt driveway and up the walls, the meager starlight reflecting off their glistening backs as they scurried for cover among the crevices.

"Do you know what time it is?" she said, rubbing her eyes.

Shoemaker held up his badge and said, "Miami Metro, Missus Castagna. Sorry for the late hour. I wonder if your husband is at home?"

"No, he's not," she replied grumpily.

"Would you mind if I asked where he is?"

"He's away on business for a couple of days. What's all this about?"

She could see he was disappointed at the news.

"Do you happen to know his partner, a Mister Hector Suarez?" detective Childs interjected politely.

"Yes, of course I do. I know Hector well. In fact, he and Bob are together right now."

"Really?" Shoemaker said with interest.

"Yes, they're sailing down to the Bahamas to view a hotel in Nassau. You *do* know they own a property company together?"

"Gold Coast Developments. Yes, we know about that," he

replied.

"Is there something wrong? Is Bob in some sort of trouble?" She sounded a bit worried now. The thought had just occurred that perhaps the boat had run into difficulty.

"Why would you say that?" asked Shoemaker.

She could see he was suspicious, alighting on every misplaced word or phrase.

"Well, why else would you call to our home at such a late hour?" Eva said irritably. "Now, is my husband okay or not?"

"We apologize for the hour, ma'am. We really do. We're just conducting a routine investigation, that's all. Your husband is not in any trouble, I assure you. And I'm quite sure he's okay."

"We'd just like to ask him a few questions when he gets back," Childs added.

"What kind of questions?" Eva squinted her eyes, growing a little suspicious.

"Ma'am, we're investigating the disappearance of a Miss Maria Gomez," said Shoemaker. "She's an employee of Hector's at the Azteca nightclub in Boca."

"I'm sorry, I really am. But I've never met her," Eva replied, showing a little concern now that she knew a young woman was missing. If they had only said so from the start, she thought.

"Did your husband ever mention her name?"

"No, not that I recall."

"Were you at the opening of the club the other night?" Shoemaker asked after a moment's silence.

"Yes," replied Eva.

"Good night?"

"Yes, a very good night," she said, growing a little tired and wondering where all this was going.

"How did Hector Suarez seem to you?"

"That's an odd question," she said suspiciously. "What do you mean by it?"

Shoemaker smiled politely. "Oh, I don't know, I was just wondering if he was in good spirits, or if he seemed to have something on his mind?"

"Look," Eva said. "It's late, detectives. I think you had better go."

Childs turned toward the car, but Shoemaker lingered a moment longer. "Okay, Missus Castagna, once again I *am* sorry for bothering you so late. But, when your husband gets back, could you please mention Miss Gomez to him?" He took out a small white contact card and handed it to her. "He can reach us at any of these numbers."

"Alright, I'll do that," said Eva.

Shoemaker shrugged before turning. "Maybe he knows something. Maybe he doesn't. But it *would* be very helpful if he could give us a call either way."

"Of course." she replied. "I'll get him to call you as soon as he returns."

CHAPTER SEVEN

THE BAHAMAS

Conor woke Bob and Hector at seven-fifteen as agreed, waiting until the *Aphrodite* was successfully anchored in the small, secluded cove. He then went down below and began making them a breakfast of scrambled eggs and a pot of hot steaming coffee. When all was ready, he left them to it, returning on deck while they showered and dressed. When they arrived at the island of New Providence earlier that morning, he had dropped two anchors, one forward and one aft, and now set about double-checking they were still holding in the shallow, stony bottom of the cove. As he smoked a cigarette on deck, he cast his gaze out across the bay. There were no other boats in sight, and no people or traffic on the visible shoreline.

The water lapping about the hull was clear turquoise and calm, so calm that Conor watched in fascination as dozens of brightly-colored tropical fish swam about the hull below him. A small school of dolphins had followed the *Aphrodite* in as she approached the island that morning, playfully leaping in and out of the water in a zigzag pattern on either side. But they turned away and swam back out to sea again when the sandy floor rose and it became shallower at the mouth of the cove.

It was beautiful there in the Bahamas. The birdsong was unique and the sounds of crickets and other insects filled the air. The sunrise over the South Atlantic had been spectacular that morning, and he had watched it alone as the island came into view on the horizon. As it grew brighter, he found Clifton Bay without difficulty, checking and rechecking the chart against his compass. It proved far too shallow for a normal mono hull yacht to traverse, whose fin-like keel would have hit bottom before it passed the breakwater. But the *Aphrodite* was a catamaran and didn't have much of a keel. She had no difficulty in shallow water and could, if she wanted to, slide right up onto the beach. But then, of course, they would be reliant on the tide to leave, and as Conor wasn't sure how long his two passengers were planning to stay, he decided to play it safe and remain a few hundred yards off shore.

It was about eight-thirty when breakfast was over and the two men appeared on deck. Conor had already lowered the large rubber dinghy into the water at the stern and had its small motor ticking over. Both of them looked a little worse for wear after the rum they had consumed the previous night, their eyes squinting painfully in the blinding white sunlight. But they were much better now that they were showered and fed, in fresh clothes, and ready to go ashore to conduct their business.

Bob was carrying the black hold-all he had brought onboard in Palm Beach, which he now handed to Conor before clambering his overweight frame awkwardly into the dinghy behind Hector. Conor passed it back down to him when he was settled, then checked they were all set before untying them from the bathing platform and pushing them off with his foot.

"We should be back by noon," Bob called out as he dropped the motor into the water and sped off noisily toward the beach.

"Don't forget to tie that dinghy above the high tide line," Conor shouted after them.

Watching through the binoculars, he waited until he was satisfied they had secured the dinghy and left the beach on foot to where a large black SUV was waiting for them. As soon as they were gone from sight, he headed straight to bed. Exhaustion was setting in and he needed to sleep before even beginning to contemplate the return voyage.

Detectives Shoemaker and Childs were slowly making their way through the maze of desks and filing cabinets in the station, heading back out to their car when one of the detectives sitting near the main door stopped them. He had a phone to his ear and was busy in conversation, but clicked his fingers sharply and motioned back toward the other end of the busy room without speaking. They both turned as one to see Captain Mendoza urgently beaconing them through the open venetian blinds hanging in her office partition window, calling them back with exaggerated gestures of her hand.

The captain was on the phone when they walked in, sitting on the edge of her polished mahogany desk. She motioned for them to sit, but continued talking to someone in Spanish. Both detectives took a seat and waited patiently for her to finish. While they did, Shoemaker scanned the office with the curious, suspicious eyes of a detective.

There were two large flags in the corners behind the captain's desk—to her left, the stars and stripes and to her right the Florida state flag, white with a red X and the state seal in its center. On the far side of the room was a glass cabinet full of various marksmanship trophies, as well as dozens of certificates and photographs lining the walls. His gaze rested on one near the window. It was a group photo taken at a charity event the previous year. Captain Mendoza was sitting at a table with the mayor of Miami Dade County and some local politicians and businessmen. It was a happy group. They were all smiling with glasses raised in toast. There was nothing special or unusual about it, except for the fact that Hector Suarez was sitting near the center, his arm around the mayor's shoulder with an enormous Cuban cigar in his mouth. Shoemaker stared into his black shark-like eyes, and at his big, fat smile. It made him want to puke.

"That was the mayor's secretary," Captain Mendoza said when she finally hung up the phone, returning to the comfort of her reclining leather chair on the other side of the desk.

"Let me guess," Shoemaker muttered. "He's complaining that we've been harassing his buddy, Hector Suarez, right?"

Captain Mendoza looked sharply at him, not appreciating his attitude. "Well?"

"What?"

"Have you? Have you been harassing him?"

"Captain, we simply asked him a few questions," Childs offered in a low, apologetic voice. "Just routine stuff."

"According to him, you were rude and disrespectful," the captain replied, keeping her gaze fixed on Shoemaker.

"Aw come on, you *know* this is bullshit," he scoffed, shaking his head at the absurdity of it all.

"Bradley, I won't have that language or tone in my office."

"Sorry."

"Now, what exactly is going on between you and Suarez? You still seem to be pursuing this personal vendetta against him. I thought we already spoke about that."

"We're just chasing up leads on the disappearance of a woman called Maria Gomez," Childs interjected. "She works for Hector Suarez in his new Boca Raton club."

"Go on."

"Coincidently," Shoemaker added. "Gomez went missing the day after she called us with information about illegal activities connected to the Suarez family. We simply called into the club yesterday to see if Hector or his boys knew anything about it."

"And what did they have to say?"

"What do *you* think?" replied Shoemaker. "They, of course, denied any knowledge of her whereabouts. Said she had probably just taken a couple of days off."

"And you don't think that is simply the case?"

"Are you kidding me?"

"Okay, so what about these illegal activities? What *exactly* was she referring to?"

There was a moment's awkward silence as both detectives considered their best response. They knew that without Maria Gomez to back them up, they had nothing to go on.

"Well?" the captain asked impatiently.

"Truth is, we never got to find out," Childs said meekly. "You see, she was gone before we could question her."

There was silence for the longest time. Captain Mendoza put a weary hand to her forehead, sighing as she closed her eyes and shook her head. She knew Shoemaker had it in for Hector Suarez and his sons. The Suarez family knew it, and everyone at the station knew it. They were all well aware of the fact that only two months previously, Bradley's eighteen-year-old daughter and a group of girlfriends had been given ecstasy tablets in one of the Suarez's nightclubs in Fort Lauderdale. Two of the young women had suffered a reaction and were taken to hospital. One had recovered, but the other, Shoemaker's daughter, had not been so lucky and was now lying in a coma.

Shoemaker wasn't born yesterday. He knew the teenagers were not forced to take the pills, that they also bore some of the responsibility for what happened. But then, there was the fact that they were, after all, only kids. Someone in that club had supplied those tablets, and he immediately set about trying to find out who it had been. Naturally enough, his initial enquiries hit a wall of silence. As often happened in a case concerning teenagers like this, no one knew anything and no one wanted to get involved.

In the beginning, Shoemaker didn't actually blame the Suarez family for the tragedy at all. The relationship between them had started out quite cordially and businesslike. They had expressed their shock and horror at what had happened and offered to help in any way they could. Yes, they had been very cooperative at first, but then things had gone south very quickly. During the course of his investigation, Shoemaker came to suspect that they were, in fact, the ones distributing the pills at their various clubs in South Florida. He questioned Hector, his sons, and numerous staff members, but they immediately closed ranks and called in the lawyers. There was a shit storm. The mayor got involved and the investigation was shut down.

Since then, Shoemaker had gone on a one-man crusade, a personal mission to prove that the Suarez family was dirty. It was, of course, a battle he couldn't win. No one could. Hector Suarez was too powerful, too well connected. The fact that Shoemaker was still trying wasn't an issue for Captain Mendoza per se. No, the problem as she saw it was that there had not been one shred of hard evidence linking them to distributing ecstasy pills, drug trafficking, or anything else illegal. For now, it was all just malicious rumor and gossip as far as she was concerned, and they were too powerful and well connected to antagonize without real evidence. Shoemaker was too good a detective to listen to that kind of talk. Far too good to waste his time on something as flimsy as hearsay and rumor.

"So," she said eventually. "Basically, what you're both telling me is that you have nothing?"

"We have a young woman missing," replied Shoemaker.

"That ought to count for something."

"Bradley, this is *not* missing persons. This is homicide."

Shoemaker took a deep breath and exhaled loudly, showing his frustration.

"Now, look, until you actually have evidence—"

"You want evidence? What about the tipoff I got last month that Suarez has someone from this department on his payroll?" he interrupted.

"Bradley, that's—"

"That was never even taken seriously, let alone investigated. Does nobody around here give a damn about that accusation? Am I the *only* one who seems to care that these drug dealing pimps are spitting in our faces and laughing at us?"

"Bradley, you know that information came from a crack addict trying to avoid jail time. A user who happened to OD shortly after talking to you."

"Once again, a very convenient let off for the Suarez family," he muttered, raising his hands in resignation. "Or once again, am I the *only* one who sees it?"

He turned his gaze toward his partner for support, but was a little disappointed to find her looking down at her feet. He sighed. Shoemaker knew he was digging a hole for himself with his stubbornness, and could appreciate how Childs was a little reluctant to get in it with him. Why would she? He knew she liked and respected him, but was also aware that she felt he was about to self-destruct. He couldn't blame her for distancing herself a little. After all, she valued her career too much to get caught up in the blast.

Thankfully for him, though, Captain Mendoza was not in the mood and let his angry remarks slide. She had heard it all before from Shoemaker and had grown tired of the accusations. Ignoring his rant, she continued what she was saying before the interruption. "Look, Bradley, until you have evidence, something concrete, I don't want to hear any more about this. Got it?"

"Yes, captain," Childs replied.

"Bradley?"

Silence.

"Bradley, I'm talking to you, goddamnit."

"Okay," he muttered reluctantly, pouting like a child who had just been told off.

The captain put her hand on a stack of folders on the desk and said, "And by the way, if you two detectives have so much time on your hands, I have plenty of unsolved cases sitting here."

Both Shoemaker and Childs shifted uncomfortably in their chairs.

"That's what I thought. Now get out of my office and go back to work."

All was quiet beneath the water. Strangely calm and tranquil. He was vaguely aware of the towering cliffs just visible overhead, of the waves crashing against the rocks. The roar of the ocean was barely audible above him as he floated there in limbo, a few feet below the icy swell. Face down, not drowning or struggling, simply hovering in the frozen no-man's land between surface and bottom. The sunlight faded as he slowly began to sink, the utter-darkness enveloping him as he descended.

In the distance, he saw a flash, a glimmer of light approaching, rising up from the nothingness. It seemed to hover below him for a time, waiting patiently in the shadows until it suddenly moved again and came into view. As the hazy figure approached, he recognized it and a sense of panic engulfed him. He tried to call out, but the frozen brine was already in his lungs. Filled with terror, he tried to swim up toward the light, but it grabbed hold of him and pulled him close. Hugging him tightly in an icy embrace, it dragged him down toward the seabed and the emptiness.

Conor woke with a start, sweating profusely and a dry sensation in the back of his throat.

When Bob and Hector returned at three o'clock, they were far more talkative than they had been earlier that morning. Still carrying the large black hold-all, they now had another see-through plastic bag, dripping water and containing three fresh lobsters. Full of chat and excitement, they went inside to freshen up while Conor secured the dinghy at the stern. The mood was a lot more upbeat now that their business had been conducted. While he raised the anchors and got underway, they ate a light lunch in the cabin and then came back out on deck to watch the island of New Providence disappear on the horizon behind them.

"You know," Hector said, lighting another fat Cuban cigar. "I've been thinking I might get myself a boat like this and go cruising down to Mexico."

"A sailing yacht?" Bob asked, a little skeptically. "Heck, I wouldn't have thought this would be your thing, Hector. I'd have imagined you'd be into something a bit more macho. With a bit more power. Like one of those big motor yachts we passed by on the way out of the marina yesterday."

"Si, si, a motor yacht," the Cuban agreed enthusiastically. He gestured toward the billowing sail above. "None of this wind nonsense."

"So then, it's speed you're after," Bob said. "But what about the thrill and majesty of moving with nothing more than the wind in your sails?"

"Fuck that shit," replied the Cuban. "While you're crawling along with the wind, my bad ass speedboat will leave you behind in its rearview mirror."

Laughing, Bob looked over toward Conor as he sat holding the wheel. "What do you say to that, captain?"

"Aye, speedboats *are* fine if that's what you're after," Conor agreed diplomatically.

Hector slapped Bob condescendingly on the back and said, "See? Even your *own* guy says it."

Laughing, Bob went below and fetched a bottle of rum and a couple of glasses, and the two men spent the afternoon on deck, talking business, smoking cigars, and drinking. Conor stayed at the helm, alert at all times, keeping them safely on course back to Florida. He was planning to call Rita as soon as he moored the *Aphrodite* back at the marina, maybe take her out for a drink. He liked the idea of having somebody to share his day with again. He only just realized that he missed having someone to come home to.

Bob started boiling the lobsters around six-thirty, and by seven forty-five the three of them were sitting in the cabin eating dinner. It was a nice meal, and Conor complimented him on his cooking.

"You can't say the military didn't teach me anything," the older man replied, smiling.

"No way! I didn't know you were in the Army," Hector said as he gulped down the last of the rum. 'You don't strike me as the military type."

"No? Why's that?" asked Bob.

"Why? Because you are too damn fat," he laughed.

"Maybe now," Bob muttered ruefully, patting his belly. "But let me tell you something, back when I was eighteen, I was pretty damn fit. I enlisted fresh out of high school, full of cum and vinegar, ready to take on the world."

Hector chuckled drunkenly.

"Oh, and by the way, it wasn't the Army. It was the Marine Corps."

Hector laughed even louder. "You, Bob? A marine? No way, my fat friend. I'm sorry. I definitely cannot picture that."

Bob didn't seem to take too much offense at the remark. He simply shrugged nostalgically and said, "Anyway, truth is, I never *did* see action. They stationed me in Bimini. Heck, I spent two years drilling on the parade ground and peeling potatoes in the kitchen."

After a moment's silence, he went down to the galley and came back with another bottle of rum. Conor left them to it and returned outside to the cockpit. The autopilot was useful, but he never fully trusted it, and would certainly never leave it for more than fifteen minutes at a time.

As the night wore on, he remained there in the cockpit keeping a careful eye on the horizon while Bob and Hector grew drunker and louder inside the main cabin. Switching on the *Aphrodite's* running lights again, he disengaged her autopilot and once again took the wheel. The sea was calm and the breeze warm, filling their sails, making it a perfect night for the return voyage. But although Conor was enjoying every minute of the trip, he still had a longing to get back to see Rita. He hadn't counted on liking her so much, thought it a bit odd that now he was finally at sea again, his thoughts were once more drawn to shore.

Around midnight, he went forward to secure a loose sheet before returning to the cockpit and settling in for the night. He sat back and looked up at the stars as he lit a cigarette, blowing the smoke toward the heavens. It was so beautiful and tranquil out there that he immediately found himself feeling guilty for enjoying it. His thoughts returned to the past and he remembered how he and Grainne would sit on deck watching those same magnificent stars. They had been so happy together back then, sharing their lives and their all-consuming passion for the sea.

But Conor's thoughts were suddenly interrupted by a burst of laughter from inside the well-lit cabin. He was glad their visit to view the property in Nassau had been successful, relieved that they were getting on again. The wind shifted and began blowing from the southwest, so he adjusted the mainsail accordingly and tightened the jib, knowing that if he maintained a steady course, he would have them back before sunrise. The lights of Miami came into view over the horizon. They were almost home.

And then it happened, and Conor's world was thrown into chaos. While he was rechecking the compass reading against the chart, a sudden explosion of sound shattered the stillness about him. It startled him, making him jump up with fright. If they had run into some floating debris, a submerged container or an empty oil drum, he knew they might only have minutes before sinking. If the blow had come directly from below from a rising whale, then they would have even less time. Either way, he knew they were in deep trouble. But then his mind focused and he quickly realized from the gentle movement of the boat that it had not been hit. No, that sound had come from inside the cabin.

Conor released his grip on the wheel and grabbed the handle of the cabin door. Flinging it open, he raced inside to find Bob standing before him with a small black revolver in his trembling left hand. He was looking at it with a strange blank expression on his face.

"Jesus, Mary, and Joseph!" Conor shouted as he pushed past the older man to find Hector's lifeless body slumped face down on the polished wooden table in the center of the cabin. "What the fuck have ye done?"

The half-empty bottle of rum was on its side in the thick, dark pool slowly spreading from beneath Hector's blood-soaked head. Conor pressed his thumb and forefinger to the Cuban's neck, but could feel no pulse. So he placed his other hand on Hector's forehead and lifted it up, only to find himself looking upon the face of death. Hector's eyes were wide open, staring lifelessly back at him. There was a large black hole where his left cheekbone had been, blood and gristle oozing from the wound. And when he looked down, he saw the white leather seat behind was covered in fragments of bone and particles of Hector's brain matter.

"You...you've killed him," he stuttered disbelievingly.

"I had no choice," Bob stammered from behind. "You don't know, Conor. He...he was going to ruin me. Heck, I had to do it. I had to."

Standing up from the body, Conor turned to Bob, put his hand out, and carefully took the gun from his sweaty grasp. The older man appeared to be in shock, motionless, not fully grasping what he had just done. So Conor put the gun into his waistband before turning toward the navigation table by the cabin door.

"Don't touch *anything*," he commanded sternly, growing angrier as his own initial shock began to wear off. "I fucking mean it, Bob. Just stay there while I call the coastguard."

As he turned his back and bent over, flipping the switches on the small VHF transmitter, something heavy and metallic came down hard on the back of his head. The pain shot though his body like a bolt of lightning, a strange, disorienting sensation that overcame his entire being. As the numbness spread throughout his neck and shoulders, he suddenly lost the power of his legs and his knees buckled beneath him. He crumpled face down onto the navigation table, lay there for a few seconds before slowly sliding off toward the floor. Unconsciousness engulfed Conor like an icy squall. Once again, he found himself floating beneath the waves. Once more being dragged down into that abyss.

CHAPTER EIGHT

Broward Memorial

He woke in the hospital to find a concerned female doctor shining a light from a pencil torch into his left eye. It felt painful, like someone had grabbed hold of his optical nerve and was squeezing it tighter and tighter.

"How are you feeling, Mister Rogan?" After a moment, when she got no response, the doctor said, "Sir, you are in Broward County Memorial. Do you remember what happened?"

What happened? At that particular moment, Conor could not even remember who he was. He blinked a couple of times, letting the numbness fade as his thoughts and coordination slowly returned. That was when the throbbing sensation hit him and he grimaced with pain. It felt as if he had been hit in the head by a swinging boom, an event that had actually happened to him as a boy while sailing a twelve-foot heron dinghy. He never forgot it. To that very day, he could still recall the blinding headache that seemed to last for weeks.

He tried to sit up as the cobwebs cleared, only to discover his right wrist handcuffed to the side rail of the bed. His left hand went up instinctively to feel a large gauze bandage stuck to the back of his head. The doctor flicked off the light and stood back with a look of mild concern on her face.

"Sir, do you know your full name?"

"Conor. Conor Rogan."

"Good. Very good. And how many fingers am I holding up?"

"Three," he replied.

"Alright then," she said with a satisfied nod. "There

doesn't appear to be any internal swelling. I'll have a nurse give you some pills for that headache." She turned for the door. But as she walked away, she added, "You can talk to him now."

It was only as she spoke these words and left that Conor noticed two figures standing silently by the window. They were not wearing white coats, and wouldn't have looked like doctors if they were. The red-haired woman's jacket was open, just enough to show she was carrying a gun in a shoulder holster. And both had their badges visible, hooked over the breast pockets of their jackets.

The tall black man stepped forward and said, "Mister Rogan, I'm Detective Shoemaker of the Miami Metro Police Department."

The nurse came in and, without speaking, gave Conor two pills and a paper cup of water. He swallowed them and downed the water in one gulp. His throat had been so painfully dry they felt like razorblades going down. The detective waited patiently until she was gone before continuing.

"Mister Rogan, this is my partner Detective Childs." He motioned to the red-haired woman who was still standing by the window, but she neither smiled nor acknowledged him. "Can you tell us anything about what happened last night?" When Conor gave no response, he added, "Anything at all?"

It was all happening too fast. Conor's mind was still groggy, his memory only starting to return as he spoke the words out loud. "We...we were sailing north toward...we were sailing..."

"Do you want more water?" Shoemaker asked, noticing how hoarse his voice sounded. He passed the empty paper cup to Childs and gestured toward the sink in the corner.

"There was a gunshot!" Conor exclaimed as the memory suddenly returned. "Yeah, that's right. I remember now. I found Bob Castagna in the cabin with a gun. He had shot Hector Suarez and then...then...then I think he must have hit me over the head with something when I went to call the coastguard."

"Just one shot?" Shoemaker asked.

"Yeah."

"You're positive about that?"

"Yeah, one shot."

"But you never *did* call the coastguard, did you?" Childs

said, as she returned from the sink and handed the paper cup back to him. As soon as he took it, she stepped back to the window.

"No...no, like I told you, he hit me with something before I could raise anyone on the VHF." He looked at both of them and realized they were not convinced. They still had questions. Well, shit, he thought irritably. So did he. "Look," he continued. "Why are you talking to *me* about this? Why don't you just ask Bob what happened?" He sat upright. "Where is that fucker anyway?" Even as he asked, he felt a wave of anger welling up inside. Bob was the one they should be questioning, not him. Bob was the one who had put him in this position. "Talk to him. That stupid son of a—" That now familiar sharp pain shot through the back of his neck again and he groaned as it ran down his spine. He took a deep breath and waited until it passed, then drank the second cup of water.

"Look," Shoemaker said quietly. "At this point we only know two things for sure. One is that Bob Castagna's yacht was found drifting off Boca Raton earlier this morning. The other is that the coastguard boarded it but only found two people, you and Hector Suarez. That is all we know at this point. You were unconscious and he was dead. There was no one else on board." After a pause to let the information sink in, he continued. "The coastguard brought the boat back to its berth in Palm Beach so that our forensic boys could conduct an examination. They have been working on it all morning."

Conor shook his head in confusion and utter disbelief. Considering the information for a moment, he tried desperately to make sense of it. But it was no use. He only seemed to come up with more questions.

"Well, if Bob wasn't there, he must have left in the dinghy," he eventually offered, more to himself than to them.

"No, sir, that is not possible," Childs replied accusingly. "You see, the dinghy was still onboard when the coastguard found you."

Conor was left speechless on hearing this revelation, even more confused than he had been before. He could feel both detectives watching his expression, hanging on his every word. They were waiting for a plausible explanation, and God knows he wanted nothing more than to give them one. But he had so many questions of his own. This was a nightmare, and his head hurt so badly. What the hell happened? He just stared at them in bewilderment, not knowing what more to say.

"Mister Rogan, can you explain why the forty-five that shot Hector Suarez was in your possession?" asked Shoemaker. "With your fingerprints on it?"

"I don't...well, because I took it from Bob. Didn't I tell you that?"

"He just handed it over to you? Is that what you're saying?"

"Sir, why on earth would he hand over his gun if he didn't want you calling for help?" asked Childs, her arms folding before her in a gesture of disbelief.

Conor could clearly tell she wasn't buying into his story. There were too many holes. Before he could say anything, however, her cell phone rang, and without excusing herself, she turned toward the window to answer it. Her voice was muffled, speaking to somebody in whispers.

"Look, Mister Rogan. Let me get this straight," Shoemaker continued in a calm, steadying voice. "You have just arrived in South Florida. Is that correct?"

"Yeah, a week ago."

"And you're from Ireland, right?"

"Yeah."

"Do you mind me asking if you have a criminal record there?"

He shook his head. "No, of course I don't."

"Of course you don't mind, or of course you don't have a record?"

"Fuck, I don't have a record. Look, I've *never* been in trouble with the police."

"Okay. So where have you been staying since you arrived?"

"With the Castagnas in Palm Beach," Conor replied. "In their pool house."

"And how would you describe your relationship with Bob Castagna?"

"He was my employer," he replied. "He seemed very friendly."

"Was? You *do* know you're talking about him in the past tense?"

"Well, I'm assuming no matter which way this goes, I'm

out of a job," Conor said through gritted teeth.

Shoemaker shrugged, acknowledging the logic. "And Missus Castagna?" he continued. "How would you describe your relationship with her?"

Conor shook his head again. Maybe it was the bang on the back of his skull, maybe the pills they had given him, but the questions were starting to irritate him. "There *is* no relationship. Eva is Bob's wife. That's all."

"Sir, we have been in contact with Missus Castagna, and she claims that you made sexual advances toward her on a number of occasions since you arrived. And also toward her eighteen-year-old daughter."

"That is pure bullshit!" he protested, visibly shocked. "Look, that's just not true at all."

"Cut the wounded innocent act," Childs said from the window as she finished her call. She slipped her phone back into her jacket, revealing more of the holstered gun hanging from her shoulder. "There has been no sign of Bob Castagna since he left to meet you at the marina two days ago. We've tried reaching him on his cell, but it's been powered off."

"Off?"

"Either that, or it's lying at the bottom of the ocean." She walked over to Shoemaker by the bed and whispered something in his ear. He kept his eyes on Conor as she spoke, nodding thoughtfully but showing no visible sign of emotion. Eventually, when she stepped back, he ran his tongue around the inside of his mouth and sighed with a gesture of resignation.

"Well, we've just got the lab report back," he told Conor. "Seems blood found on the deck of the boat is a positive match to Bob Castagna."

"What? Fuck. No way."

"Can you explain, or offer *any* reason as to why *his* blood is on the deck and he is nowhere to be found?"

Conor took a deep breath and exhaled loudly in disbelief. "I... Look, please, there has got to be some mistake."

"And by the way, the gun in your belt had actually fired *two* shots," Childs added with a grunt. "Not *one* as you claimed."

As Conor paused to digest this latest bombshell, he suddenly felt his heart beating faster than it had ever done before. A dull faintness came over him and his head began to swim and throb. Shoemaker took out his notebook, flipped it open, and began reading.

"Conor Rogan, you have the right to remain silent. You have the right to an attorney. If you cannot afford an attorney, one will be provided..."

He was given time to dress under the watchful eye of a uniformed police officer whom the detective called in when he had finished reading him his rights. Shoemaker instructed the officer to take a seat in the room and wait for a doctor's signature on the hospital release form. After that, he was to take Conor to the station in Miami for formal processing and more detailed questioning.

"Alright, George, I'll leave you to it," Shoemaker told him as he and Detective Childs left the room. Then, turning to Conor, he said, "Rogan, we'll talk later down at the station."

Officer George Henderson was an overweight man who looked close to retirement. He didn't say much to Conor, just sat in the corner drinking coffee from a thermos, reading the sports section of the Miami Herald. The headline read: *Gator's Debut New Quarterback Against Kentucky.* Conor wondered if the taxi driver from the Azteca approved. *Funny how the mind works when it's under stress,* he mused. *How thoughts can wander when drowning in a sea of duress.* It had taken hours, but when the release paperwork finally came through that evening, Officer Henderson wasted no time.

He led Conor down the main corridor with hands cuffed behind his back. It was a surreal experience for him. He could feel all those accusing eyes on them as they passed, staff, patients and visitors, yet noticed none of them actually making direct eye contact with him. It seemed they had all seen the news on TV or at least heard about it on the radio by then. He supposed that, as far as they were concerned, he was a dangerous killer, not to be messed with.

Officer Henderson brought him to a stop when they reached a service elevator at the end of a long, fluorescent-lit hall that reeked of antiseptic. They were on the sixth floor and rode it all the way down in silence. When the big metal doors finally creaked open before them, the officer motioned him out with a nudge. They found themselves alone in the underground parking garage where his patrol car was waiting nearby, a white Dodge Charger with a long green and gold stripe on either side and a narrow bank of emergency lights bolted to the roof.

"Watch your head," he said automatically as he guided Conor into the back seat. Conor imagined that he must have said that phrase a thousand times over the years. "Legs in the vehicle."

He slammed the door behind Conor with a loud *clunk* and adjusted his gun belt and nightstick before climbing into the driver's seat in front of him. He started the engine and immediately went straight for the radio. As Conor waited helplessly behind a black metal grill, Officer Henderson proceeded to call in.

"Control, this is David Three Seven Nine, over."

Silence.

"Control, David Three Seven Nine. Come in."

A few seconds later came a low, crackled response. "Three Seven Nine, this is control. Hey, George, what's your twenty?"

"Just leaving Broward Memorial with a prisoner. ETA forty, forty-five-minutes," he told the female controller on the other end of the radio.

"Roger that. Traffic's building up on the turnpike. Might be better to take the Interstate."

"Will do," he replied. "Over and out."

He replaced the handset, turned the key, and headed toward the exit booth at the other end of the darkly lit parking garage. As he did, Conor settled into the back seat in preparation for the journey, still full of confusion as to what was actually happening to him. Under the circumstances, he could see why the detectives were suspicious of his story. But he just couldn't understand *why* they thought he would do something like that. What possible motive could they think he had?

Then he remembered Detective Shoemaker's comment about him making advances toward Eva and Abi, and immediately felt another knot tighten in his stomach. Was *that* supposed to be his motive? Jesus Christ, he thought. One was a married woman, the other a young girl. Had the women actually said that, or was Shoemaker just making it up, he wondered, trying to get a reaction from him? The thought of Eva lying about such a thing, he *could* believe. He remembered how the last time he saw her she was pretty mad. As far as he recalled, she had told him to go fuck himself. And, although he didn't know her that well, the notion that she could be so vindictive and spiteful did not come as any surprise. But Abi, he thought. Jesus Christ! No way could he ever imagine her saying *anything* like that. No way. Not unless her mother had forced her to.

He took a deep breath and decided to put it from his mind for now as it just wasn't doing him any good. He resolved to remain as calm as possible in the hope that he might remember something else of the previous night. Anything that might give a clue as to what happened. But after a while, it felt like he was like trying to piece together a jigsaw puzzle with no picture reference. There were far too many grey areas. Too many unanswered questions.

So he went over it again and again in his mind, desperately trying to make sense of it all. First off, there was the shot, then the look on Bob's face when he entered the cabin. Had that look of panic been real? Conor wondered. He definitely *seemed* to be in shock after killing Hector. And then he suddenly remembered something Bob had said about Hector going to ruin him. Yes, he definitely *had* said that. He tried to recall some of the different conversations the two men had on the voyage. Hector had been goading Bob on and off the whole trip. He had come across as being an arrogant, unlikable man. He belittled Bob whenever he got the chance. But that was ridiculous, Conor thought. Everyone knew people like that. And although they might want to, they certainly didn't go around actually killing them for it. No, there had to be more.

Then Conor remembered the black hold-all they had carried back in the dinghy from their inspection trip. He made a mental note to ask the detectives if it had been found. Were the two men really viewing property on the island, he wondered, or were they up to something else? Were they, or had they ever been, partners in a property development company? But his head still felt sore, too painful to try to unravel all the pieces just yet. He sat back and sighed heavily. He would need a pen and paper to write it all down.

As the patrol car pulled away with a jolt, Conor started wondering if everything had been a lie from the start, even before he got on the plane in Ireland. Was he such an idiot that he never saw what was happening? Maybe he was reading too much into it, but he wondered if the whole thing had been staged by Bob, or if it was just something that occurred unplanned. At the time it happened, he had just assumed the killing had been due to the effects of too much alcohol, an argument that had gotten out of control. But now. Now he wasn't so sure.

Conor did know *one* thing, though. One thing that was *not* a gray area. He knew, without doubt, that he had not fired that gun the previous night. And he also knew with certainty that he had not killed anyone. And that's when he remembered Rita. He suddenly felt sick to his stomach at the thought of her hearing the news.

The sudden violent collision knocked the wind from his sails and sent him flying sideways to his right. He banged his head against the inside of the door and ended up lying on the back seat surrounded by shards of broken glass. The patrol car had been rammed at speed by a large black Jeep with thick, silver bull bars. It crashed into the driver's side of the Dodge Charger just as they began exiting the parking garage ramp, sending it careering sideways into the low concrete lane divider.

Officer Henderson shouted something so inaudible that Conor wasn't sure if it was a command for him to stay down or just a general curse at the suddenness of the crash. He had been incapacitated by the airbag, which deployed from the steering wheel in front of him, and was struggling to wriggle his arms free. He only barely caught sight of the two masked men who sprang from the Jeep and ran toward him. His window had been smashed in the crash, so there was nothing between him and the sawn-off shotgun one of them brought directly up to his temple. Conor pulled himself upright again, just in time to see the officer struggling to get his gun from its holster. Due to his size, however, and the flopping white airbag that had pinned him in his seat, Conor could see he had no room to maneuver.

Officer Henderson looked at the barrel of the shotgun and began to say something as it went off in his face. The sound was deafening in the cramped confines of the patrol car. His head exploded like a watermelon squashed by a heavy sledgehammer. Bone and brain fragments sprayed the interior, and Conor screamed in terror as his face, neck, and upper torso were instantly stained red by his blood.

Before he knew what had happened, the back door of the patrol car was wrenched open and the second man reached in and grabbed him by the shoulders. He tried to fight, but with hands cuffed behind his back, it proved to be a one-sided struggle. As soon as his head and shoulders were pulled through the door, the man who had killed Officer Henderson reached over to help his companion. Kicking and shouting, Conor was dragged violently from the back seat and bundled roughly into the back of the Jeep.

They placed a dirty cloth sack over his head so he couldn't see where they were taking him. It smelled of oil and grease and made him wretch. He tried to shake it free and right himself in the seat as they sped off, but without warning, felt a bone-crunching thump as the butt of the shotgun came down hard on his right temple. The blow wasn't severe enough to put him out or fracture his skull, but it was sudden and painful, and it dazed him, knocking him into quiet, drowsy submission.

Detective Bradley Shoemaker left Childs waiting in the car, filling out overdue progress reports, while he walked through the revolving door of a steel and glass building on the outskirts of Fort Lauderdale. The surrounding grounds were landscaped, with an impressive water fountain shooting up from the center of a small lake near the open-air parking lot. The grass was bright green and well cared for, watered by countless buried sprinklers whose spraying jets stuttered in circular motions across the lawn. Beds of brightly-colored flowers bordered the area with islands of pink Bougainvillea Shrubs and Cabbage Palms placed at precise intervals around the grounds.

Childs sat for a while in contemplation, watching the various groups of people strolling about the gardens before her. The patients were all wearing white dressing gowns, while those members of staff keeping an eye on them were dressed in light blue hospital uniforms. Some of the patients seemed lucid, chatting amongst themselves in small, intimate groups. Others, she noticed, appeared more sedated. They were the ones sitting quietly alone on the benches or in wheelchairs, staring blankly into the distance as if lost in their own troubled worlds.

Inside, Shoemaker walked briskly down a wide, brightly lit corridor leading to the private wards. There were countless signs to direct visitors, but he had been here before and knew his way around without looking at them. When he came to an intersection, he turned left and walked straight up to a small nurse's station down the end of the hall. The middle-aged lady behind the counter looked up at him over her horn-rimmed glasses and smiled warmly. "Good after-noon, Bradley. And how are you today?"

"I'm fine, Marlene. And you?" He took a pen from the counter and proceeded to sign the visitor's book.

"Davey has been accepted into the police training center in Miami." She beamed proudly. "He asked me to say thank you for putting a word in."

Davey was Marlene's teenage son who had left high school a year earlier, but was now struggling to find a job due to the downturn in the economy. He seemed like a good kid to Shoemaker, one who genuinely wanted to work. Shoemaker had felt like telling him to pick another career when they spoke a few weeks earlier, that if he wanted to have any kind of a normal existence, he should choose something else. But he didn't. Instead, he gave him the rou-tine lecture about how police work was not just a job, but was, in fact, a way of life. About how people would treat him differently once they knew he was a cop, never fully trusting him in case he was taking note of everything they said.

He then proceeded to give the kid the statistics on the high suicide rates among members of the force. But it didn't seem to dissuade him. Shoemaker soon came to realize that Davey wasn't really taking it in. He had seen too much TV and wanted nothing more than to get his hands on the gun and the uniform. He was looking for an exciting challenge. Shoemaker didn't hold that against him, though. Most of the young recruits were like that. At least, in the beginning.

"Naw, tell him he's welcome, Marlene," he said, waving the thank you away with his hand. "All I really did was give the kid a character reference. The rest was his doing."

Shoemaker turned and went straight for the door at the end of the corridor. He stopped for a second and took a deep, steadying breath before opening it. Inside, the curtains were closed and the room was in darkness. He immediately went to the window and drew them open to let the light in. As he turned back, though, his gaze went painfully toward the young woman lying in the bed. She was in a coma, a plastic tube coming from her mouth to a ventilator, another from her arm to a drip hanging from a metal stand. There was a heart monitor on a table to her right that beeped intermittently to show she was still alive.

Alive, Shoemaker thought. *Jesus, who in their right mind could call* this *alive?* He leaned over and lovingly kissed his daughter's forehead, sat back in the hard bedside chair, and then remained there for a few seconds. The flowers on the locker were dying, and he made a mental note to bring fresh ones. After a while, he took a book off the locker and began reading from where he'd turned down the page on his last visit. The book was called *Baby Goes to SeaWorld*, one of Alisha's favorites when she was a little girl. He used to read it to her by the light of her pink bedside lamp, tucking her in, sending her off into a safe, peaceful sleep.

Shoemaker remembered those times well. They were the happy years when he still had a family. When he and his wife, Diane, took trips to the beach or the park at weekends. Alisha loved the sea. She was only about four or five, as he recalled, but he would put her on his shoulders and walk through the white sand for hours. Then he got promoted to detective and everything changed.

He remembered celebrating the good news with Diane. They cracked open a bottle of red wine and stayed up half the night talking about what they would do now that he was finally on a half decent salary. The first thing she wanted was to put down a deposit on a house and move out of their crummy apartment. A house with a garden for Alisha to play in, she said. He had been content in that old rundown apartment, even happy, but he went along with the plan and started viewing houses with her up in Boca. After a while, the houses all started to look the same to him, and he and Diane began arguing about how most of the ones she picked out were over their budget.

Then his caseload started to get on top of him and he was forced to put in a lot of overtime if he wanted to keep his job and pay for the new house. Of course, it wasn't long before he wasn't there weekends anymore. The trips to the park and beach became scarcer until they eventually petered out and stopped altogether.

Shoemaker finished reading a chapter and folded the corner down for next time. He stood up, kissed his daughter's forehead again, and whispered, "See you next Friday, baby."

As he walked down the corridor, back out to his waiting partner, he reflected on the night about two months ago when Diane called him at work to say Alisha had been rushed to hospital. That was one of the darkest times of his life. He remembered arguing with the doctor in the ER who informed them Alisha had suffered a reaction to an ecstasy tablet she'd taken, while Diane just sat there crying. Their daughter was a good, respectable young woman, he had told the fresh-faced doctor who just looked back at him like he'd heard it all before. She was an intelligent girl who would never be stupid enough to take drugs. She was too smart for that, had gotten good grades, and knew exactly where it led.

But then the tired young doctor led him behind the curtain to where she lay unconscious on a gurney, showing him the toxicology report that had just come back from the lab. There was no doubt about it, her blood contained MDMA, MDEA, amphetamines and traces of LSD. But there were also traces of Atropine, a prescription drug that could be harmful if overdosed. How had he missed it? he wondered. How in God's name had he not seen the signs? He, a detective of all people, who dealt with that sort of thing every day of his working life?

As he exited through the revolving door into the blinding white sunlight and back down the steps toward the car, he sighed wearily to himself. He may have known all about what signs to look for, but in truth, he had not been at home enough to have seen them. He and Diane had drifted apart since he had begun spending almost every waking hour at the station or out on the road. The only time he saw Alisha was when they would bump into each other like strangers in the night. She was in her mid-teens and difficult to read. They would say a quick, awkward hello before continuing on their separate ways. He was usually just back home to grab a fresh shirt, heading off again on some case or stakeout that couldn't wait. Diane had started drinking around then, but he didn't blame her. No, there was only one person responsible, and that was himself. Him, he thought as the rage built up inside, and also those evil scumbags who were becoming rich off the misery of others. That's when he resolved to find out who was responsible for dealing the pills and bring them to justice.

"Everything all right?" Childs asked, looking concerned when he climbed back into the passenger seat.

"Fine," he replied.

"No change?" She placed the stack of unfinished reports on the back seat.

Shoemaker put on his seatbelt and sighed. "Nope, still the same."

"That's a shame." Childs started the engine of the Ford Marauder and headed slowly toward the main gate. "Hey, you want to head back to the station and question that guy Rogan some more?"

"Sure, let's do that," he replied.

"So...what do you think *really* happened?" she said matter-of-factly as they exited the gate and turned out onto the road. "You think he did it?"

"Who knows," sighed Shoemaker. "I've seen so much shit go down in this town that nothing would surprise me anymore. But you know, given that the Suarez family is involved, I just can't help thinking things may not be as cut and dry as they seem."

"So, I take it you won't be sending flowers to Hector's funeral?" she said, casting him a glance to see his reaction.

But Shoemaker didn't smile as she thought he might. In fact, he didn't show much emotion at all, just shrugged.

"You know the old saying?" Childs said.

"No, which one's that?"

"You live by the sword, you die by the sword. Right?"

"Guess in this case it's true," Shoemaker replied.

"You're damn right it's true."

"But you know what?" he continued. "I think I prefer, if you spit in the air, it will hit you in the face."

"What? Did you just make that up?" she chuckled.

"No, I didn't, it's a real saying."

"Yeah? So what does it mean?"

Shoemaker shrugged. "Who knows? But I think in Hector Suarez's case, it kind of means something like, what goes around comes around."

CHAPTER NINE

CARLOS AND ERNESTO

When Conor regained full awareness, it was with a loud gasp. A bucket of ice-cold water was thrown over him and the greasy cloth sack removed from his head by someone standing behind. He was bound to an old wooden chair with silver duct tape, his ankles fixed to its front legs, his hands still handcuffed behind his back. The dead officer's blood and gristle was stinging his eyes, caked in his hair, and dried onto his face and chest.

"What's going on?" he gasped, spitting out water. "Who's there?"

Silence. As his eyes adjusted, he cast his gaze around the room in an attempt to face his captors. One was behind, the other standing in the shadows just out of view to his right. He quickly scanned his surroundings and saw he was in a dark, filthy basement with a metal door barely visible to his left and a small window beyond it in the far corner. It was too high to reach, he decided, and probably too small to climb through even if he could. The bare flickering bulb overhead gave off a dull yellow glow, but in the half-light, he could just make out something moving on the floor about ten feet in front of him. It puzzled him for a second or two. Curious, he squinted his eyes and leaned forward to see what it was, only to emit a loud, terrified scream as a ferocious-looking alligator lunged from the shadows and snapped its razor-sharp teeth within inches of his feet.

"Mother of God!" he shouted, rocking the chair from side to side in sheer panic as the monster sprang toward him once again. This time, he actually felt the rush of air as its enormous jaws snapped down before him. Its breath was foul, and the stench lingered in his nostrils even when it took a few steps back and receded into the shadows.

He inhaled a deep gasp of air and let out a sigh of relief as it retreated, just catching sight of a chain tied around its neck as it disappeared into the darkness. The chain was wrapped around a bolt in the wall, and he realized it had been just long enough to allow the creature to move forward without actually biting him. Whoever tied it there had intentionally done so to strike terror into his heart, purposely and sadistically leaving only inches to spare.

He frantically looked to the other side of the room for another way out, but found nothing there except dozens of heavy metal beer kegs stacked haphazardly against the wall near the window. There was also a wooden pallet on the floor opposite, packed with cardboard boxes, partly covered by a dusty tarpaulin. The entire place reeked of stale beer and urine. But that was not all. No, there was another, much stronger odor he couldn't quite make out. It smelled of rotting flesh down there, similar to fish guts decomposing in the sun, yet more pungent and nauseating than anything he had ever encountered.

As he tried to work out what the smell was, Carlos Suarez stepped from the shadows to his right. As soon as Conor saw him, his heart sank. He knew they must be in the cellar of one of the nightclubs, and with a sickening feeling in the pit of his stomach, finally understood what this was all about. If Carlos was the one who threw the water over him, he concluded, the other man standing behind must be his brother, Ernesto. They were the masked attackers who murdered the police officer and abducted him. They were out for revenge. It all began to make sense.

"Listen to me," he said with as much calmness as he could muster under the circumstances. He knew he had to remain calm, to explain the misunderstanding. "Please, you have got this *all* wrong. I swear to Christ, I had absolutely *nothing* to do with your father's death."

If Carlos had spoken, Conor thought he would have felt a bit better. At least then they might have discussed what transpired the night before. Maybe he would get the chance to explain all he knew, and maybe, just maybe, they would believe him and let him go. But Carlos approached him in stony silence, ignored his protestations, and calmly placed a strip of silver duct tape over his mouth. It was clear he did not want him talking just yet.

As Conor jerked his body to-and-fro in protest, Ernesto leaned over from behind and looped a noose of electrical cable around his neck. He tugged it back so tightly that the front legs of the chair left the floor with a loud creak. Conor suddenly found himself leaning backwards, staring up toward the light bulb as if in a dentist's chair waiting to be examined. The noose pulled tighter around his throat, biting into his skin and forcing him to start gagging for breath. All the while Carlos just stood there looking down at him, saying nothing, showing no visible sign of emotion.

Then Conor caught sight of Ernesto moving away to his left and realized with dread that the cable was tied to something behind the chair. He was now left suspended in limbo, leaning backwards in a most precarious and unnatural position. It was the most horrible, nauseating sensation. There was something weighty behind the back legs of the chair, something stopping it from falling back any further. Perhaps it was a concrete block or one of the heavy beer kegs, he pondered. Either way, he quickly understood its purpose. It was a cruel device, only allowing him breath if he remained perfectly still with the chair balanced awkwardly on its two back legs. For if he struggled or tried to move in any way whatsoever, the chair would automatically fall forward and the cable would tighten unbearably around his neck.

But Conor realized something else. Slow strangulation was the least of his problems at that point in time, because as he sat there balancing on the two back legs, he caught a brief glimpse of the alligator's snout peeping out from the shadows. It was chewing on something. Gnawing. There was a blood-soaked hand protruding from the corner of its jaw— pale, thin fingers tipped with blue nail polish. His stomach retched and he tasted vomit in the back of his throat.

As he quickly swallowed it back, Conor caught sight of Ernesto kneeling on the floor to his left and felt his canvas shoes being removed to expose his bare feet. The Cuban clipped something sharp and spiky onto his right big toe, then did the exact same thing to his left. It was only when he moved back and there was a flash of bright sparks nearby that Conor finally understood what was going on. Shouting muffled protests through the duct tape, he strained his head down as far as he could to get a better look. To his absolute horror, he found Ernesto kneeling over a large semi-truck battery on the floor.

The pain was more intense than anything he had ever experienced in his life. When the Cuban touched the cable to the positive terminal, a surge of electricity shot through Conor's body like a bolt of lightning. It felt like a red-hot dagger being plunged back and forth into his spine. The sensation was unbearable. His body gyrated uncontrollably and he began shaking like a worm impaled on a fishing hook. The chair fell forward and the noose yanked painfully at his throat. He bit his tongue.

After a few minutes, Ernesto took the cable away from the terminal. The sparking electricity stopped immediately, yet it took a full minute for Conor to stop shaking. But he was choking now, gagging for air. When the alligator came into view again and lunged forward with mouth open wide, it required every ounce of strength and willpower he possessed to quickly kick his toes off the floor, leaning the chair back just in time to save himself. The chain around the beast's neck snapped taut and stopped it in its tracks. Almost as if it knew the routine, it shuffled reluctantly back into the darkness to await another chance.

But at least now Conor could breath, even though it was only through his nose. The sharp, stabbing pain had subsided, but it was immediately replaced by a cold numbness. He tasted blood in his mouth, running down his throat, felt dizzy and totally drained of energy.

Then, without warning, Ernesto stood up behind him and placed a plastic bag over his head. He squeezed it so tight around Conor's neck he could not catch his breath. He tried desperately to inhale through his nostrils, but began gagging and spluttering as the plastic was sucked up into them. His airways became blocked. He felt his lungs bursting for oxygen, the veins in his neck throbbing and his eyeballs bulging in their sockets. Conor's head felt like it was imploding, his body thrashing to-and-fro like a fish out of water desperately fighting for breath.

When Ernesto removed the bag a few seconds later, Conor turned his head helplessly to Carlos, his burning eyes pleading with him to stop this madness. But the Cuban had been standing no more than two or three feet away to his right, talking on his cell phone the whole time. He was watching the show as if he had no great interest in its outcome. It was as if Conor's pain and suffering meant nothing to him. There wasn't the slightest hint of emotion showing on his square, chiseled face.

Conor then saw him blink his eyes to Ernesto to signal "again," and he emitted a pitiful, muffled scream to stop. It was no use, though. Ernesto touched the cable to the battery and the pain surged through him once more. This time, the agony went on longer until, just as he began to pass out, Ernesto broke the circuit and stepped back. Again, even though the electricity stopped, he continued shaking uncontrollably for the longest time. When the pain eventually subsided and his body fell still, Carlos finally stepped closer and ripped the duct tape from his mouth. There was an acrid smell of burnt flesh, and although he couldn't see or feel them, Conor knew it was coming from his toes.

"Donde esta la bolsa?" Carlos said coldly.

"I...I don't know what you're talking about," Conor replied through chattering teeth.

"Where is the bag?"

"What bag? Please, Carlos, I don't know anything about a—"

"Where is the bag?"

"Please. If you'd just tell me—"

Carlos nodded toward Ernesto and it began again. Without the tape covering his mouth, Conor's agonizing cries were so loud they drowned out the crackling sound coming from the sparking battery. He blacked out for what seemed like an eternity, yet when his senses returned and he opened his eyes, Carlos was still in the exact same position before him and he realized with utter dejection that it had only been a few seconds.

"Once more," said the Cuban. "Where is that bag?"

"Please, Carlos," he groaned. "For the love of God, I don't know anything about a bag." He saw him signal to Ernesto once more, but shouted, "No! Stop! Just stop and I promise will tell you everything. I swear to God, I will tell you."

There was a pause as Carlos considered his words. Shaking, Conor prayed with all his might that the Cuban would not signal to his brother again. He knew his body could take no more.

"Alright then," he finally said without emotion. "Start by telling us why you killed our father."

"But it wasn't me!" stammered Conor. "It was Bob Castagna."

"Castagna's dead," Ernesto growled angrily from behind.

"No," Conor cried. "He's alive. He's alive. I swear."

"Castagna, that weasel," Carlos muttered beneath his breath, his eyes opening a little wider at the prospect that Bob might actually not be dead. "I should have known he had *something* to do with this."

Conor felt his spirits raised for a split second. If they believed him, there might at least be a glimmer of hope.

"So, if what you say is true, where is he?" Carlos asked coldly.

Conor swallowed hard. "Look, I don't know where he is right now. He must have gone into hiding. I heard a shot in the cabin and found him standing over your father with the revolver in his hand. When I tried to call for help, he knocked me out. The police think I killed them both because he was gone when they got there. That's why they arrested me. But he *is* alive. I swear to you."

Carlos considered this for a moment, before saying, "Then if you're telling the truth, where is the bag?"

"What bag are you talking about?" Conor caught the look of anger and impatience on the Cuban's face. "Please, Carlos. What bag?"

"The bag of cocaine our father and Castagna carried back from the island."

"Huh?" he moaned. He was struggling to remain conscious, but this revelation jolted him awake. In his mind, he made the connection at long last. It was a piece that finally fit into the jigsaw. If there *had* been drugs in the bag, then that changed everything. He was now certain the black holdall was not on the yacht anymore, that Bob now had it. Was *that* what this was about? Had Bob killed Hector Suarez and framed him for a lousy bag of drugs?

"Donde esta la bolsa?" Carlos repeated irritably, growing more and more impatient by the minute. "Tell us where it is or you will suffer like you cannot imagine."

"Bob must have it," he replied, stuttering as he caught sight of the alligator's snout coming out of the shadows.

"Very well. If that is so, then tell us where he is," he said again as he raised his hand.

"But I told you, I don't know. Please."

Carlos motioned for Ernesto to begin again, but before he could connect the battery, Conor shouted, "Wait, Carlos! There *is* something else."

The Cuban raised a hand for his brother to hold for a moment.

"I...I think he may have had help."

"What do you mean? *Who* would have helped him?"

"Look, I don't know," he moaned. "But the detectives said the dinghy was still attached to the *Aphrodite* when they went onboard."

"So what?"

"Don't you see? Bob could *not* have gone ashore without that dinghy. Not unless he had help. Not unless someone else came out in another boat to get him."

Carlos pondered this new information for a few moments, his brain sifting through the various scenarios. Conor knew instinctively what he was thinking. There weren't many people he could think of who would knowingly help Bob Castagna kill his father and steal his cocaine. Anyone familiar with the Suarez family was aware that they would stop at nothing in their search for retribution. That much even Conor had learned, even though he was only a newcomer. Their reputation had been forged in violence and intimidation ever since Hector came over from Cuba in the late fifties. Escaping Castro's revolution, he got into the nightclub business in Miami and had built it up into the successful enterprise it was today by commanding fear and respect among his rivals. But if there was even a hint of a coup...

No, Conor felt he knew exactly what was going through Carlos' mind as he looked down upon him tied to the chair. Which, if any, of his local competitors would have the balls to make such a move? Hector's actual murder had been carried out by Bob Castagna, alright. He knew Carlos believed him about that. He knew he didn't like or trust Bob from the first time he saw them together at the club. But if it *was* true that someone else had helped, he knew Carlos would desperately want to know who it was. Because that opened up a whole new avenue of scenarios and possibilities. The way powerful men kept control of their empires was by staying one step ahead of those who would take them away, so if there was even a *hint* of a conspiracy, he needed to know about it and he needed to know fast.

Either way, Conor thought, Carlos would stop at nothing until he found Bob and the cocaine. No matter what it took, no matter who stood in his way, and no matter what he had to do. And when he *did* locate him, he knew he would first find out who had helped him and then take great pleasure in killing him. That thought didn't bother Conor at this point. Bob had put him in this position and he hated him for it. He wanted him to suffer.

"You might as well tell us where he is," Carlos said quietly after a pause.

"What? Weren't you listening? I have told you everything I know. You've got to believe that I am just a victim in this like your father. I have absolutely no idea where Bob is."

"Maybe so," Carlos said quietly. "Perhaps you *are* telling the truth."

Conor breathed a little sigh of relief.

"But still, I don't really think you are telling us every-thing," he continued. "There has got to be more."

It wasn't the reaction Conor was hoping for. He was counting on them freeing him so he could help locate Bob.

"I swear to you, Carlos, on my life, I don't know where he is."

"My friend, let me be clear about this. If you do not start telling us the whole truth, you will not leave this room alive. But if you tell us where Castagna is, and also who else is helping him, the pain *will* stop. I promise you that. It will not be so hard on you if you tell us what we want to know."

"This is crazy," Conor gasped disbelievingly. "I had abso-lutely nothing to do with this. I know you know that. All I want to do is find Bob Castagna the same as you."

He sensed Carlos knew he was telling the truth, that he genuinely didn't know any more. But Carlos was a man who knew no pity. He must have figured out that if Conor was involved, he would probably not have remained on the boat with the body of his father.

"Last chance to talk," he said.

"Please, no more."

"Donde esta Castagna? Donde esta la bolsa?"

"Please, no more. I'm begging you."

Conor saw him nod to Ernesto to continue the torture.

Danny McNamara had been sitting for over an hour in the waiting room of the Miami Metro Police Department when a voice finally called out his name. It had taken an awful lot for him to voluntarily enter a police station after Detective Shoemaker phoned asking him to come down. Police stations were definitely not among Danny's favorite buildings. They were not environments where he felt comfortable. In the past, the only time he had actually been in one, he had either been beaten up in the interrogation room or locked in one of the basement cells. They were not happy memories, and even just sitting there among the other waiting victims and witnesses made him feel extremely uncomfortable.

He rose and went over to meet the red-haired woman by the desk who had just called his name. Detective Childs eyed him distastefully and a little suspiciously, but shook his hand cordially enough and asked him to follow. Without explanation or small talk, she led him down a corridor full of stacked box files and through a large set of double doors. She then brought him across the huge, open-plan office to a desk by the window, one that was buried beneath stacks of manila folders and loosely stapled papers. Detective Shoemaker was already sitting there, and without standing, motioned for Danny to sit. He asked him if he wanted coffee, but Danny declined, immediately asking to see Conor.

"When is the last time you spoke to him?" Shoemaker inquired, ignoring Danny's request.

"When? Couple of nights ago," he replied. "But I can guarantee you both, he had absolutely nothin' to do with any of this."

Childs pulled up a chair and sat down at the other end of the desk. "So how did you find out about Rogan's arrest? Has he been in touch with you?"

Danny explained how he heard them talking about it on the local radio station that afternoon. About how Hector Suarez was pronounced dead at the scene and how Conor had been charged with the murder. Also, there was something else about a local businessman called Bob Castagna, who had seemingly gone missing and was feared drowned.

Shoemaker sat forward in his chair and told Danny not to believe everything he heard on the radio. He said the report of Conor's arrest was true enough, but the investigation itself was not as cut and dry as the earlier news reports suggested. Danny asked him to elaborate, but he refused, saying he was "unable to comment at this time."

"Look, events have taken what you might call *an unexpected turn* in the past couple of hours," he said quietly. "But right now, we need to know when *exactly* is the last time you spoke to him?"

Danny also sat forward in his chair. Squinting his eyes, he said, "What the fuck's going on here? Why can't I see my friend?"

"Because you're not here on a social visit," snapped Childs. "Now sit the fuck back. You are here for one reason, and that is to answer our questions."

"You're a bit of a spiteful bitch, aren't ye?" Danny replied, folding his arms in defiance. "Well I'm not sayin' another goddamned word until you let me see Conor."

Shoemaker sighed in resignation, considering the best way to handle the situation. "Alright then," he said quietly after a pause. "Look, here's the deal. At approximately six-thirty this evening, there was an incident at Broward Memorial."

"An incident? What the hell are ye talking about?"

"An officer from this department was killed while transporting your friend, Rogan, to the station."

"You're kiddin'," exclaimed Danny, a look of genuine disbelief on his face.

"Trust me, I would not kid about something like that," growled Shoemaker. "I knew the officer personally. He was old school and well liked around here. He didn't deserve what he got." He leaned further forward and stared Danny accusingly in the eye. "Believe me when I tell you, McNamara, I will stop at nothing until his killers are brought to justice."

"Hey now, I hope you don't think I had anything to do with it," Danny said.

"Your alibi held up," replied Shoemaker. "We have witnesses and security footage putting you and your girlfriend in your bank manager's office on Commercial Boulevard at the time of the killing."

"Well okay then." Danny nodded with satisfaction, thinking it was the first time a bank's security camera had actually been beneficial to him. The irony was, the last time he was caught on one, he went away for five years. "So what about Conor?" he asked. "You know there's no way he had anything to do with it either."

"Yeah? We're not so sure," replied Childs. "Now where is he?"

"But that's just fuckin' crazy. Conor Rogan is one of *the* most honest people I know."

"I'd imagine it's not hard to gain that distinction in *your* world," she said sarcastically. "Given the caliber of criminals and scumbags you associate with."

"That has nothin' to do with Conor," snarled Danny. "He's as straight as the day is long."

"Really? Well if he's *so* honest and law abiding, what the hell is he doing hanging out with low-lifes like you and Hector Suarez?"

"Bitch."

"I'll ask you one more time, where the hell is he?" snapped Childs.

"And what in God's name was he thinking, getting mixed up with the Suarez family?" Shoemaker added a bit quieter.

"There was no sign of him when the officer's patrol car was found," Childs said when Danny made no response. "So we are now wondering if he didn't mastermind all of this. If he hasn't escaped, freed by his accomplices."

"That's bullshit!" Danny roared, springing to his feet so quickly he startled Shoemaker. The detective sat back with a fright and instinctively brought his hand to his gun holster.

"Sit the fuck down!" he shouted through gritted teeth. "Right now! Or so help me, I will shoot you where you stand."

Danny slowly sat back down with fists clenched tightly on the desk. He was angry that anyone would accuse Conor of such a thing. If it was himself, he could understand. Hell, he had done some crazy, evil shit in his day. But not Conor Rogan.

He owed a lot to Conor and had sworn to repay it one day. He felt he had always been good to his sister, Grainne, and had helped him personally through some tough times. And not just lending him money and shit. Sure, he had bailed him out on more than one occasion, but more importantly, Conor had visited him in Mountjoy Prison in Dublin and had offered his support when most of Danny's so-called friends and even his family simply abandoned him. Over the years, he had been a good friend to Danny, helping him move to London when he got out, and even helping him get a job. In fact, in many ways, Conor had probably saved him from himself.

"Now get this and get this straight," Shoemaker continued in a low, controlled tone. "Either one of two things happened here. First, your friend is an innocent in all this, as you would have us believe. If that *is* the case, he may have been framed and then abducted at the hospital today for reasons we don't yet know."

"Or?" asked Danny.

"Or he is party to multiple homicides, and as Detective Childs already said, was freed by accomplices during a rescue attempt."

"No way has he got anything to do with this," repeated Danny. "As far as I'm concerned, he's in trouble and needs help. And to be honest, I want to know what exactly this excuse for a police department is going to do about it?"

"We will do what we have to," Shoemaker replied. "And watch your mouth or I'll have you locked away and bury the paperwork so that you never see daylight again."

"Well, all I know is he's innocent." Danny sighed heavily. "Soon as I heard Hector Suarez was pals with his boss, I knew it wouldn't end well. I fuckin' warned him."

"Well, it's too late now," said Shoemaker. "Either way, there is also the fact to consider that someone tipped off the killers about him and Officer Henderson leaving the hospital at that precise time. It can't have been coincidence that they sprung their attack precisely where they did, in the one blind spot where there are no security cameras."

"Well that's your problem," muttered Danny. "Conor is all I'm concerned about right now."

"Alright then," Shoemaker said thoughtfully. "So, in a nutshell, you're telling us you haven't spoken to him in a couple of days, and that you have no idea where he might be?"

"No, none. I swear it."

"Alright then. So let's say we believe you, it goes without saying that we want you to call us if you hear from him."

"Sure, no bother. But hey, I want to hear from you too if you locate him."

"Okay. You may as well go home then. Thanks for coming down."

As Danny rose to leave, Shoemaker stood up with him.

"Look, McNamara, if it's any consolation, I'm not totally convinced myself that Rogan did it," he said. "I'm not a big fan of the Suarez family and would like nothing better than to find out they have something to do with this. Anyway, I aim to find the sons of bitches who are responsible, one way or the other. And when I do, I will personally hang their balls from the station flagpole. That is a promise."

Shoemaker sat back down and folded his arms, watching thoughtfully as Childs led Danny back across the office toward the door.

"Conor Rogan," he whispered to himself. "Where the hell are you hiding?"

As he sank deeper beneath the waves heading toward the seabed, he finally felt at peace with himself. He surrendered. He stopped struggling and let his body drift down into the blackness without fighting the current. It wasn't so bad. He felt a calmness wash over him now as he descended ever deeper, had almost given himself to it when the hazy white figure rose up again from the depths. It moved slowly but with purpose through the icy water, grabbed hold of him, and began pulling him closer. He blinked his eyes open to see her face directly before his. Her skin was bleached pale, her dead shark-like eyes staring deep into his soul. He knew her!

Conor regained consciousness in the silent semi-darkness of the basement. He was still tied to the chair, which in turn was still balanced at an angle on its two back legs. The Cubans were gone for now, but he was certain they would be back before long to resume his torture. Either that, he decided, or to finish him off for good. The fact that he was still alive probably meant one of two things. Either they believed he could still be of use for information, or else they simply wanted to take their time killing him. As soon as they returned, however, he knew with certainty that he was dead. There was no way Carlos or Ernesto Suarez were letting him go now.

Every muscle in his body ached from the electric current that had passed through it. His feet throbbed and were blackened and burnt raw, his throat stinging from the hard plastic cable still cutting into it. The problems hanging over him with the police were serious—Hector Suarez's death, Bob Castagna's disappearance, and the officer's murder at the hospital. But he didn't have the luxury of pondering any of them right now. At that moment in time, the most pressing problem Conor faced was how to get himself out of this nightmare. That was more serious. If he was to survive the night, he knew he had to act fast. He had to focus, as if he were guiding a yacht through a storm. There was no way he could go through another hour of torture. He knew that with certainty. His battered body just wouldn't take it. So he decided he had to proceed with calmness, as if at the helm, fighting alone against the waves. That was the only way to survive, he decided. He had to clear his mind of fear, blank out the pain and think. Figure some way out of this hell.

Talking his way to freedom was not an option. He knew from painful experience that the Suarez brothers were not the type of men to engage in debate. They were vicious animals who showed no empathy, who could not be reasoned or bargained with. There was talk of missing cocaine, and he knew that, to evil scum like them, getting it back took precedence over all else, even the death of their own father. He knew they would not let him leave this basement to tell the authorities, no matter what helpful information he gave them. He had seen it in Carlos' eyes at the end. Even when he started to believe his story, it made no difference. So he knew he did not have much time. If he was ever going to get out of this, he would have to rely on his own wits. And above all else, he would have to act now before they returned.

Keeping a close eye on the shadows where his nemesis, the alligator, was still lurking, Conor decided his first course of action must be to get out of the noose gripping him so tightly and restraining his movement. That was his first priority. And to do that, he had to figure out a way of getting the chair to go fully backwards. That was the key. He thought about this for a while before realizing there was really only one way open to him. So, without further delay, Conor began rocking the chair from side-to-side on its two back legs, all the while terrified it would lurch forward and strangle him. He moved slowly and carefully at first, then picked up speed and moved faster and more violently, until finally, its wooden mortise joints began to creak. After another two minutes, the wood eventually split under the strain and gave way completely. The back legs collapsed beneath him and he crashed painfully to the floor. As if alerted by the sudden noise, however, the beast suddenly sprang forward from the darkness with its teeth showing. Conor barely managed to roll onto his side, pulling his feet away a split second before its jaws snapped shut in front of him.

Still bent over in a sitting position, hands cuffed behind his back and ankles taped to the front legs, he turned around and began working his head out of the unforgiving noose. As he gripped it with his teeth and shook it loose, he saw how it had been tied to a six-inch nail in the wall behind him. The back legs of the chair had been screwed to a large plank of wood, which in turn had been nailed fast to the floor. It was an ingenious, yet sadistic contraption. The wooden brake had stopped him falling backwards in the chair, and the tightly secured cord had prevented him going forward with its threat of strangulation.

The blood froze in Conor's veins, however, when he suddenly thought he heard a noise outside the door. They must have heard the crash of splintered wood, he decided. His heart skipped a beat at the mere thought they might be coming back to finish him off. His mind raced in terror; sweat dripping from his brow as he waited nervously to be discovered. It seemed an eternity, but when no one came in after a few nervous minutes, he finally shook himself back into action and continued freeing himself from the chair.

Giving his hungry adversary a wide berth, he hopped over to the beer kegs stacked near the window. Except for its lack of back legs, the chair was still intact. So he lay down on his side and wedged the backrest between two of the heavy metal canisters then began pushing and twisting with all his might. It was extremely difficult and painful to maneuver with his hands cuffed behind him, but finally, after what seemed like an age, Conor managed to snap the back of the chair away from the seat. After that he had no difficulty getting the front legs and base to separate. It was simply a matter of prying them apart using the same method.

Still lying on his side, Conor now swung his arms down behind his back and stepped into the loop. With his hands finally in front of him, he was at last able to tear open the duct tape on his ankles and release himself from the two front legs of the chair. The sight of his blackened toes caught his eye and sickened him to the core, but he ignored them and quickly slipped on his shoes.

He fell to his knees with a sense of urgency and frantically began searching the dirty concrete floor for something to open the handcuffs. When he eventually found a small metal staple sticking out of the wooden pallet, he muttered, "Thank you, God" as he twisted it free. He wasted no time after that, hobbled over to stand in the dim yellow light directly beneath the tiny window, and set about bending the staple using a narrow crack in the wall. It took about five minutes to pick the lock on the handcuffs. He had done it before. It was a trick Danny and some of his criminal friends back in Dublin had taught him some years earlier. At the time, Conor had simply learned it as a joke, planning to use it as a party trick himself, never in his wildest imagination dreaming that it would someday save his life. As the lock clicked open and the cuffs fell away, he made a mental note to thank Danny if he ever got free. But he was not out yet. He knew only too well that the danger was only beginning. The yacht had not cleared the storm. He still had a long way to go.

Right now, Conor had one thing on his mind. Rubbing his wrists in an effort to get the blood flowing again, he grabbed one of the chair legs to use as a weapon. If the Cubans returned, he resolved to go down fighting. He was painfully aware that he was in no physical condition to put up a fight, and that they would probably be armed. But he swore to himself on everything sacred, he would rather die fighting than fall into their sadistic hands again.

With this in mind, he rolled one of the metal beer kegs from the corner to rest beneath the window and stood up on it in the hope of climbing out. But the attempt was in vain. As soon as he got high enough to see, he was confronted by an iron window grill bolted to the outside ledge. There was no way through it. So, without wasting any more time, he lowered himself to the floor and hobbled back toward the door. As he did, the alligator shifted on its bed of straw and followed him with its dead eyes, watchful for a chance to strike if he got close enough.

Once at the door, he listened carefully for a few minutes with his ear pressed against the cold metal panel. He wondered if he dared see what was on the other side. The thought of opening it terrified him beyond description. There was music coming from somewhere beyond, but it was muffled and distant. He couldn't wait. With time running out, he decided he had no other option but to go for it.

A quick inspection revealed there was no handle or keyhole on the inside panel. The door was locked, however, so there was obviously a bolt on the other side. But he noticed the hinges were facing him, which allowed it to open inwards. Using the handcuffs as a makeshift chisel and the chair leg as a hammer, he began working on the metal pin holding the bottom hinge in place. It took an age, and every bang put him more in danger of being discovered, but he was eventually able to knock the pin upwards so that it peeped out the top of the hinge. Once he could get at it, he used the teeth of the handcuffs to pry it out. As he had hoped, the structure of the door was compromised as soon as it was removed. At last now he had a chance. A glimmer of hope

Conor pulled the door open from the bottom left hand corner, using the handcuffs to get a grip at first, then when he was able to get his fingers in, with both hands. The top hinge bent slightly under the strain and there was a loud creaking sound outside as the metal deadbolt was twisted and pulled away from its bracket. The heavy door grinded against its frame until he was finally able to squeeze through the opening. He found himself glancing back at the alligator as he left the basement, saw its cold, lifeless eyes following his movement, watching him go with hungry disappointment.

With his improvised weapon in hand, Conor now moved cautiously out into a dark, narrow corridor. To his relief, he found it deserted except for a few stacked beer kegs and wooden crates lining the opposite wall. There was another metal door to his right, and at the far end, about thirty feet away, a thin glow of white light beaconing to him in the darkness. It was shining through a gap beneath the main exit door that was raised up above a set of old wooden steps. That was where the music was coming from, he realized, not relishing the prospect of opening it to find out who or what was on the other side.

So he turned his attention to the nearer door first. Squinting in the darkness, Conor approached it with caution and put his ear to the panel. He listened for a while, but could hear no sound coming from the other side except for a low, curious whimpering. So he opened it carefully and crept through into the darkness. As soon as he switched on the overhead light, he was shocked to find three young Asian women huddled together in a square metal dog cage by the far wall. Dressed only in t-shirts and panties, they sat upright when the light went on, looks of sheer terror on their tear-stained faces. He put his finger to his lips to tell them to be quiet, but the sight of an approaching man covered in blood and carrying a wooden chair leg sent them into a state of panic. They began sobbing and wailing even louder, holding each other tighter for protection. He tried to pacify them, but it was no use. The closer he got, the louder they became.

"Shhh," Conor whispered toward them, putting the weapon on the floor and raising his palms in a gesture of friendship. "I'm not here to hurt you."

One of the girls grabbed hold of the cage with both hands and began shaking it violently while the other two started screaming.

"Please," he said in a raised voice. "If you don't stop, they'll hear you and come back."

But it did no good, simply made them scream even louder. He reached down and picked up the chair leg again. Seeing there were no windows in the room, and realizing the captives would surely give him away with their racket, he hurriedly exited back into the hall and closed the door behind him. He knew that trying to help them right now was pointless. They were too scared and traumatized to be reasoned with. He figured the only way he could possibly save them would be to get clear and raise the alarm. And at that moment, he vowed even harder to get free. The Suarez family was into more than just bars and nightclubs. They were the lowest of the low in his eyes, drug smugglers and sex traffickers, trading in misery, in human flesh and addiction to make a profit.

Against his instinct and better judgment, Conor now headed for the main door at the end of the corridor. There was nowhere else left for him to go, he concluded, no other possible way out. But as he hobbled painfully toward the light, the music coming from the other side grew louder. He held his breath as he waited for someone to come bursting through at any moment. If they did, he told himself he would at least be ready for them with his makeshift club in one hand and the pointed end of the handcuffs in the other. Although he would be no match for an armed adversary, he was prepared to swing and stab without mercy if anyone came through that door. He told himself not to hesitate as he got closer to it. Gritting his teeth, he swore to give no quarter. Conor now felt like a wounded animal set to be slaughtered. Cornered, frightened, driven to the point where he would do absolutely anything to survive. He would have to be prepared to kill or he knew he would surely die.

His thoughts turned to Danny and to how he would handle the situation. The big man would not be afraid. He would probably get mad and kick open the door, pouncing on anyone unfortunate enough to be on the other side. But then, Conor knew he was not Danny. He didn't have that violent streak in him. But regardless of that, scared as he was, he resolved that whatever happened, he would not be captured again.

As he reached the steps below the door, however, its handle suddenly began moving downwards. Despite his resolve to fight, when the moment of truth actually came, Conor's knees went uncontrollably weak. A man speaking Spanish in a loud voice started to come through, his shoulder just visible in the opening. Although he had sworn to go on the offensive, Conor's blood felt as if it had suddenly left his body and he simply froze there in terror. Paralyzed with fear, his heart stopped beating as the door creaked open before him and the light from the other side began streaming into the hall. He was caught in no-man's land, frozen stiff like a rabbit in the headlights of an oncoming car. But then the man stopped for a moment in the half-open doorway to shout back to someone on the other side. It was only for a split second, but just enough time for Conor's senses to return to him. As soon as they did, he turned his head and noticed there was another inner door just ahead to his left that had been hidden by the staircase, one he had not been able to see before in the darkness.

Ernesto Suarez moved nonchalantly down the creaky wooden steps into the hallway, heading back to continue Conor's torture after taking a short coffee break. But on seeing his prisoner's silhouette darting through the other door, he let out an angry roar and quickly pulled a revolver from his belt. Conor slammed the door shut behind him and leaned against it as a bullet smashed through the wooden panel and whistled by his ear. He searched frantically around the frame in the darkness as another bullet ripped through the door and ricocheted off the wall behind him. With trembling hands, he came across a bolt halfway down and instantly slid it into place. Just as he did, Ernesto grabbed the handle and tried to open it. The door shook violently as the enraged Cuban began battering it down with his shoulder, screaming threats and obscenities in Spanish as he did so.

Conor turned on the light and found himself in a small toilet with a shit-stained bowl and a cracked porcelain sink pulled away from the wall. But he paid no attention to the squalor, instantly turning his gaze to a small window above the urinal. As he did, the door buckled inwards as Ernesto rammed it again. The bolt creaked under the strain and began coming away from the frame. Conor's heart skipped a beat and he prayed the screws would hold for just a few seconds more as he leaped up onto the toilet and forced open the rotten-wooden window. To his utter relief, there were no bars blocking his way this time, and he gratefully whispered, "Thank you Lord," as he climbed up and frantically scrambled through.

As he made his escape, the door exploded inwards behind him and Ernesto dove across the room to grab his ankle. He was left in limbo for a brief terrifying moment, hanging helplessly from the window as the Cuban tried desperately to get hold of his other leg and pull him back in.

Conor screamed like a madman, kicking out with all his might until he found Ernesto's chin with the heel of his shoe. The big Cuban let out a roar of pain, releasing his grip as he fell backwards to the floor. Seconds later, Conor dropped down into the deserted alleyway behind the building and began hobbling away.

It was night and there was a lightning storm off in the distance. Not the kind of storm he was familiar with back in Ireland, usually hidden by clouds and only glowing in the darkness for a split second. This was a spectacular sub-tropical lightning show common to South Florida, especially in the overpowering heat of the summer.

The flashes came quick and strong as he limped his way to freedom, his eyes frantically scanning the maze of alleys and turns that ran left and right about him. As the loud cracks turned night to day, he suddenly paused for a second to catch his breath and decide which way to go. But even as he did, he heard Ernesto shouting after him from the open window and ducked as another bullet whizzed past his head and smashed into the brickwork above. Then Conor heard another raised voice approaching from behind to his right. He couldn't see him, but he was certain it was Carlos. The other Cuban knew he had escaped and was now coming after him.

Wiping the blood and sweat from his eyes, he immediately darted away toward the end of the alley to his left, hopping and grunting as the pain shot up through his feet. Every time he reached a junction or a turn, he knew the choice he made was a matter of life and death. But he couldn't think about that right now, in the same way he couldn't dwell on the pain. There was no time to waste. He knew if he hesitated again, they would be on him, so he kept running as fast as he could.

Reaching the end of the alley took less than thirty seconds in the darkness. When he got to the far end, however, he discovered it led out onto a wide, dimly lit road that was not too busy with traffic. He thought about rushing out and waving down a passing motorist, but decided against it. First, he would probably be run over as he couldn't see anyone in their right mind stopping for a bloodied, crazy-looking madman. Second, he had not forgotten about his arrest and how the detectives didn't believe a word he said. He knew Carlos and Ernesto would deny everything and he would probably be left holding the bag for the officer's death as well.

Conor was a stranger in this foreign place, had no money and nowhere to go. But then his thoughts returned to Danny and he immediately decided he had to get to a phone. It was his only hope. If Danny would help him, shelter him for a while, maybe he could catch his breath and figure out the best course of action to take. His eyes fixed on a Chevron gas station about a hundred yards up ahead on the opposite side of the road. The pumps were sheltered by a large blue overhang. The office and store were about ten feet behind them with a sign over the entrance reading "Food Mart." It was well lit inside, like an oasis in the darkness. Conor knew he had to act fast.

Tossing the chair leg and cuffs into an open dumpster, he sprang out of the alley and sprinted across the road, all the while praying they were not close enough behind to see which direction he had taken. Using the undergrowth along the verge for cover, he quickly made his way to the station. He tried to look as inconspicuous as he could when he arrived, limping across the busy forecourt until he reached the side of the building. Once there, he quickly ducked around the back and hid himself in the shadows, panting and retching as he tried to catch his breath.

A few seconds later, the Suarez brothers raced across the forecourt and stopped by the pumps, scanning the area like wolves. Conor broke into a cold sweat, sure they had seen him. He held his breath and immediately regretted discarding his weapons. His heart started beating faster, so much so he feared it would burst in his chest. But thankfully, they only stopped for a moment, catching their own breaths before taking off at speed again in the opposite direction. He exhaled a deep sigh of relief.

About five minutes later, a white Lincoln Navigator pulled up close by and a large woman climbed out and disappeared into the store. Conor moved quickly, opened the unlocked SUV door, and slipped inside. On seeing the keys were not in the ignition, he grabbed a cell phone lying on the dash and immediately disappeared back into the shadows behind the building. He held his breath as he waited for Danny to pick up. The phone rang for what seemed like an age, but to his dismay, there was no answer. He tried again, certain he was dialing the correct number. Still no answer. Eventually, just when he was about to give up, the phone started vibrating in his hand. Unknown number.

"Hello?" he said quietly, certain it must be for the woman in the store.

"Is that you, Conor?" a woman asked in a broad Southern accent.

He hesitated for a moment. "Who...who is this?"

"Shawna. It's—" There was a rustling noise and muffled voices before Danny came on the line sounding very concerned. "Con, where the fuckin' hell are ye? Have you *any* idea of the trouble you're in? The cops are watchin' me in case you come by. I'm not sure if they're tappin' my phone, so I had to get Shawna to call you back on hers."

"Look, I don't have much time," Conor interrupted. "I know I'm in trouble, Danny. Believe me, even more than you know." He paused when he saw the fat woman get back into the Lincoln with a couple of plastic shopping bags, reverse, and then drive away. When she was gone, he moved further around to the other side of the building in case she discovered her phone missing and came back. He crouched down in the long grass. It was darker and more secluded here and he felt safer. An article he had read in a magazine on the flight over warned visitors to avoid long grass and areas of waste ground in Florida due to the threat of snakes, but right now, that didn't bother him in the slightest. At that moment in time, he was more concerned about a different type of snake.

"Danny, I need help bad. I'm hurt and I need you to pick me up. Can you do that? Please?"

"Shit," the big man said in frustration. "These fuckin cops are up my arse right now."

"Please, Danny. I won't last the night."

"Give me a second."

"Please."

"Just give me a second while I think. Okay, look, I want to help you. I've just got to figure out the best way." Then, after a short, thoughtful pause, he said, "All right, I've got it. Tell me where you are and I'll get Shawna's brother, Anton, to pick you up and bring you to his gaff. You remember him, don't you? You met him outside the club the other night."

"Are you sure you want to involve him?" Conor asked. "This isn't just petty shit, Danny. There are guys after me. Killers. This is serious."

"Anton is family," Danny reassured him. "Don't worry. He and I are like brothers."

"Okay, but I'm not sure where *exactly* I am. The street sign says One-Hundred and Sixty-Fifth," Conor said. "I'm hiding out the back of a Chevron station."

"Any landmarks?"

"I can see a Wynne Dixie and a Pizza Hut down the end of the street on the opposite side."

"I'm pretty sure I know where you are then. As far as I can tell, you're in Boca, close to where we met the other night."

"You mean the nightclub? The Azteca?"

"Yeah."

"That makes sense," muttered Conor. "It makes sense that they would bring me there."

"Huh?"

"Look, tell Anton to pull right up to the Food Mart behind the pumps. I'll be waiting at the side by the air pump. Out of sight."

"Good man," said Danny. "Keep your head down 'cause your face is all over the fuckin' news. I'll get him to head over there right now. It should only take him about fifteen or twenty minutes. Think you can hold on that long?"

"Yeah, I think so."

"Grand. Just sit tight so."

"Wait!" Conor shouted before Danny could hang up. "I forgot to ask what make of car he'll be driving?"

"What the fuck does that matter?"

"Just so I'll know it's him," Conor said.

Danny laughed heartily. "Believe me, Con, Anton's got a style all his own. There's no way you're gonna miss him!"

CHAPTER TEN

POMPANO BEACH

When Anton Washington finally pulled up to the Food Mart, he was driving a bright red Cadillac El Dorado convertible. Conor suddenly realized what Danny had meant. Shawna's brother certainly did have a style of his own, but could not have been any more conspicuous if he tried. He seemed oblivious to the surrounding danger, however, and beckoned welcomingly to the bloodstained Irishman who scurried around from the side of the building and jumped into the passenger seat. The Suarez brothers were nowhere to be seen for now, but Conor kept low until they were well out of the neighborhood. He observed Anton as he drove. Wearing a white string vest and dark blue pants, Danny's friend wore so much gold jewelry he could have opened his own store.

"Man, you look like you havin' a *bad* night," he said in a broad Southern accent. "Anyhow, don't you worry no more, my man. I'm bringing you to my place in Pompano. Cassandra, my woman, is out of town for a couple of days, so there ain't no one gonna bother you there."

"Thanks for doing this," Conor whispered through gritted teeth. Now that he was clear of immediate danger, he was beginning to become aware of the searing pain throughout his body. "You've just saved his life."

Anton simply smiled and said, "No big thing."

"So where's Danny?"

"Relax, he'll be over in time. Soon as he's sure them cops ain't following." Anton paused as he turned a corner, then swung around and said, "Hey, man, I know it ain't none of my business, but I've got to ask if what they sayin' about you is true? On TV, I mean."

Conor told him it wasn't. He didn't mind talking about it. In fact, he welcomed the opportunity to discuss the recent events with someone, to get it off his chest and maybe, just maybe, distract him from the pain he was in. He finished his tale ten minutes later as they drove down I-95 toward the ramp for Pompano Beach.

The lightning storm had ended and the night was now still. The sky was black and starless, but the streetlights gave an eerie orange glow to the deserted roads and sidewalks. It was still very hot, but at least the convertible allowed the oncoming air to cool him down.

"Man, you are in some *deep* shit," Anton exclaimed when Conor finished talking. "But I'll tell you, brother, if *anyone* can help you, it is our man Danny."

Conor noticed he spoke about Danny with genuine respect and admiration.

"We been working construction together for a couple of years now," he told Conor. "And he's been dating my sister, Shawna, for 'bout a year and a half. Hell, we're almost related. Now, I ain't sayin' Danny's a saint. He ain't. But compared to how he used to be before she put the leash on, shit, man, he's pretty much housebroken these days."

"Yeah?"

"Straight up, brother. My little sis has finally tamed his big Irish ass. They even bought a house together." He laughed about it for a while, then began telling Conor various tales, recounting some of the crazy things he and Danny had done before his reformation.

Conor sat back as he spoke, closed his eyes, and let the oncoming wind cool his face for a while.

"Hell, they look like shit," Anton exclaimed when Conor slipped off his shoes a few minutes later to examine his burnt toes. "But everything's gonna be okay when we get to Pompano, man. Trust me. I got a first aid kit and a bottle of bourbon that'll fix you right up. Right up."

Detectives Shoemaker and Childs had been watching Danny McNamara's terraced house in Oakland Park for over two hours when he and Shawna finally stepped outside and walked around toward the small un-lit parking lot at the side of the building. They hadn't eaten since lunchtime and were in the process of deciding what take-out they might order if the stakeout turned into an all-nighter.

There was a discussion about George Henderson's upcoming funeral and whether or not his estranged wife and kids would make the trip down from Wisconsin. Childs thought they should organize a whip around at the station, maybe make a donation to the local peewee softball league. Sports were one of George's passions, and he had been a coach for one of the junior teams.

As they watched Danny and his girlfriend climb up into a black Ford pickup, they suddenly forgot their hunger and prepared to follow. It was so dark in the parking lot, however, they did not notice when Danny slipped back out of the passenger side, rolling expertly into some nearby bushes. Shawna pulled away slowly and headed off in the direction of Miami with the unmarked police car not far behind.

Danny waited until they had left the street and the coast was clear before driving Shawna's old blue Chevrolet down to Pompano. It took less than ten minutes as traffic was light. Once there, he parked out back and entered Anton's house through the rear patio door.

"Holy fuck!" he exclaimed when he walked in to find Conor lying shirtless on Anton's brown leather sofa. There was a bag of ice on his head and his shoes were kicked off. He had just taken a shower and Anton was applying some sort of antiseptic cream to his toes before bandaging them with gauze and tape. There were numerous cuts and bruises on his arms and ankles, as well as what looked like rope burns on his neck.

"What the fuck happened to you?"

Conor told Danny the entire story from start to finish while Anton got the bourbon and poured them all a glass. After he knocked it back, Anton made him a bologna and cheese sandwich and Danny poured another glass.

Danny flew into a rage and cursed angrily when he heard what Carlos and Ernesto Suarez had done to his friend. With eyes bulging, he swore on his grandmother's grave that he would make them pay dearly, even if he had to call every ex-IRA man living in Florida. He said if the Suarez brothers wanted a war, they would get one. But Conor quickly calmed him down, telling him the most important thing to do first was to try and find Bob Castagna so he could clear his name.

"My main priority is to get square with the police," Conor told him. "Castagna is the key to proving my innocence. After that, you can do what you want to the Cubans."

"Yeah, okay, that makes sense," Danny agreed. "You were always the smart one, Con. So, whatever way you want to do this, just say the word." He glanced toward Anton. "Right, bro?"

"Shit, man, I'm already in," replied Anton.

Conor thought about it for the longest time, pacing up and down as Danny and Anton looked on in silence. He was trying to think of something, anything that might help. It occurred to him to go back to the house in West Palm Beach to try to talk to Eva and Abi. He desperately wanted to question them, to ask them *why* they had lied to the police about him making advances toward them. More importantly, he thought, to ask if they had spoken to Bob or knew of his whereabouts. But he quickly disregarded this idea as a bad one. The chances were they would not speak to him and simply call the police. After all, he *had* been arrested for Bob's murder, and he *was* still a wanted man. Also, he would be naive to imagine the house was not under some sort of surveillance.

Then, after another round of pacing and wracking his brain, he began to recall the man Bob had met in the parking lot that second day. The one he had given an envelope to. He realized it was a long shot, and that she would probably tell him to go to hell, but he picked up the stolen cell phone and reluctantly called Rita.

"Hello?"

"Hello, Rita. Please don't hang up!" he said in desperation.

"Conor?" She sounded groggy, and he realized it was the middle of the night and he had woken her up. "Conor, is that you?"

"Yeah, it's me," he replied.

"We saw you on TV. They're saying horrible things."

"I know, Rita, but I swear to you that none of it is true," he said. He felt terrible about calling her. She had only just met him and now he was trying to drag her into his mess. "I'm sorry for calling you. Look, I know I have no right to ask, but I *really* need your help to clear my name of this."

"What can I do?" she asked.

"I need you to go down to the marina tonight and look back over the parking lot security footage from Tuesday morning."

"What?"

"Will you do that for me?"

"Tonight?"

"Yes, I'm sorry, but it really can't wait."

"Why would you want the security footage?"

"I don't know. It's probably nothing, but the other day Bob Castagna met a man there. A red-haired man driving a green Jeep. I saw them passing an envelope. I didn't think anything of it at the time, but now I'm wondering if it could have something to do with what happened."

There was a pause. Silence on the line. He thought for a moment she had hung up.

"Rita?"

"I'm still here. Look, Conor. What *exactly* is going on?"

"I don't know. So help me God, I really don't. All I can tell you is that Bob shot Hector Suarez when we were on our way back from Nassau. I swear I knew nothing about it. Then he disappeared, leaving me unconscious to take the blame. Now I've just found out that they were smuggling a bag of cocaine back into the country."

"Jesus!"

"These guys are serious criminals," he continued. "They're into drugs and sex trafficking and God only knows what else. And now they're after me."

"Did you know about any of this when you got involved?" she asked.

"I swear to you, Rita, on my life. I didn't know *anything* about it. And I didn't do *any* of the stuff they're saying."

"I believe you, Conor. I do."

He sighed with relief. To hear her say the words meant so much to him. All of a sudden, he felt some of the weight lift off him and he could breathe a bit easier, think a bit clearer. "Thanks for that. You don't know what it means to hear you say it."

"So, what are you going to do?" she asked after a pause.

"First, I need to find Bob Castagna to clear my name," he told her. "Don't ask me how, but I'm certain he's still around. I can feel it."

"So what do you want me to do with the security footage?"

"I just need you to see if you can get the license number of the red-haired man's car. It was a strange-looking vehicle. But be careful. I don't want you to put yourself in any danger. If anything happens or you get a bad feeling, just forget about it and leave."

There was another silence before Rita whispered, "Okay, Conor. I'll get my neighbor to watch Emilio and head over there right away."

Conor felt another wave of relief. If she had been standing in front of him, he would have hugged her and kissed her. "Thank you, Rita. I don't know what to say."

"Listen, give me a couple of hours and I'll call you back on this phone."

"Okay," he said as she hung up. "Thanks again."

When he turned to Danny and explained what was happening, the big man told him that Shawna had a girlfriend in the DMV who could trace the license tag. But it could take a little time, he warned.

"I'll ask her to see if she can have her friend on standby," he told Conor. "If you *do* get a license number, I'll pass it on to her straight away, see what comes up."

Conor nodded in gratitude. It was up to Rita now. He knew his fate lay in her hands. If nothing came of this, he didn't know what else to do but go to the police and hand himself in.

"You should get some rest," Danny said, looking into his blood-shot eyes. "You really *do* look like shit."

So Conor lay on Anton's bed for a while in an effort to get a few hours sleep. But it was not easy coming. He had taken some painkillers with the bourbon and it was only when they finally kicked in that his eyes shut and he started to drift off. Stress and exhaustion had taken their toll on his battered body and troubled mind. But he knew he was among friends now. He felt safe in their care. So he surrendered to the exhaustion, letting himself drift off into a deep sleep. He didn't dream or even toss or turn for a good two and a half hours.

The young clerk behind the counter of the Chevron service station eyed them a little nervously. It was late at night and the Food Mart was empty now except for the two scary-looking Cubans who had just walked in. He knew they weren't looking for gas because they had driven their Jeep across the deserted forecourt and pulled right up to the store. The shorter one immediately started walking down the food aisles toward the freezers and beer section, as if looking for something in particular. The taller one with the pock-marked skin walked directly toward the counter.

"Hi, how are you tonight?" the young man said with a nervous smile. As he did, he caught sight of the shorter man approaching from behind the aisles to his left. Seeing nothing in his hands, the thought occurred that he hadn't been looking for beer after all, but was instead checking that there were no other customers in the store.

He had been leaning on the counter reading one of his college books, last minute revision for a test he had in the morning. The night shift was ideal for that. It wasn't usually busy and allowed lots of time to catch up on his classes. But as usual, he had also been keeping one eye on the monitor to the left of the register. Its screen was divided into four sections, each one a view from one of the security cameras. Three were of the forecourt outside. Two of them showed the pumps from different angles while the third gave a full view of the storefront. The fourth camera was directed inside the store, taking in the automatic glass entrance door as well as the counter nearby.

"We want to see the tapes from earlier tonight," Ernesto Suarez said in a gruff Cuban accent.

"I'm sorry? The what?"

"The security footage from earlier tonight," he repeated. "Show it to us."

The young guy behind the counter stood up straight, looking puzzled. "I'm sorry, but who exactly are you?"

Carlos Suarez was also at the counter now after ensuring there were no other customers in the Food Mart. He stood beside his taller brother and calmly pointed toward the monitor. "That one. Top left. The one showing the front of the store."

"Look, if you could come back and talk to my boss in the morning. His name is Rick. He should be here about eight-thirty."

Ernesto reached over and grabbed the kid by the collar with both hands. Before he knew what was happening, he was pulled up over the counter and sent crashing to the floor at the Cuban's feet. He shouted something about calling the police, tried to get up, but received a violent kick to his ribcage.

Five minutes later, all three stood in a small storeroom behind the counter. The young clerk was being a lot more cooperative now, and had kindly offered to show them the footage from earlier that evening. He sat down nervously at a small desk by the far wall, and with the Suarez brothers standing behind him, powered up the computer and began searching through a folder called "security footage files." He could feel them looming threateningly over him as he pressed fast-forward and let them see the view of the forecourt. Their breaths were hot on the back of his neck. Intimidating.

"There!" Carlos shouted after a few minutes. "Go back. Go back."

The clerk pressed rewind until the Cuban slapped a hand down on his shoulder. "There. Play it from there."

As the Suarez brothers watched the playback on the computer, they saw a bright red El Dorado convertible pull up to the front of the Food Mart. Seconds later, a shadowy figure darted out from behind the store and climbed into the passenger seat. It was a grainy picture and they couldn't make out his face, but they knew it was the Irishman they were after. They watched as he ducked low in the seat and they drove away. But it was not the face they were looking at now, rather the vehicle itself.

"Can you pause and zoom in on the tag?" Carlos asked.

The young man shook his head. "I'm sorry, I don't know how. I only know how to play the files. That's all."

"Then rewind and pause so we can read it."

The clerk played around with the pause and rewind for a moment or two until he got the most promising frame. "There. That's the best you're going to get."

He felt suffocated, starved of oxygen as both men eagerly leaned forward on either side of him. The smell of sweat and aftershave was overpowering, but he dared not move. Neither of the Cubans spoke for a moment, just stared closely into the screen, trying to make out the letters and numbers on the pixilated frame.

"Is that a three or an eight?" Carlos asked, pointing to one of the numbers.

"It's not clear enough to make out," said Ernesto.

"I think it's a three," offered the clerk, forgetting himself for a second as he became engrossed in the puzzle.

Eventually, Carlos stepped back and said, "Rewind back to where the car pulls in. Maybe we can see the driver."

The kid did as he was instructed, rewound, and then hit play again. As soon as the El Dorado came into sight, he hit pause.

"Shit. He looks familiar," Carlos muttered thoughtfully, studying the screen with squinted eyes. "Where have I seen him before?"

"Yes, I remember!" Ernesto suddenly cried. "That is the negrito son of a bitch who sold us a case of tequila last year. Said it fell off the back of a truck on the highway in front of him."

"That's right," Carlos muttered. "He was with a big Irish motherfucker, wasn't he? I remember them because they got complimentary VIP tickets for our Miami club and then showed up drunk and started a fight with security."

"Anton something," Ernesto said, more to himself than out loud. "Anton Washington."

Carlos took out his cell phone and started making some calls. Ernesto directed the clerk back outside the storeroom as his brother began talking to someone, looking for an address to go with the name. The kid looked anxiously from Ernesto to Carlos before looking back again to Ernesto, who was now hovering dangerously near him by the cash register. He knew if they were going to kill him, they would do it now.

"Look, man, whatever's going on, it's none of my business," he said nervously to Ernesto. "I won't tell anyone about this. I swear."

Ernesto said nothing, just kept his gaze on Carlos who was still deep in conversation on the phone. After a few minutes, Carlos finished his call and headed toward the door.

"Washington lives in Pompano Beach," he said as he walked out.

Ernesto leaned menacingly across the clerk, who cringed in terror when he saw him drawing closer. But the big Cuban simply took a pack of chewing gum from the display behind him. Without saying a word, he took out a dollar and dropped it on the counter. As the young man watched, the two brothers left the store without another word. They climbed into their Jeep, reversed with a screech of rubber, and then sped off into the night in the direction of Pompano.

Detectives Shoemaker and Childs finally said enough was enough when the black Ford pickup circled the Sun Life stadium in Miami Gardens for the third time that night. Shoemaker knew the area well and had come to suspect something was not right. The stadium was home to the Dolphins football team and the University of Miami Hurricanes as well as, until recently, the Florida Marlins baseball team. Shoemaker remembered going to a couple of games with his father in the late eighties when it used to be called the Joe Robbie Stadium. Then, back in the day when they were still a family, he had taken Diane and Alisha. It was a place of happy memories for him, but right now, he was not feeling very happy.

"This is bullshit," he growled angrily to Childs. "I'm pulling them over."

He was tired and hungry and his lower back muscles ached from sitting in the car too long. So, when the Raptor pulled over to acknowledge their flashing light, he walked up to the driver's door in an already bad mood. The tinted electric window came down slowly, revealing immediately that Danny McNamara was not in the passenger seat.

"Goddamnit!" he bellowed out loud, slamming his hand down hard on the roof.

Childs was watching from the passenger seat of their car as she spoke on her cell phone. She saw his animated reaction and muttered, "Fuck."

Shawna Washington played it cool, keeping both hands on the wheel as she looked out at him with a polite, innocent smile. "Good evening, officer. What seems to be the problem?"

"Wake up, man," Danny said as he nudged Conor in the side with the palm of his hand. "Your phone's ringin'."

Conor had been in such a deep sleep, the buzzing and vibrating on the bedside locker had not even registered with him. But now awake, his mind shot into overdrive and he sat up and grabbed the phone with urgency.

"Rita?" he gasped as he rubbed the sleep from his eyes.

"Have you got a pen?" she asked quietly, not expressing much emotion.

He had a pen ready and wrote down the number as she called it out. As he did so, Danny was standing over him on his own phone, calling it out to Shawna.

"Thanks," he said when she was finished. "I owe you *so* much."

"Just promise me you'll sort this out," she said after a few seconds. He could hear the emotion in her voice now, knew she was holding back the tears.

"I will. I promise."

"I know you didn't do those things the police said. You're a good man, Conor. I know you are. So if you need any more help, I'm here for you."

"Thanks, Rita, but you've done enough. I don't want to involve you anymore in my mess."

"No, I mean it, Conor. I want to help you get out of this in any way I can. If you need anything else, just call me."

"I promise you, I *will* fix this," he assured her. "And when I do, I also promise I will find some way to say thank you."

"Shawna's mate came through with that address," Danny exclaimed excitedly when his girlfriend rang back about five minutes later.

Conor opened his eyes and sat up again. He had lain back down on Anton's bed after Rita hung up, lost in his own thoughts. But now, when he opened his eyes and glanced up, he noticed for the first time a large mirror on the ceiling overhead. The state of his battered body was not a comforting sight.

Danny spotted him looking up at the mirror and said, "Kinky little bugger, isn't he?"

"What was that you said about an address?" Conor asked as he slipped on a clean t-shirt he'd borrowed from Anton.

Danny proceeded to tell him how Shawna's contact had traced the tag to a guy named Benny Levinsky who lived in Sunset Lake, a neighborhood just north of Miami and close to the Florida Everglades. Conor was delighted with the news, but even more so when Danny smiled and continued.

"Turns out this Levinsky guy is a bit of an amateur forger who did time up in Wakulla for passin' bum welfare checks. But now he's out, they say he's becomin' one of *the* top guys in the state at forgin' documents and passports. Seems he learned a thing or two in prison. Refined his skills, so to speak." He smiled broadly. "You *do* know what that means, don't you?"

"Yeah. It means he might have been making new papers for Bob," replied Conor.

"Bingo. That's exactly what I was thinkin.'"

"But if that is the case, it would mean Bob had this whole thing planned before we even set sail for Nassau. Why else would he be getting false papers?"

At that moment, he didn't know *what* he was feeling. Joy that they had been given a lead, or anger that he had mis-judged his employer so badly.

"We're gonna take Shawna's Chevy and pay this Levinsky guy a visit," said Danny. "It's not the best, needs a service, but we can't take Anton's new ride cause it sticks out like a sore fuckin' thumb."

Conor slipped on his shoes and splashed water in his face as Anton turned off the lights and locked up the house. He closed all the curtains to avoid sun damage to the furniture, saying Cassandra would have his balls if she came home and found them open. Then, as he came out of the bathroom, he stood on a stool and opened a panel in the living room air conditioning unit. Seconds later, he removed a couple of hand guns and tossed one down to Danny, followed by a couple of spare clips.

"Jesus," Conor whispered as he stepped into the room.

"Hey, we might need these if things go bad," Danny told him.

Conor nodded. "I know. I know. It's just that. Well, I feel like I've dragged you both into this mess. I'll never be able to repay you."

"Fuck that."

"No, I mean it. Before we go any further, I just want to say that I am really grateful to you both."

"No need," said Danny.

"No, there *is*. I mean, I don't even want to think about what I would have done without you."

"Hey, put those tampons back in your handbag." Danny grinned. "You'll have us all cryin' in a minute."

He and Anton both laughed as they motioned for Conor to follow them out to the car parked around back. It was get-ting brighter outside, the sky in the east glowing yellow as

the sun grew higher above the rooftops. It was already starting to get hot.

As Anton locked the front door behind him, Danny and
Conor headed toward the car. The big man put a reassuring
arm around Conor's shoulder, pulled him close, and said,
"Look, Con, don't worry about it. We'll sort this mess out. I'm
here for you no matter what happens. Just like in the past
you were there when I needed you."

"But this is different," Conor replied. "This is dangerous
stuff."

"The danger is what keeps things interesting," Danny
laughed.

Conor just shook his head and said nothing.

"Look," Danny continued. "All jokin' aside, no one on this
earth is gonna fuck with one of my pals and get away with it."

"Thanks, man."

"Besides. Anton and I have nothing better to do today!"

Against Danny's advice, Conor used the stolen cell phone
to call Detective Shoemaker as they turned right onto the
Sawgrass Expressway and headed south toward Sunset
Lake. As the temperature began to rise, the Florida Everglades became more visible to their right, a sun-scorched
grassy swampland stretching out as far as the eye could see.
He called the Miami Dade police department and was
patched straight through to the detective as soon as he revealed his identity.

Shoemaker was surprised to hear from him and immediately demanded to know where he was and who had killed
George Henderson at the hospital. Conor refused to answer
the first part of the question, saying he was going to clear his
name before he turned himself in. But then he told him in
detail how Carlos Suarez and his brother Ernesto had murdered the officer in cold blood, and how they had tortured
him in an effort to find Bob Castagna and a bag of missing
cocaine that he and Hector Suarez were smuggling back into
the country.

"Not only that," he continued. "But they also have a couple of young women caged in the basement of their club in
Boca Raton. It looks like they're into sex trafficking as well as

drug smuggling."

This revelation immediately got the detective's attention. He cursed the Cubans beneath his breath and muttered something about finally getting the proof he needed and not resting until they were brought to justice.

"Call the captain and get a search warrant for the Azteca nightclub in Boca," he excitedly told Childs, unable to hide his eagerness as he placed his hand over the phone so as not to be overheard. "Seems we finally have something concrete on the Suarez brothers."

Conor wasn't sure if he was supposed to hear that, but he did, and it made him feel a hell of a lot better. At least now it sounded as if the detectives might be starting to believe him.

"Look, Rogan," Shoemaker said in a more sympathetic tone. "I won't lie to you. You still have a lot of explaining to do. But I sure as hell can't even begin to help you unless you turn yourself in."

"I can't do that," Conor replied, catching an agitated glance from Danny that he really needed to hang up. "Look, I think Bob Castagna is still here in Florida. But I also think he may be planning to leave the country soon. Without him, I am screwed, and you know it."

"You're not screwed if what you're saying about them is true."

"Well then, I'll let you chase after them while I track down Castanga."

"You're making a big mistake," warned Shoemaker. "You need to tell us where you are right now. Because, trust me when I tell you, Rogan, if the Suarez brothers are after you, you won't last very long out there. That's not a scare tactic, it's a cold, hard fact."

Danny made another urgent hang up gesture, so Conor ended the call and, without saying another word, pulled the SIM and battery out of the phone and tossed the whole lot into the burnt grass verge as they sped past. Before the Chevy was even out of sight, an army of black ants began crawling all over the alien objects which had just invaded their territory.

Cassandra returned a day early from visiting her girl-friend, Lorraine, in Jacksonville. They had gotten into a stupid argument about Lorraine's three kids. A teacher from the local elementary school had called to complain about their disruptive behavior, and when Cassandra innocently pointed out there was some truth in it, Lorraine had screamed at her, telling her to "get da fuck out of her house."

It was the early hours of the morning and she was exhausted from the drive, so when she saw Anton's new El Dorado parked outside, she assumed he would be asleep in bed. Anton worked construction with his friend Danny, and depending on how far away the site was, they would sometimes have to get up in the middle of the night to make the drive. As work grew scarcer these days, that was becoming a more regular occurrence.

She turned the key in the front door and stepped straight into the hall, slipping off her flat driving shoes before heading quietly toward the bedroom. The curtains were closed, so the house was in darkness, but she knew her way around and had no trouble feeling her way past the various chairs and cabinets scattered in her path. When she reached the bedroom, she gently eased the door open and tiptoed inside.

"Anton, baby. It's me. Are you awake?"

Her heart skipped a beat when she flicked on the bedside lamp to find a strange Latino man sitting on the end of the bed with one of Anton's golf clubs on his lap.

She screamed and turned to run out, only to discover the door blocked by another strange man. In sheer terror, she tried to pound him out of the way with her fists, but he didn't even flinch. Grabbing her by the wrists, he swung her tiny frame around and threw her down onto the bed. She drew her knees up to her breasts and backed up to the headboard like a frightened animal surrounded by vicious wolves.

"Where is Anton?" Carlos Suarez demanded angrily from the door. "Your boyfriend?"

"You get the fuck out of my house," Cassandra screamed.

She reached for the telephone on the bedside locker, but Ernesto swung the golf club and smashed it violently to the floor, narrowly missing her fingers. As she screamed again, he stood up from the end of the bed and hovered menacingly over her with the club in both hands.

"I'll say it again," growled Carlos. "Where is Washington?"

"I don't know."

"Give me your cell," he commanded.

He decided a phone call to Anton was all it would take. As soon as the negrito heard they had his woman, he would give up the Irishman without any trouble. But as soon as Cassandra took her cell out, she quickly turned her back to them and started hurriedly tapping at the keypad. Ernesto reached down and, after a brief struggle, grabbed it from her hands. He quickly scrolled through the open contact list.

"Shit. She's deleted his number," he exclaimed.

"Fuck you!" Cassandra cried defiantly.

"That was not a very smart thing to do," Carlos muttered coldly. "Now we will have to get it out of you the hard way."

Ernesto's eyes shone with excitement as he raised the club and started swinging.

CHAPTER ELEVEN

THE SEA OF GRASS

Benny Levinsky was vegetating on his couch, eating cold Chinese food from a greasy white paper box when his doorbell rang. It was ten-fifteen and the early morning sports review had just ended, so he flicked off the TV and shuffled wearily toward the front door in a light blue tracksuit and bare feet. Grumbling to himself and scratching an itch down the front of his pants, he got within four or five feet of the door when it exploded inwards beneath the weight of Danny's right shoulder. Benny's heart skipped a beat and he screamed, falling backwards to the stained carpet with a look of sheer terror on his face.

Danny was on him in a flash, even before the flying splinters and pieces of broken doorframe came to rest. He grabbed Benny by the scruff of the neck as he frantically tried to escape backwards, hoisting him up in one effortless movement. He carried him screaming into the lounge and then flung him violently backwards onto the smoked-glass coffee table. There was a deafening crash that filled the room, leaving Benny moaning, lying on his back in a mound of broken glass and spilled egg noodles. Conor and Anton entered seconds later, shutting the busted front door behind them.

"What the hell is all this about?" Benny cried as he tried to get to his feet.

"We're lookin for your buddy," Danny snarled threateningly. "Bob Castagna."

"I've never heard of him," Benny replied a split second before Danny's fist caught him square in the face, breaking his nose. Danny lifted him up by the shoulders and flung him onto the sofa. Then he moved back a pace as Conor stepped forward.

"Do you know who *I* am?" Conor asked.

"Dude," replied Benny, using the sleeve of his tracksuit to stem the blood pouring from his shattered nose. "You're the guy from the news."

"Then you know Bob Castagna is trying to frame me for Hector Suarez's murder."

Benny waved a hand in front of his face and said, "Hey, dude, you've got to believe me. That has nothing to do with me. I swear."

Danny slipped his revolver from his belt, letting Benny see it as he said, "Tell us what you know, you piece of shit."

"Look," Benny said quietly. "I really don't want any trouble."

"Well trouble is what you've got," Danny grunted. "Now talk."

"Dude, if it got out that I had given information on a client, I'd be out of business," he replied. "You can appreciate that, can't you?"

Without warning, Conor suddenly snatched the gun from Danny's hand and pointed it directly into Benny's face. "I'll tell you what *you'd* better appreciate," he growled angrily, so out-of-character that it even startled Danny. 'You'd better appreciate that my life is over if I don't find Bob Castagna. So the truth is, I really don't give a flying fuck about your business. Now, if you don't tell us where he is in the next ten seconds, I swear to Christ, I'm going to spray you brains all over this sofa."

There was a tense, silent pause as Benny looked up at him and considered his options. Conor must have looked like he meant business to him, appearing desperate enough that he could in fact pull the trigger. He sensed Benny reasoning that he could continue protecting Bob and risk a bullet to the head, or he could just tell them everything he knew and worry about the consequences later. Eventually, Benny chose the latter, raised a hand between the gun and his face and said, "Okay dude, okay. Everything's cool. I'll tell you what you want to know if you promise not to shoot me."

He proceeded to tell them how Bob Castagna had contacted him through a mutual acquaintance called Scott, a guy who ran a web design company for him up in Palm

Beach. It seemed Scott was a buddy of Benny's, but was a bit slow in the head, probably from smoking too many drugs. He was, however, a real genius when it came to computers. Like a savant Bill Gates, said Benny.

"Get on with it," Danny snarled, losing patience.

Benny took a deep breath before telling them that Bob had wanted a couple of new passports. One for him and one for a woman. He assured them that Bob never once told him what was going on, and he never once thought to ask. Anton was interested in how much the passports cost, and Benny informed him they ran at two thousand a piece.

"Motherfucker, that's daylight robbery!" exclaimed Anton. Then, looking toward Danny, he said, "We're in the *wrong* business, brother."

But Conor had barely been listening to a word since Benny announced how he had also forged a passport for a woman. Maybe now he could find out who Bob's accomplice had been. Who had picked Bob up from the *Aphrodite* while he lay unconscious in the cabin? Just who the hell was helping him?

"What did this woman look like?" he asked. "Was she a blonde? Good-looking, in her forties?"

"What woman?"

"The one you made a passport for."

"Oh, *that* woman," Benny said. He shrugged and squinted. "I really don't know, man. Bob just gave me two passport-sized photos. I honestly can't remember what she looked like 'cause, well, the truth is, I really didn't pay much attention."

"Do you have a copy?" Conor asked.

"No way, dude! The first and last rule of my trade is *no* copies." He chuckled to himself at the absurdity of the suggestion. The blood had started to congeal so he was now able to take his sleeve away from his nose. "The cops would have a fucking field day if they ever got a warrant and found copies."

Danny stepped forward and pointed a finger at him. "Alright, cut the crap and tell us where Castagna is. And no bullshit mind, or I swear to Jesus, we will be back to finish you off."

"Cool, man. But you've got to give me your word you won't say I told you."

"You've got it," Danny said quietly. "Just tell us where he

is and you won't see us again."

"Alright, now get this," Benny said after a pause. "First off, I met him on Tuesday morning at the marina to pick up the photos and half the money up front. But he called me yesterday morning in a panic, saying he would pay an extra two grand if I could have them ready within a couple of hours. Well hell, I was almost finished anyway, just had to laminate them. So I agreed, and the dude came by and picked them up a few hours later."

Conor couldn't believe what he was hearing. "Bob was *here?* Yesterday? In person?"

"Yeah, man. Yesterday afternoon."

He turned away in disgust, cursing beneath his breath. If Bob already had his new passport, he could be long gone. He took a step away from the sofa and stood with his back to them, his face in his hands. Bob was gone. That was it. It was over.

"Yeah, man, it's a bummer for you," Benny sympathized, sounding as if he felt genuine empathy for Conor's plight. "I really feel for you, dude. I really do."

"Did he say *anything* about what he was plannin' to do? Where he was fixin' to go? Anything at all?" Danny asked, seeing Conor's dejection but trying to squeeze every last drop of information out of Benny before the momentum was gone. He knew from experience, when someone under questioning started to talk, you had to keep them going or they could quickly dry up. Once they started thinking about the information they had just imparted, about the consequences, the moment was gone. Once that happened, you lost them. And when that happened, nothing you did or said could get them started again.

"Well he *was* acting kind of strange," Benny offered. "You know, nervous and shit. I hadn't heard the news at the time, so I didn't know what had gone down."

"You know more than you're letting on!" Danny roared accusingly, so sudden and unexpected it made Conor turn back around with a start.

The conversation had seemed to be winding down. As far as he was concerned, they had reached a dead end with Benny. He was beginning to resign himself to the fact that Bob was gone forever, that he would have no other option but to turn himself in to the police. But the look he now caught on Benny's face was odd. Danny was right, he thought. Benny *did* know more than he was telling them.

"Look, I don't know anything else, man. I swear."

Danny made a lunge toward him with his fist raised menacingly.

"Okay, okay. Don't hit me. Although I don't know where *exactly* he is, I think I *might* have an idea."

Conor took a deep breath, realizing he hadn't been breathing for a while now.

"Go on," Danny snarled.

"Okay, but please, just don't hit me in the nose again."

"Go on," repeated Danny.

"I don't know if you're aware of this, but it seems Bob has got a small hunting cabin somewhere in the Everglades. Somewhere by a lake."

"The Glades cover one and a half million acres," Danny said angrily. "You'll have to do better than that, you fuck."

"And what makes you think he's there now anyway?" Anton added.

"Oh, I'm pretty sure he's there," he continued. "You see, first of all, he needs to stay off the grid. His face is all over TV, so if he tries to check into a motel or wander out in public, he'll be spotted straight away. But secondly, and most important of all, when he was here yesterday, he asked me to contact some dealers I know. Seems good old Bob is interested in offloading a sizable quantity of coke."

"No shit."

"But I have to warn you, the guys I put him in touch with are serious players. Man, I mean *serious* players. Not to be messed with, dude. I met them when I did some time in Wakulla. Scary niggers out of Jacksonville." As soon as he spoke the word, he turned sheepishly toward Anton. "Sorry, man, my bad."

Anton said nothing, just stood in the doorway with arms folded.

"Anyways, after I made a few calls, he got talking to them on the phone. He didn't know I was listening from the other room, but I overheard him arrange to meet them at the cabin sometime today. But there is something else."

"What's that?" asked Danny.

"Before he left, he paid me and said that once the deal was done, he's leaving the country for good."

"And you've no more information on where this cabin is?" Conor asked.

Benny shrugged apologetically. "Dude, I swear, I just overheard him talking about it on the phone. I've told you everything I know."

"So, what about these guys you know from Jacksonville? How about getting them on the phone for *us*?"

Conor saw Danny looking over at him as he spoke, shaking his head to indicate it was a bad idea. There was no way in hell those kind of people were going to tell them where they were planning to conduct their drug deal. He realized then that contacting them would probably also tip them off, and thereby ruin any chance they had of catching up with Bob.

But at least there was still something keeping Bob in South Florida, he mused. That bastard Castagna had used him from the start, but if he could only just find out where this cabin was, he could turn it all around and make sure he got what he deserved. He suddenly realized that he was still holding the gun, and immediately handed it back to Danny who lodged it in his belt once again.

"Dude, believe me. These Jacksonville guys won't talk to you. And they would surely kill me if they even *thought* I had told anything about their business."

"You'd better be tellin' us the truth," Danny warned him as the three of them headed toward the door. Then, turning back before he followed Conor and Anton outside, he said. "And by the way. Don't even think about tippin' them off that we're coming, or so help me, we *will* be back. And next time, we won't just break your nose.'

"Believe me, dude, I won't be telling them anything. If they knew I'd spoken about this, I'd have more to lose than you."

"Alright so," Danny said as he walked away.

"Hey, man, you owe me for a new door!" Benny shouted after him. "And a coffee table!"

An hour later, Conor, Danny, and Anton sat in a rest stop off the Sawgrass Expressway, sipping cold drinks and eating warm burritos they had just bought from a roach coach parked nearby. There were a couple of regular customers gathered around the rusty food truck, eating a late breakfast while standing in the shade of its large tin awning. They were in a loud, heated conversation, interrupting and talking over each other as they argued the latest news and sports stories of the day, putting the world to right with shouts and animated gestures. The truck seemed to do a pretty good business from these passing tradesmen and long distance drivers who used the Expressway. Mornings were especially busy.

Danny was sitting on the hood of the old blue Chevy. He had just gotten off the phone with Shawna, having agreed for her to pick him up at the rest stop in the next few minutes. He told Conor they had another meeting that morning with their bank manager to discuss refinancing their mortgage loan, how the downturn in the economy had seen them fall behind on the payments.

"Should be back within the hour," he told him reluctantly. "Fuckin' bank manager's been callin' Shawna at work, so now she won't leave me alone until we sit down with him. Pain in the ass, but if I backed out now, she would make my life a livin' hell!"

Anton made a whipping noise beneath his breath.

"Don't worry about it." Conor nodded understandingly. "Do what you've got to do."

"I'll be straight back here when we're done," Danny assured him.

"Yeah, man, don't sweat it. We ain't goin' nowhere," said Anton.

Conor was sitting on an upturned wooden box near the car while Anton sat in the driver's seat with the door open, his legs hanging outside in the long burnt grass at the verge. Before Shawna called, they had been discussing their next move and had come up with a plan that Conor was not at all happy with.

"Con, you've got to face facts," Danny had warned him. "If we don't find out where that cabin is, this thing is over. Bob will be gone forever, and you, my friend...well, you will be well and truly fucked."

"Man, you've just *got* to do it," Anton agreed as he tossed his empty soda can into the long grass. "Ain't no other way."

"What about the land registry office?" Conor had suggested. "There must be some record of the building and where exactly it is in the Everglades?"

"Is that right?" Danny said sarcastically. "So just who the fuck do *you* know in the land office to get that kind of information?"

"Hey, man, even if you knew someone, time is not exactly on your side," added Anton.

"Besides," Danny continued. "It may be just a shack and not a proper registered property. The Glades are full of them."

Conor nodded his understanding, but sighed wearily. He hadn't touched his food. The thought of what lay ahead, of what he had to do had killed his appetite. He looked down to see the ground moving under his feet. Hundreds of small black ants milled about, carrying bits of leaves and burrito crumbs back to their nest.

"Come on, Con. You *know* there's no other way." Danny told him. "Besides, man, she went to the marina in the middle of the night for you. What does that tell you? And didn't she say she was there if you needed any more help?"

"Yeah, she did," Conor replied quietly, still looking down at the ants. "But help is one thing. This is *way* beyond anything I can ask of her."

"Brother, she sounds like a mighty fine woman to me," Anton added. "Ain't too many of those about these days."

"Con, she *likes* you, man," said Danny. "And it's not as if it's *that* dangerous. She'll be in and out in a couple of minutes. All she's got to do is stick to the story and she'll be alright."

As he spoke, Shawna pulled up beside them in Danny's black Ford Raptor.

"Come on, baby. We late," she shouted impatiently as the window rolled down.

"One second," he called back. Then, turning to Conor before he left, he said, "Do it, Con. Do it. You don't have a choice."

Conor took a deep, steadying breath, exhaling slowly as he watched Shawna pull away with Danny in the passenger seat. When they were gone, he stood up and took Anton's spare phone from his outstretched hand. Without speaking, he walked a few feet away from the Chevy and stood in the long grass with his back turned to Anton. This was going to be one of the hardest phone calls he'd ever have to make. But he had no choice. Deep down, he knew that. Anton had been right when he said that time was not on his side. So Conor took another deep breath and started dialing the number.

"Hi, Rita. It's me again."

Abi Castagna walked into her mother's bedroom to find her packing. Eva was startled when her daughter walked in on her, but composed herself quickly and continued without speaking. After drinking the last of the scotch, she had placed a large pink suitcase open on the bed and was in the process of filling it. Abi looked puzzled and immediately asked where she was going, but Eva did not reply. She just sat down on the edge of the bed and started crying. Abi hurried over and sat down beside her, placing an arm around her mother's shoulders to offer her support.

With breath smelling of whisky and tears welling up in her eyes, Eva told how she couldn't take it anymore, how she was going mad just waiting there in the house. Every time the doorbell or the phone rang, her heart would skip a beat before racing again at twice the speed. It was like being on a rollercoaster. The police had been to visit a couple of times, but the last time they were there, they had warned her and Abi to "prepare for bad news."

"Bad news!" she exclaimed, sobbing. "I've been getting bad news my whole fucking life!"

Abi squeezed her tighter. She knew the story of her mother's troubled past, had heard it a dozen times before.

"First my parents died, leaving me alone, barely in my teens. Then my only living relative, Aunt Lilith, took me in. But I swear I would have been better off in an orphanage. She was the coldest, meanest bitch I've ever known. And when she found out I was pregnant with you, she just threw me out without a second thought. She spent more time with her head in the fucking Bible than in the real world."

"But you had me," whispered Abi, trying to stay strong for her mother. Eva wasn't really listening, though. In her drunken despair, she could only focus on those negative events that had befallen her, not on the positive ones.

"Even when the old bat died, and I thought *finally* I would come into my inheritance money, that at long last we could get out of that rat-infested trailer we were living in." She paused for a second as the tears of despair turned to anger. "Even *then* I got bad news from the lawyer. I swear he was grinning to himself when he told me how that shriveled up spinster had left everything she owned to the church! Ha! The church, for Christ sakes. Her only niece penniless and starving, with a young child to support, and she ups and leaves it all to the church. Every fucking cent!"

"But you survived," said Abi. "You always do. You always make it through the tough times. Don't you always tell me that?"

Eva shook her head as she leaned out of Abi's embrace and started drying her eyes with a handkerchief. Her mascara was smudged and her eyes red. "I don't think I can take any more, baby," she whispered. "When Bob came along, I really thought our luck had changed. He loved me and he was a good father to you. We finally had money and a nice home."

"Hey now, we still have each other. And the house," said Abi, gesturing her hand at the beautifully decorated bedroom they were sitting in.

"No, baby, we *don't* have the house," sighed Eva. She paused, saw the look of puzzlement on her daughter's face, and said, "Bob's business has gone from bad to worse these past eight months. He's up to his neck in debt. The house has been remortgaged and we're months behind with the payments. He owed every bank in town and couldn't get any more credit. Even his life insurance policy has been signed over to them. They're circling like vultures as we speak."

Abi looked stunned at the news.

"That's why I'm packing, you see. I want to be ready when they come to take the house. But I won't leave anything of value behind for those carpet baggers." She stood up and opened one of the dresser drawers to continue packing. "You need to start packing too, baby. We'll get all our things ready to go, and then we'll sell or pawn anything that's not nailed down. Unfortunately, the bank owns the cars, but there's lots of other stuff. Jewelry, Bob's golf equipment, and all his fancy guns."

Abi was speechless when Eva fell silent. She remained quiet for a few minutes, before whispering, "So, you're saying we have nothing?"

"No, not nothing," replied Eva. "Like you said, I guess we

still have each other."

Detective Bradley Shoemaker stood with a triumphant look on his face as Carlos Suarez angrily examined the search warrant he had just handed him. Ernesto stood menacingly beside his brother with his arms folded, glaring back at Shoemaker as if he was ready to kill. Detective Childs and two uniformed officers had gone down into the basement a few minutes earlier to investigate the recent allegations, to search for torture chambers and alligators, dead bodies and captive sex slaves. But Shoemaker wanted to stay up here with the two brothers. He felt this was his moment of vindication and he wanted to watch them squirm, to see their faces, to savor every last moment of it.

It had not been easy to convince Captain Mendoza to get the warrant in the first place, but she had eventually capitulated on one condition. Sitting in her office less than an hour earlier, Shoemaker had to swear to her that this was the last time he would ever go after the Suarez family. In truth, he was just amazed she had gone along with it, and really would have been prepared to swear to anything if it meant getting that piece of paper in his hands.

"If this proves to be another false lead," she had warned him. "You will never again mention their names in this department. Is that clear?"

"My informant *is* reliable," he replied.

"Alright then," she had said. "But, Bradley. I mean it. Never again. And so help me, if you cross me on this, you will be writing parking tickets on Sunrise Boulevard until you retire."

A loud burst of swearing from Carlso Suarez brought Shoemaker's train of thought back to the present, to the task at hand.

"Bullshit! This is plain and simple police harassment," the Cuban snapped as he crumpled up the warrant and tossed it to the floor at Shoemaker's feet. "We will be instructing our lawyer to prepare a lawsuit over this."

Shoemaker just smiled at him and said nothing as he stood there waiting for Childs to report back. After a few minutes, one of the young uniformed officers leaned around the basement door and beckoned him over. There was a concerned look on the man's face as the detective approached.

"Well, what have you got?" Shoemaker asked.

"Detective Childs wants to see you, sir."

"Okay," he replied, a little puzzled. "You stay out here and keep an eye on these two while I'm gone."

"Yes, sir."

"And stay alert," he warned the young officer quietly. "This isn't a random search. These guys are hardcore, so you need to be ready for anything."

Leaving Carlos and Ernesto behind in the club, he descended the wooden steps and made his way down into the basement toward the end of the hall where he could see the other uniformed officer standing. As he did, he noticed the broken door immediately to his right and what looked suspiciously like two bullet holes in it. But he didn't stop to examine them, just continued walking toward the end. When he got there, the officer stepped aside to allow him to pass.

The metal door leading into the basement was barely hanging from its top hinge and had been strangely twisted out of shape. He raised his eyebrows as he walked through, putting his hand over his nose to block out the stench that greeted him as he entered. Detective Childs was standing in the center with a flashlight in one hand and the other holding a handkerchief over her nose and mouth. She was shaking her head.

"Well?" he asked, turning his gaze around the room, scanning the darkened corners for anything they might use as evidence.

"Not a goddamned thing," she replied. "If dirt and stink was a crime, the Suarez brothers would be guilty of a felony. But as far as a torture chamber is concerned, I'm sorry, Bradley, we've got nothing."

Shoemaker was visibly disappointed. "And the Asian girls?"

"There *is* some sort of animal cage in the other room alright, but no sign of captive women."

"The goddamned informer has beaten us to it again," he snarled. "Soon as we went looking for a warrant, they cleaned the place out."

A lone figure watched from the small coffee shop on the opposite side of the street as the two detectives left the club fifteen minutes later and returned to their car. Danny McNamara sat over an untouched coffee and donut by the window, quietly observing their unmarked Ford Marauder and the patrol car pull away from the curb outside. As soon as they were gone, he left the shop and crossed the street, then made his way down the alleyway behind the building. Wearing a Florida Marlins baseball cap that covered his eyes, he had a small black laptop bag swinging from his shoulder. But on closer inspection, the bag seemed a little bulkier than normal. The ordinary passerby probably wouldn't have noticed though. Nor would they have spotted how he was holding on to it more carefully than usual, his right hand preventing it from banging against his side as if it contained something very delicate.

When he reached the small, low down toilet window at the rear of the club, Danny stopped with his back to the wall and scanned the area to ensure he was alone. Seconds later, he kicked it open with his heel, bent down, and quickly crawled inside. He was gone for less than five minutes before emerging without the bag to walk back across the street again. He made for the narrow alley beside the coffee shop and stepped unnoticed behind one of the two dumpsters sitting there. When he was certain he was not being overlooked, he casually stuffed two wads of cotton wool in his ears before withdrawing a small remote control unit from his pocket. He extended the slim metal aerial and pointed it toward the other side of the street, held the small silver box in both hands, and flicked on the power button. As soon as the red light flickered to life, Danny took a deep breath and pressed the center button, watching with a sense of calm and pride as the second floor of the Azteca nightclub erupted in a flash of flame and smoke. The explosion was sudden and ear-shattering, instantly blowing out all the glass windows and taking off a small section of the building's roof.

As the burning debris fell to the road outside, a dozen car alarms began sounding off at the same time, a deafening crescendo that only added to the confusion. Horns blared and bells rang, panic-stricken people emerging screaming from nearby offices and shops, their hands covering their heads for protection. As plumes of thick, dark smoke began pouring from the upper windows of the club, Carlos and Ernesto Suarez suddenly exited the main door with their clothes torn and their faces and hands blackened. Coughing uncontrollably, they appeared to be in a state of shock at the devastation, just standing there in the center of the street as a noisy crowd gathered outside to observe the destruction.

With a look of satisfaction, Danny calmly closed the remote unit's aerial and then casually tossed it into the dumpster before turning to leave. As he walked away from the ensuing chaos, he plucked the cotton wool from his ears and flicked it into the gutter. The sounds became clearer to him now and he could suddenly hear fire engine sirens approaching in the distance. Carlos and Ernesto had just received a taste of their own medicine, he thought as he reached Shawna waiting nearby in the black Ford pickup.

He didn't say a word as he climbed up into the passenger seat, just leaned over and kissed her affectionately on the cheek. He hadn't told anyone but her what he was planning to do, and still wouldn't tell a soul now that it was done. It wasn't about that to Danny. It was about him being able to sleep at night, about him knowing he had stayed true to himself and his friends.

No one fucked with him or his and got away with it, he had advised Conor the previous night. And now, as Shawna pulled away from the curb and headed off into the traffic, he leaned back into the headrest and glanced out the window with a look of satisfaction etched on his face. No one threatened or messed with his family without paying the price. No one. No matter *who* they were.

Abi answered the front door at noon to find an olive-skinned woman standing before her on the porch with a briefcase in her right hand. Wearing glasses, her raven black hair was tied back in a ponytail and she was dressed in a dark blue pinstriped skirt and jacket over a white silk blouse.

The woman smiled at Abi and said, "Hello, you must be Abi?"

"Er, yes. Can I help you with something?"

"I'm Rita Morales, from Sundown Life Insurance. Is your mother home?"

"I'm afraid she's sleeping."

"Abi, I'm very sorry to hear about your father," said Rita. "I'm sure the past few days have been absolutely horrible for you both."

"Things have not been good," Abi confirmed solemnly. "Could you come back after five?"

"Well, look, I certainly don't want to disturb either of you. Perhaps I could just leave a few papers for her to sign? If you ask her to call me when she does, I'll come straight back to pick them up. Oh, and if you could just tell her that the sooner she does, the sooner we can make payment on your father's insurance policy."

She balanced her briefcase on one knee and clicked it open, then started fumbling about inside as if looking for something. After a few seconds, she stopped and looked up at Abi with an embarrassed smile. "I know the darn things are in here somewhere. I wonder, would it be a very big imposition if I came in for just a minute? I really need to put my case down to find these papers."

Abi looked unsure and hesitated for a moment.

"I promise, it will only take a minute." Rita smiled.

Abi led her into the lounge and they sat in the coolness of the air conditioning while Rita opened her briefcase on the coffee table and started flicking through some of the paperwork inside. It was a big, open-plan room with imported Italian floor tiles and a white leather suite positioned in a circle around a low mahogany table.

Abi, of course, didn't realize that the so-called "paperwork" Rita was examining were in fact specifications on a new extension to the marina. She sat back politely while Rita explained how her father's life insurance policy could be paid out without a death certificate, just as soon as the police report and signed paperwork was filed back at her office.

"I'm sure your mother would welcome that," said Rita.

"But I thought the policy had been signed over to the bank?" Abi said, sitting forward with a hint of confusion in her voice.

Rita hesitated for a second, not knowing quite how to respond. But then she gathered herself and pretended to examine some of the documents before saying, "No. Definitely not *this* one. Perhaps your father had more than one life poli-cy? That wouldn't be unusual for a company director."

That seemed to satisfy the young girl, who just nodded her understanding before sitting back in the plush white arm-chair opposite. After a short pause, Rita asked if she could use the bathroom.

"Of course," Abi replied, leading her back out into the hall and pointing toward the end. "It's the second door down on the right."

"Thank you so much. I'll just be a minute," Rita said, smiling as she headed off down the hall.

She stepped inside the bathroom and closed the door, waited a few seconds, then opened it again, making sure Abi had gone. As soon as she saw the coast was clear, she slipped out and entered Bob's office, which just happened to be the next door down. Conor had explained the layout to her on the phone, so she knew exactly where to go and what to look for. He told her Bob had shown him his gun collection that was kept in a locked glass case beside the bookshelf.

But Rita wasn't looking for guns or books. Following Conor's instructions, she made straight for Bob's desk to sift through his paperwork. Finding the drawers locked, she quickly used a silver letter opener to pry them open. It didn't prove too difficult to budge, as it wasn't a heavy-duty lock. After a few seconds, there was a loud *snap*, and to her relief, the top drawer slid open by itself. Rita hurriedly scanned through the folders and envelopes inside, trying to get an address or even just a rough location for the hunting cabin.

Her heart was beating furiously in her breast for fear of being caught. This was all new to her. Not the kind of thing she was used to at all. But Conor's life was in danger and she was determined to do everything in her power to help him. After an initial period of shock and doubt when the news broke, she had quickly come to suspect that someone was framing him. Even before Conor phoned to explain and ask her to review the security cameras, she knew in her heart that he was innocent. She felt she had met someone who was spe-cial to her, someone who was different from the other men she knew. She decided to trust her judgment of him, and re-solved to do whatever it took to help him prove his innocence.

When she came up empty-handed in the last drawer, Rita let out an exasperated sigh. There was nothing but old work files, invoices, and some pornographic DVDs in the desk. *Teenage Tits and Ass on Parade* was definitely *not* what she was looking for. So, after a few more minutes of searching, she reluctantly gave up and headed for a small filing cabinet by the large bay window overlooking the pool. There were three unlocked drawers and she examined each one with the same meticulous vigor. But once again, try as she might, the search proved fruitless. She took out her phone and called Conor.

"Rita," he gasped anxiously. "Are you okay? How's it going there?"

"I'm sorry," she whispered despondently. "But there is nothing here."

"Did you check the desk?"

"Yes, and the filing cabinet by the window."

"Well that's it then," he gasped, unable to hide the disappointment in his voice. "Look, please just get yourself out of there, Rita. Thanks for trying. You did your best. But you've got to leave now."

"There has got to be somewhere else—"

As she spoke, the door opened behind Rita with a low creak. Panic-stricken, she dropped the phone back into her pocket and slid the drawer closed with her knee as she turned. Standing there in the doorway facing her was Abi, hands on hips, looking less than pleased.

"What are you *doing* in here?" she snapped irritably. "This is my father's office. *No one* is allowed in here."

"Oh, I'm so sorry," Rita stammered. "I...I was just admiring the house and peeped in the door. When I saw the beautiful pool outside, I couldn't help myself from taking a closer look."

"Well you need to get out now," Abi said sharply.

"Yes. Yes, of course. I'm sorry."

Abi led her back to the living room in a stony silence. The mood had changed considerably. There was tension between them now that would not be broken by talk of insurance payouts or important forms. Rita didn't even sit down when they got there, just leaned over her case and muttered, "Oh, you know what? I don't know what's wrong with me today. I seem to have left those papers back in the office."

Abi said nothing. It was obvious she was very suspicious now. "What did you say the name of your company was again?" she asked.

"The name? Oh, Sundown Life," Rita replied, grateful and also amazed she could remember the name under such pressure. "I'll tell you what. I'll head back to my office and pick them up. And then, perhaps I'll come back later today when your mom is awake. Would that be okay?"

"Yes, I think that would be best," Abi said coldly. "Come back after five."

She was glad to be rid of the woman. As they reached the front door, she quickly opened it and stood aside to let her leave, anxious to see the back of her. But Rita stopped a few paces short and began admiring the row of photographs lining the hallway.

"That's interesting," she said, pointing to one small photo in particular near the door. "Is that your father?"

Looking displeased, Abi stepped back to see which one she was pointing to. "Yes," she answered impatiently. "That's him out hunting in the Everglades with one of his clients. Now I think you had better—"

"It looks so beautiful there," Rita said. "Would you believe I've lived in Florida all my life, but I have never actually been to the Everglades? Oh, what is that small grey building behind him?"

"Building?" Abi looked closer. "That's just his hunting cabin."

Rita tried to look calm and only mildly interested. Holding in her excitement for fear of giving herself away, she said, "Boy, it looks so peaceful there. Is that a lake beside it?"

"Yes," replied Abi. "Now I think you should—"

"It's beautiful. Where exactly is it?"

"It's the one by Monument Campground."

The Tamiami Trail cut South Florida in half, running directly through the Everglades from Miami on its eastern gold coast, due west to the city of Naples on its sun coast. Anton turned Shawna's old blue Chevy off onto a narrow asphalt track about halfway across when they came upon a large brown road sign reading, "Monument Lake Campground."

Conor had never seen or experienced anything quite like the Florida Everglades before. It was a vast ocean of swaying grass, an interwoven-mixture of damp marshes and sun-scorched prairies. The largest wilderness east of the Mississippi, the Everglades was a place where Cypress trees towered high above the flatlands, scattered in clumps like small desert islands, their roots evolved over centuries to survive below the thick, green, swampy water. Mangrove forests sprung up where fresh water from Lake Okeechobee in the north made its way down to Florida Bay where it mixed with salt water from the Gulf of Mexico. It was a living, breathing place with alligators, manatees, Florida panthers, snail kites, and sea turtles, not to mention the ever-present mosquitoes. There, they were the rulers of all they surveyed, swarming unchallenged in the wettest, hottest summer months.

They left the Chevy hidden from view in a densely grown hammock of cabbage palms, then made their way on foot around the lake through the undergrowth. The heat was exhausting, the insects everywhere. But they beat a path through the brush for half an hour until finally emerging into a clearing to find the cabin sitting on the edge of the swampy lake. It was a small, wooden structure with a flat, corrugated tin roof. The boards had rotted to a silver color with a small overhanging porch falling down to one side. But most importantly, at least as far as they were concerned, there was an old blue pickup and a black mud-stained SUV parked outside by the water's edge. And even more importantly, a tiny telltale wisp of smoke rising from the blackened chimney pipe. They were not too late.

Danny told Conor to wait there while he and Anton checked it out, then slipped off through the bushes around the back of the building. He returned a few minutes later by himself, revolver in hand, looking very serious.

"Con, we've got a bit of a situation," he said quietly.

"Is he there?" Conor asked anxiously.

"Yeah, I think so." Danny nodded. "There *is* a guy matches your description. Problem is, there are also two bad-ass-lookin' black dudes, and they are packin' some serious hardware. Must be Benny's mates. One's got an Uzi hangin' from his shoulder, the other looks like he's holdin' an M4 carbine. I left Anton behind the cabin to keep an eye on them."

"So what do you want to do?" Conor asked nervously.

"There's no way I'm letting Bob leave here. If I can just get closer and identify him, we can call the cops and put an end to this once and for all. As soon as they have him in custody, it should be over. I'll be in the clear."

Danny thought about it for a moment and said, "Look, Con, I know clearin' your name is the number one priority, but there *are* different ways to go about it."

"What are you saying?" Conor asked with a sudden look of suspicion.

"Okay, just hear me out," continued Danny. "Them black gangbangers gotta be those Jacksonville lads here to buy the cocaine, yeah?"

"So what? Look, I don't care about them, Danny. I only care about Bob."

"Just hear me out," he repeated a little louder. "Now, I've been thinkin', if we do this my way, it could be a win-win situation for us all."

"Jesus," Conor muttered, realizing what was coming next. "You want to go after that cocaine for yourself, don't you?"

"No, man, not *just* the cocaine," Danny replied with a glint in his eyes Conor remembered only too well from the old days. "What I'm sayin' is, if we do this the right way, we can walk out of here with Bob, as well as the cocaine *and* the cash. Win-win for all of us. You can clear your name with the cops *and* have enough money to buy your own boat again." He looked directly at Conor, knowing what buttons he needed to press to convince him. "Look, I know you're broke, Con. You're nearly thirty and don't own shit but the clothes on your back. Hell, even that t-shirt you're wearin' belongs to Anton."

"So?"

"Well, all I'm saying is you're lookin' at takin' orders from poxy fuckers like Bob Castagna for the rest of your life."

"Danny, I don't *want* the money. I just need to confirm that it's Bob in there, then call the cops and get this nightmare over with."

"Well then think of me and Anton," Danny snapped irritably. "Jaysus, Con, we've put our fuckin' necks on the line for you, no questions asked. We were not lookin' to make anything out of this, you *know* that. But, holy fuck, man, we'd be mad to turn down this chance." He lowered his voice a bit, changing his tone. "Listen, Con, I never mentioned any of my own troubles 'cause, well, you had enough of your own. But things have not exactly been goin' good for me and Anton of late either. This recession has all but killed off the construction game down here. People are losin' their jobs and their houses left and right. And the way things are goin', well, me and Anton won't be far behind them. And that's the truth, brother."

Conor sighed wearily, put a hand to his forehead, and said, "Okay, Danny, I get it, I get it. But please, just promise me *one* thing."

"Yeah?"

"Promise me there won't be any killing. And no matter *what* happens, we call the cops as soon as we have Bob."

"You've got it." Danny smiled. "I promise you, Bob is our number one priority. Soon as we've got things under control, Anton and I will split with the gear and the cash, and you can wait here for the cops. Okay?"

As soon as Conor agreed, Danny led him through the undergrowth to where Anton was waiting out back, gun in hand, looking tense but highly excited. Danny flashed him a glance, which Conor knew was his way of telling his friend that they had the green light. Danny then handed Conor a small rock and told him to count to twenty before smashing it through the back window as a distraction. He and Anton immediately headed around to the front of the cabin.

"Eighteen, nineteen, twenty." Conor hurled the rock as hard as he could and the dirty bug-covered glass shattered into a million pieces and fell inwards. While the three men sitting inside stood up and turned toward it in surprise, Danny and Anton kicked open the front door behind them and charged in firing.

Bob Castagna screamed in terror, crouching down on the floor with hands shielding his head. But Danny and Anton knew exactly what they were doing and ignored him, only taking out the two armed men as they had planned. The smaller one with the M4 carbine went down immediately, shot two or three times in the chest, but the taller man with the Uzi swung it quickly around his midriff in an attempt to fire back. He didn't manage to get a single shot off, however, before a hail of bullets cut him down and sent him sprawling backwards against the wall. As Conor reached the front door and stepped inside, the black man's legs buckled beneath him and he slumped down in a heap beside the stove.

Conor was speechless, but he knew there was absolutely nothing in the world he could do about it now. Things were out of his control. Danny was acting like the wild man he knew of old, doing his own thing with little regard for the consequences. He was as violent and unpredictable as he had always been. That, after all, was what got him into so much trouble over the years.

In a way, Conor felt as if he had made a pact with the devil or, at the very least, one of his demons. But, he asked himself, what else had he expected when he asked Danny for help? He was not just an innocent in all this. He knew well that people could probably die. He had only been too aware of what could happen the moment he saw them with those guns in Anton's house. He had no choice but to go along with this now. Yes, he thought, things *were* out of his control. But then, he realized, they probably had been ever since he arrived in South Florida.

"Hey, Danny! This mother's still alive," Anton exclaimed in astonishment as he stood over the smaller man who had been wielding the M4 carbine, prodding him in the ribs with his toe.

Danny casually walked over, and without the slightest hesitation, pointed his revolver at the man's head and put a bullet in it.

Conor turned away in disgust. But he knew there was no going back now. As Danny and Anton examined their spoils on the table, giddily counting the money and packs of cocaine like children on Christmas morning, he walked across to Bob and stood directly over him. The terrified businessman was still huddled in a ball, whimpering with fear.

"Don't kill me. Please, just take the bag and go."

"Relax, Bob. We're not going to kill you."

Recognizing his voice, Bob lowered his hands and looked up in amazement, still trembling. "Conor? Is that *you*?"

"I'll bet you never expected to see me again."

"I'm sorry, Conor. I had no choice."

In a rage, Conor grabbed him by the collar and dragged him to his feet. He stood for a second with fists clenched tight, but as Bob started to repeat how sorry he was, he hit him square in the mouth with all his strength. It was powerful enough to knock the older man down, sending him reeling back over one of the wooden chairs. He squealed in pain and clambered to his feet with one hand on his bloodied mouth and the other in front of him for protection.

"Sit the fuck down!" Conor shouted, grinding his teeth in anger. "I said sit down, or so help me I'll hit you again."

Bob found a seat, still shaking and holding his split lip, never taking his eyes from Conor's. After a moment, he gestured to the money and cocaine on the table and said, "Look, why don't you all just take it and go? You can have it all. And I won't say anything, I swear. You'll never hear from me again."

Danny finished counting the money and announced there was close to three quarters of a million in cash as he stuffed it into the black hold-all on top of the cocaine. He zipped it up and immediately handed it over to Anton. "Oh we are *definitely* takin it all." He smiled. Anton headed outside to put the bag in the back of the drug dealer's SUV, struggling to balance as it was now so heavy. "But you, Bobby boy, you are stayin' here with Conor to wait for the cops." On saying this, he placed his revolver and Anton's spare cell phone on the table in front of Conor. "Hey, are we good, man? You know we had no choice, don't you? We had to kill those lads or they would have hunted us down. Those Jacksonville gangsters live by the feud. You know, kill or be killed? Believe me, if we didn't tie up the loose ends, it would surely come back to bite us on the ass."

"Please," Bob begged with a tremor in his voice. "You don't have to call the police. Just take it all and let me go my way. I have nothing left now. Calling in the authorities would serve no purpose for any of us."

"Yeah, right. In your fuckin dreams," muttered Danny. Then, looking down at Conor and placing a hand on his shoulder, he said, "So, man, what about it? Are we good?"

Conor nodded slowly, resting his hand on the cold metal gun. He had been sitting there looking at Bob in silence, feeling contempt for him, but also an overpowering sense of relief that it was finally over. In the weeks to come, he knew he would relive the horrors of the past few days, but for the moment, he was content to just sit there, quietly looking into the older man's frightened eyes.

Danny and Anton dragged the two dead bodies out to the SUV. Shortly after, they set about cleaning up the blood-stained floor with a bucket and mop they had found on the porch. Danny told Conor they would drive back down the track to where the Chevy was parked. He said they would go back to his house to wait for Conor. Anton would follow Danny home in the SUV, but that on the way, they would dump it and the two bodies into one of the many swamps that surrounded the area, never to be found.

He then asked Conor to wait about thirty minutes before calling detective Shoemaker, which he calculated should be enough time to get to the Chevy, dump the SUV, and drive back to his house before the police arrived at the cabin. He assured him that part of the money was his. Insisted upon it.

"Enough to buy a boat with a bit of change left over." He smiled before telling Conor to deny they were ever there.

"So what should I say?" asked Conor.

"Best tell them Bob mentioned the cabin while you were stayin' at his house," he advised. "Say that you came out here on a hunch of your own. Oh, and by the way, make sure to tell them you hitched a ride. That will explain how you got here without a car. But most important of all, Con, whatever Bob says about money or cocaine or black dudes gettin' shot, just fuckin' deny it all and say he must be crazy. There is nothin' they can do if you stick to that story, understand? Nothin' at all."

Conor nodded and said, "Okay, I've got it."

"This piece of lying shit is goin' behind bars," Danny scoffed, gesturing toward Bob. Then, looking directly at him, he said, "You fucked with the wrong paddy, you asshole! Now you're goin' straight to jail. Oh, and guess what? I hear those Suarez boys have lots of horny amigos in there, just lickin' their lips at the thought of getting their hands on a nice piece of white meat like you!"

At that moment, Anton popped his head in the door and advised Danny they should get going, before waving good-bye to Conor with a salute of respect and genuine heartfelt gratitude. He had gotten involved in this for friendship, not money. Conor could see he felt good about himself for that. But now Anton looked like he was over the moon, like someone who had just won the lottery and wouldn't even have to pay the taxes.

When they were gone, Conor and Bob sat across the table from each other in silence. Bob's lip was still bleeding and starting to swell a little. Conor's left hand was resting on the phone, his right firmly gripping the gun. Bob knew he was going nowhere. After a while, he looked to Conor, sighing wearily as he said, "So, don't you at least want to know *why*

I did it?"

Conor shrugged nonchalantly. "I know why you did it, Bob. Because you are a greedy fat fuck. That's why."

"You don't know anything about me," replied the older man. "Or my situation."

"I think I know everything I need or want to know."

"You don't know anything about it," he growled. "How would you like it if everything you worked for your whole life was about to be taken away from you? And all the while, you were being pushed into a corner and could do nothing about it?"

"Bob," grunted Conor. "After what you have just put me through, I really don't want to hear it."

Bob sighed again, nodded his head in appreciation of the irony. After a pause, he looked toward Conor and said, "You know, all my businesses *were* doing well. I really wasn't lying about that. All my dealings were straight and above board until that evil bastard Hector Suarez came along." He stopped for a second and thought about it before continuing. "Heck, I should never have gotten involved with him. I know that now. But, well, it seemed like such an innocent partnership at the time. And lucrative too. It was an opportunity I just couldn't refuse. He had the money and I had a line on a piece of real estate that was ideal for one of his nightclubs. Anyway, we both made a lot of money out of the deal. Then one thing led to another. We joined forces and began buying more and more properties together to sell on."

Conor looked at the phone and saw it had been almost fifteen minutes since Danny and Anton left. Ten more, he decided, and he would call Detective Shoemaker with the good news.

"Anyway," Bob continued. "I won't bore you with the details, but when this recession hit, things went south quickly. Very quickly. We suddenly began losing money instead of making it, and Hector promptly informed me that I owed it to him, that he only invested on the strength of my personal guarantee." He smiled wryly to himself, shrugged, and said, "What could I do? Heck, he started threatening my family. I couldn't go to the police. My credit line at the bank was maxed out. The stress was unbearable, and all my other businesses began to suffer. So eventually, I went to him and I asked him *how* we could square things up and make them good again.

And that's when he came up with the idea of buying a yacht and transporting cocaine into Miami for some Columbian friends of his. He claimed it was only going to be two or three trips a year at the very most, that's all. But there was huge money in it and very little risk. And the beauty of it was that, if for any reason the coastguard came close, he said all we had to do was drop the bag overboard so they couldn't prove a thing. It was his idea that I buy the *Aphrodite* and front a new charter business that, for all intents and purposes, would be legitimate. And it *was* a real business, Conor. I didn't lie to you about that. Any money made from charters would be split down the middle between us. All I had to do was hire a captain and..." He looked at Conor and said sheepishly, "Well, heck, I suppose you know that bit."

"Bob, you played me for a fool from the very beginning," Conor spat venomously, dialing Shoemaker's number as he spoke. "I have no sympathy for you at all."

The phone rang for a few seconds until a familiar voice said, "Shoemaker."

"This is Conor Rogan," he announced triumphantly, gun at the ready in case Bob suddenly tried to run for it. "I have him, detective!"

"What?"

"I have Bob Castagna alive and well and sitting right here in front of me."

"Holy shit!" Shoemaker exclaimed. "If you are telling the truth, Rogan, I swear, I will be the first in line to shake your hand and apologize."

"Good enough."

"Now, are you going to tell me where the hell you are?"

Conor explained where they were, giving precise directions. With great excitement, the detective ordered him to sit tight, saying he and Childs were near the Sawgrass Expressway and could be there in fifteen minutes. Conor told him to hurry and then hung up and breathed a deep sigh of relief. It was over at last. Against all the odds, he had Bob in front of him and could start to relax, start to think about the future.

"Well," Bob said with an air of resignation. "It looks like you are in the clear, Conor."

"Looks like it," he replied with contempt.

"But tell me, how can you be *so* sure your Irish buddy is not going to double cross you and keep the money and cocaine?"

"First off, Bob, not *everyone* is a back-stabbing arsehole like you," Conor told him angrily. "And second, I really don't give a damn about the money and cocaine. *You* are what I came for. You. Nothing else."

"Okay, okay, if that's the way you say it is, I believe you," Bob replied with a shrug of the shoulders. "Anyway, since we're both stuck here, I might as well continue."

Conor looked on with indifference.

"Where was I? Oh yes, my arrangement with Hector was that he would give me fifteen percent of what he was getting from the Columbians. I swear I was going to tell you all about it in time. Even cut you in on the profits. But then, three days ago, just as everything seemed to be going to plan, I learned that he and his sons were starting to think they didn't need me anymore. As soon as the charter business was up and running and our trial run to Nassau was complete, those greasy back-stabbers were planning to step in and take over the *Aphrodite.* Those double-crossing bastards were actually going to leave me out in the cold. You see, Hector advanced most of the money to buy the boat, so legally, he holds the ownership papers." He paused for a while to reflect on all that had happened. When he continued, it was in a much more somber tone. "Anyway, I really wish you would believe me when I say that I *am* sorry I got you involved. Heck, I didn't intentionally set out to do it. It just kind of happened the way it happened, you know? I had my back to the wall and, well I was facing total ruination. I was facing being left with nothing"

"You must be an idiot," Conor said angrily. "You wouldn't have had *nothing*. You would still have had your family. A beautiful wife and an amazing daughter."

"Ha!" Bob grunted sarcastically. "My wife? Look, as I told you already, Conor, you don't know anything about me. Do you actually think that what you witnessed at my house was a scene of wedding bliss? If so, then think again, my young friend." He sat forward and put his hands on the table. Conor sat back in response, gun at the ready in case he was planning something. "Let me tell you about my perfect loving wife," Bob continued with a look of hatred in his eyes. "First of all, I may have neglected to mention that I met Eva at a swinger's party up in Tallahassee when I was still married to my first wife. Oh yes, Eva is my second, and a real party girl, as I'm sure you noticed."

Conor said nothing, beyond caring at this stage.

"Well, boy, did she get my juices flowing. But at the same time, she also got her money-grabbing claws into me. Manipulated me. Before I knew it, I was divorced from my first wife and remarried to her. Then, within months of the wedding, she made me a laughing stock among all my friends and business acquaintances by sleeping with each and every one. And I'm not just talking about the men! It was as if she purposely set out to humiliate me, you know? To ruin my good name. And money? Oh boy, Conor, let me tell you. She went through my cash like it was nothing. Nothing. Only the best and most expensive would do for my Eva. You know, she is the main fucking reason I got myself into such financial difficulties in the first place. If it wasn't for the pressure *she* put me under, I never would have considered getting involved with Hector." He stopped for a moment to catch his breath, to let his blood pressure go down. After a few seconds, he swallowed hard before continuing. "And then, listen to this and see if it doesn't take the biscuit. Do you know that recently she actually accused me of making advances toward Abi? What a spiteful, vindictive cunt! I mean, come on, you met her. Abi? Of *all* people. Heck, if only that sweet, innocent little girl knew how evil her mother really is."

Conor still said nothing, but knew from experience that Abi was not as sweet and naive as Bob maintained. He may have been right about Eva. She *was* a scheming bitch, no doubt. But Abi was certainly not the innocent Bob thought her to be.

With the sound of an approaching car engine and the crunching of tires on stones outside, Conor felt a wave of relief that at last Detective Shoemaker had arrived. Sitting opposite Bob was becoming more than he could bear and he was actually beginning to feel nauseous.

Seconds later, the engine died and Detectives Shoemaker and Childs climbed out of their Ford Marauder with guns drawn. They looked around for a few minutes to be certain there were no surprises waiting, that they weren't walking into an ambush, before stepping up onto the creaky porch and inching slowly inside. Shoemaker was first, but when he saw the revolver in the Irishman's hand, immediately let out a roar and ordered it to be placed on the table. As soon as Conor's hand left the gun, Detective Childs leaned across and snatched it away from him.

"Is there anyone else here?" she asked loudly, still on alert. "Rogan, godamnit. I said is there anyone else here?"

"No one," he replied. "Just us. Just me and Bob."

Amazed at the sight of the two men sitting calmly at the table before him, Shoemaker holstered his weapon and just stood there for a moment with hands on hips, observing them as he shook his head in disbelief. Conor was sitting back now with arms folded, looking extremely satisfied with himself. And why wouldn't he be? For sitting opposite him was the elusive Bob Castagna. The man who, up until now, was presumed dead and lost at sea. The "resurrected" victim was simply sitting quietly at the table, expressionless, staring straight ahead, showing no emotion.

"Well I'll be damned," Shoemaker muttered beneath his breath. Then, looking at Bob, he said, "Mister Castagna. It is *so* nice to see you back from the dead. You *do* realize that the coastguard and half the police force have been out looking for you?"

Bob cast him a disinterested glance and just shrugged a little, still saying nothing.

"And as for *you*," he continued, turning to Conor. "It seems I owe you an apology."

"Accepted," Conor replied, smiling with satisfaction. "Does that mean I am no longer under arrest?"

"It does," said Shoemaker. "But I'm afraid the same cannot be said for your friend, Mister Castagna, here."

Childs turned to him and said, "Bradley, I'm going out to the car to call this shit in."

"Fine. Go ahead and do that," he answered without looking at her. "Oh, and by the way, might be no harm to get a patrol car up here. Get a couple of uniforms to do a proper sweep of the area."

When she was gone, he leaned both hands on the tabletop and just stood there smiling. This was a dream come true, a moment to savor. After all his failed efforts to get proof, he knew Castagna had the goods on the Suarez operation and was in no position to keep quiet about it. With Carlos and Ernesto undoubtedly after his blood, he would now have no choice but to spill the beans in exchange for

protection. It was either that or prison. And prison was definitely not a place to hide from thugs like them. On the contrary, it would be like offering himself up to them on a plat-
ter. Yes, Shoemaker felt like all his paydays had come at
once. After all this time trying to get something on them, he
had finally hit the jackpot. And that jackpot was sitting right
in front of him.

"So, what's it to be?" he finally said, looking down at Bob
with raised eyebrows. "You want to talk to me now, or would
you rather wait until we get back to the station?"

"I have nothing to say until I speak to my lawyer," Bob
replied without making eye contact.

"You see, that's where you're making a mistake," advised
Shoemaker. "Since you will be charged with the murder of
Hector Suarez, your lawyer can do nothing to keep you out
of jail. And after the stunt you just pulled, there is no way
he's going to convince a judge that you're not a flight risk. So
the reality is that there is no way in hell you will be making
bail any time soon. All he *might* do is eventually negotiate a
lighter sentence in exchange for your cooperation. But even
that could take weeks."

Bob looked up and squinted his eyes. He began to com-
prehend what the detective was hinting at, was now more
interested in what he had to say. "Go on."

"Well, seems to me," Shoemaker continued. "Since you
murdered their father, the Suarez brothers will want you all
for themselves. Fact is, they will get their pound of flesh
whether you end up in a cell back at the station or in the
county lockup. Trust me, you will be like a fly in a glass jar to
them, just waiting for someone on their payroll to slit your
throat or stick a shiv in your liver."

Bob sat back and folded his arms. Conor watched his expression change as the conversation progressed. Realizing
now that even in police custody he was not safe, Bob was
beginning to seriously consider his only real option. Shoemaker could see this, decided to lay it on a little thicker.

"Could be anyone, anytime. But I *do* know for a fact that
they have police officers on their payroll, probably prison
staff too. Anyhow, I'll bet even if you sleep with one eye
open, you will never see them coming."

"Okay, okay," Bob gasped in desperation. "So what exactly do you want me to do?"

Shoemaker leaned down and stared directly into his eyes. "First off, you need to tell me everything you know about the Suarez operation. And I mean everything. Drugs, human trafficking, the whole nine yards. Even shit you probably don't even know you know."

"Okay, okay, but I genuinely don't know that much."

"You know enough to get things started," Shoemaker said.

"And then what?" asked Bob.

"Then I will need you to agree to testify to it in court. In the flesh. You will have to agree to sit before a judge, look those bastards in the eye, and put it all on record. You think you can do that, Bob?"

"Heck, I don't see that I have any other option."

"That is correct, you don't," Shoemaker agreed. "Now you're being smart."

Bob just nodded without looking up.

"Alright then, first thing we do is call in the FBI. Metro's not safe for you. I want to sign you into witness protection so that you are kept under wraps while I bring Carlos and Ernesto Suarez down to their knees."

"This all sounds very personal to you," Bob observed quietly.

"It is," Shoemaker grunted. "And it's lucky for you, because if anyone else had found you, they would probably throw you to the wolves. And by wolves, of course, you know I mean the Suarez brothers. Although I actually see them more as hyenas or jackals."

"Vultures more like," Bob agreed with a hint of bitterness in his voice.

"Alright then, let's do this," Shoemaker said.

He placed a hand on the back of Bob's chair and, pulling it away from the table, motioned for him to stand. Once he was on his feet, he told him to put his hands behind his head and began patting him down. It was procedure, and if nothing else, Shoemaker was a stickler for procedure. Just then, as he was finishing his search, his hand came across a hard object in Bob's back trouser pocket.

"What the hell have we got here?" he muttered with interest as he pulled out two dark blue US passports.

On seeing them, Conor figured they were Benny's handiwork, but said nothing, realizing it would only open up a can of worms best left alone.

The detective stepped back from Bob, who was still standing with hands on his head, and began inspecting the bogus documents. "Mmm, nice work. Really, really nice. Remind me to get the name of your forger." He checked the name at the bottom. "Mister Preston." He flipped the passport shut, opened the second one, and began leafing through its pages until he stopped cold. "No way. Well, will you look at—"

The gunshot was loud and unexpected, resonating from the open doorway behind throughout the confines of the cabin like an explosion, forcing them all to duck their heads in fright. The forty-five-caliber bullet left the muzzle of the small Glock revolver and entered the wall less than six inches above Shoemaker's head. He shielded himself as the splinters flew about him, instinctively reaching for his service revolver as he turned.

"Drop it, Bradley!"

Detective Childs was standing in the open doorway, her body silhouetted by the intense white daylight behind. She was holding her revolver in both hands, aiming directly at him. "I really don't want to kill you, but I will if I have to."

There was a coldness about her tone that Shoemaker had never heard before, a look in her eye that told him she meant business. He dropped his weapon to the floor and kicked it toward her. Conor had jumped away from the table at the sound of gunfire, but was motioned to sit back down again when she waved the muzzle of the glock at him in a downwards movement. She picked up Shoemaker's revolver and put it in the waistband of her skirt, directing him and Bob to join Conor at the table.

Looking dumbfounded by this new turn of events, Bob picked up the passports Shoemaker had dropped on the floor. He slipped them back into his pocket as he sat down. All three men now had their hands on the tabletop before them. Conor and Bob were confused by it all, pawns being played in someone else's game, but Shoemaker wasn't. He appeared enlightened. Finally, it all made sense to him. His eyes followed Childs with bitter disdain as she slowly circled around them.

"So what's going on, Childs? You acting off your own bat on this, or are you working for the Suarez brothers now?"

"They've finally had enough of you," she said coldly.

"They wanted me to put you down, Bradley, but I have just talked them out of it. I've just spoken to Carlos on the phone and he said to tell you they are willing to give you another chance. All they want is Castagna and what belongs to them."

"Oh really, is that all?"

"You can walk away from this, Bradley. You *and* Rogan. There's no need for any trouble between us."

"Fuck you," he replied angrily.

"And after I talked them out of killing you." Childs was behind him now and pushed her gun hard into the back of his neck. "Take out your handcuffs and your cell, Bradley." Then, when Shoemaker placed them on the table, she said, "Now cuff yourself to Rogan and give me the key."

As soon as this was done, she relaxed a little. Taking their cell phones from the table, she walked over to the soot-covered stove and tossed them into the smoldering ash. She began searching around the cabin, opening the cabinet doors by the sink, and then dropping to one knee to check under the cot in the corner. After a fruitless search, she returned to the table and addressed Bob. "So where the fuck is the bag?"

Shoemaker shot a puzzled glance to Conor. This was the first time he had heard anything about a bag. Conor looked back at him, blinked once, and nodded to show that he knew what she was talking about. Bob also turned to him, but not in puzzlement. His look was one of accusation.

"Ask *him*," he said. "His buddy took it. Danny something. Big Irish guy."

"McNamara," Childs muttered irritably. She turned the gun and pointed it directly into Conor's face. "Okay, Rogan, so where did he take it?" When Conor didn't reply, she cocked the hammer back to show she meant business.

"I heard him say he was going to Pompano," Bob offered, trying to be as helpful as he could, searching for a deal, desperately needing a way out. "Please, detective. Go there and get the cocaine if you want, but please, I beg you, don't hand me over to the Suarez brothers. You know what they'll do to me."

"*You* deserve everything you get!" she spat, lowering the gun from Conor's face.

"Well there is something else you don't know," he continued in desperation. "Something that could prove extremely beneficial to you. Maybe we could make a deal?"

"Go on."

"What if I told you there was three quarters of a million dollars in cash that Carlos and Ernesto know absolutely nothing about?" He proceeded to tell her about the murdered drug dealers and how Danny now had both the cocaine and the cash in the hold-all. "Give Carlos and Ernesto their cocaine. Fine. They're welcome to it. But can't you just take the money for yourself and let me go? You'll never see me again. I swear."

Childs said nothing. Instead, she flipped open her phone and called a number. When Danny answered, she told him who it was, then immediately handed the phone to Conor. "Tell him to meet us at the junkyard off South Dixie Highway and Tenth Street. Near the railway tracks. Get him to bring the cocaine *and* the money, and you can walk away from this unharmed. Otherwise, tell him you will die now and the Suarez brothers will come looking for him within the hour. He knows what they are capable of. Remind him there is nowhere he can go where they won't find him."

"Danny, did you hear that?" Conor said, putting the phone to his ear.

"Yeah, I heard," Danny grunted. "Tell her I said she's a fuckin' bitch!"

"This is a one-time offer," Childs added, knowing Danny could hear. "Tell him if he is not there when we arrive in half an hour, the offer is gone and he will be dealing directly with Carlos and Ernesto."

"Danny?" Conor waited for a response, listening to silence on the other end of the line for what seemed like an age. "Danny?"

"Put her on," he eventually said.

Childs took her phone back and listened as Danny told her he would meet her. But he had conditions. He said she must personally guarantee Conor's safety as well as rescind his arrest warrant and drop all charges against him. She must also clear it with the Suarez brothers that once they got their bag, they would promise not to pursue the matter with him or Conor any further. She assured Danny that once the cocaine and the cash was in the bag, Carlos and Ernesto would be content. She said Castagna would answer for their father's death, which would satisfy their thirst for revenge, and that he and Rogan could then get on with their lives without fear of reprisal.

"Okay then, you've got a deal," Danny said. "I'll be there in half an hour."

Shoemaker stood up begrudgingly when she motioned for the three of them to head out to the car. Cuffed to Conor's right hand, he followed slightly behind as they walked toward the door, staring venomously at Childs as he passed her by. Understandably, Bob was the most reluctant to get up and leave, and as she pushed him forward at gunpoint, he began whimpering.

"I thought we had a deal?"

She nudged the gun into the small of his back and snapped, "Move it, fat boy!"

Then, as they drew up to where Shoemaker and Conor were standing in the doorway, she turned to her partner and said, "Don't eyeball me like that, Bradley. You're *no* saint yourself."

"Now I know why you were on that goddamned cell so much," he muttered bitterly. "You were passing information to them the whole time."

"Yeah, well, in case you've had your head up your ass these past few years, times have gotten tougher and our pay hasn't exactly kept up with inflation. Shit, even our own department treats us with contempt these days, like we're glorified traffic wardens. Since we are out here every day risking our lives, we should at least be properly compensated. Don't you think? Besides, everyone in the department has dipped their fingers in the cookie jar at one time or another."

"Speak for yourself, Childs. In all my years on the force, I have never once taken a dime."

"Yeah? Well maybe you *should* have. Maybe then, you would still have your family."

Shoemaker stopped angrily in the doorway, pulling Conor back from the porch in mid-stride. "It was *you* who tipped them off about the hospital, wasn't it?"

Childs made no reply, still pushing the gun into Bob's back to keep him moving along.

"You were responsible for George Henderson's death. You know that, don't you? You may as well have fired that shotgun yourself."

"Come on, move it outside."

"And while we're on the subject, I wonder what part you played in Maria Gomez's disappearance." On seeing the look in her eyes, he continued. "Christ, you *did* tip them off about her, didn't you? You know, Childs, I know it means absolutely nothing to you, but you are a disgrace to that badge and everything it stands for."

"Please," she snapped sarcastically. "Give it a rest, Bradley. I'm sick to death of your constant whining and moaning. Get down off your soapbox and join the *real* world. The one with mortgages and car payments and credit card bills."

"*Your* world? No thanks."

Shoemaker stood firm for a tense moment, shaking his head in disgust, blocking the doorway so she couldn't leave. Childs stood facing him, eyeball to eyeball for a few seconds. Then, eventually pushing Bob to one side, she turned the gun toward him.

"Bradley, I swear to God, if you don't walk through that fucking door and get in the car right now, so help me, I will forget we were ever partners and drop you where you stand."

CHAPTER TWELVE

South Dixie Highway

The drive north to Pompano was not a pleasant one for Conor. Bob was locked behind them in the sweltering trunk, shouting and banging incessantly, while he and Detective Shoemaker sat cuffed together in the back seat. Shoemaker was still pissed. He was fuming obscenities beneath his breath at his partner's betrayal. But Childs simply ignored him, turning off the police radio as they drove at speed toward the rendezvous.

"So, Childs, just how much are they paying you?" he muttered.

"Bradley, if you keep your mouth shut for five minutes, I might split some of it with you," she replied as she slowed down at an intersection and came to a stop for a red light. "Why don't you play it smart for once in your life? They are only interested in Castagna and the cocaine. They don't have to know anything about the cash Bob spoke of."

"Fuck you," he growled beneath his breath.

"Then what about Alisha?" she said after a pause. "Hell, I know it hasn't been easy, that those medical bills have been crippling you."

"Don't you mention her name," he shouted angrily. "Drug peddling scum like Carlos and Ernesto are the reason she's *in* hospital in the first place, and greedy traitors like you are the reason they keep getting away with it."

"You really believe that?" she asked, catching his eye in the rearview mirror.

Shoemaker didn't really believe it, and they both knew it. Childs knew him all too well. The truth was, deep down,

Shoemaker believed *he* was the main reason for his daughter's condition. Sure, maybe the pushers and the peddlers and the Suarezes of this world were responsible to *some* degree, and for that she knew he would do his damnedest to bring them to justice. But Childs knew how Shoemaker believed it was also his own fault. He was haunted by guilt. If only he had been a better father, a better husband.

"Alright, Bradley, suit yourself." She shrugged when he didn't reply. The lights went green and she took off again. "You keep telling yourself that it's everyone else's fault."

They passed a bright yellow school bus going in the opposite direction, ferrying pupils from a local middle school for a day out in the Glades. The children's faces were pressed excitedly against the glass windows, sticking out their tongues and waving to anyone who looked over. Conor saw them gesturing to him as they passed, but just couldn't bring himself to raise a smile back at them. All he could think about now was Danny. He knew there was no way he was going to give up the hold-all without a fight. Not a hope. Conor knew him too well, and the prospect of what he might do scared him.

They turned onto South Dixie Highway and passed a large retail mall on their left. He watched shoppers unloading carts into the trunks of their cars, families walking hand-in-hand out of the scorching heat into the welcoming air-conditioned mall inside. They were just normal everyday people going about their normal everyday routine. It was, after all, just another summer's day for most of South Florida's population. Conor wondered if he would ever have that kind of life again. If, after all he had endured in the past couple of days, and assuming he would survive, he could ever put this behind him.

His thoughts were suddenly broken by a sharp elbow to the ribs. He turned to see Shoemaker motioning toward the door handle with his eyes. It seemed insane to Conor, but the detective was suggesting that they make a break for it. He jerked his head back and shook it fast in a gesture of disagreement, but Shoemaker just scrunched up his face and showed his teeth to indicate that he was not asking for permission. The truth of it was, Shoemaker knew *exactly* what lay in store for them. Childs had been working for the Suarez brothers all this time, lining her pockets while selling out people like Maria Gomez and George Henderson. Conor may not have fully appreciated it at the time, but Shoemaker knew she had blood on her hands, and could therefore not let either of them live to tell about it.

They were in a desolate, rundown part of town now, full of rows of used car lots, storage lockers, and distribution warehouses. There was minor road work up ahead, and the traffic became slowed to just one lane by a series of large red and white cones. Shoemaker suddenly yanked on the handcuffs to let Conor know that this was their opportunity, gesturing his head to show they were driving parallel to a set of railway tracks.

Before Conor could protest or do anything to dissuade him, Shoemaker pulled back the handle and shouldered open the back door, pulling Conor out onto the grass verge that ran down to the tracks. It was a bumpy, unforgiving ride. They hit the hard, dry ground with a thud, knocking the wind from their lungs as they fell. Even as Childs screeched the car to a stop and shouted after them, they rolled awkwardly down the embankment and out onto the hot metal tracks. Shoemaker was first up, standing upright on the gravel as he helped Conor to his feet beside him.

"Are you okay?" he shouted.

But Conor was dazed for a moment and said nothing.

"Rogan, are you hurt?"

Regaining his senses, Conor looked down, examining himself carefully before eventually nodding that he was alright. His trousers were ripped at the knee and there was a streak of dirt running down his shoulder as far as his grazed left elbow. But he was okay. There were no broken bones.

"Let's go," Shoemaker cried. "It won't take her long to come after us."

Even as he spoke, Childs was ramming the pickup ahead of her in an effort to push it forward, then reversing hard into the car behind to make room to drive out. She swung the Marauder off the road and onto the grass verge in one motion, its tires emitting a loud screech of rubber as they left the hot concrete with speed and bounced over the incline. She let the vehicle slide down the embankment until it hit the gravel along the tracks with a shudder, then pressed her foot full force onto the accelerator and sped after them like a woman possessed by the devil.

"This way," Shoemaker roared to Conor as they ran across the tracks and ducked through a narrow gap in the corrugated metal fencing on the other side.

At first, Conor was dragged along by the detective, but on seeing the approaching vehicle closing on them, picked up the pace and began matching him for speed. Childs smashed the car through the corrugated fence behind them, but immediately found herself spinning out of control. After a few seconds, the Marauder came to rest facing in the opposite direction in a cloud of dust, with her at the wheel, frantically trying to restart the engine as her two escaped prisoners continued running. They turned a corner into an old abandoned used car lot, probably once filled with brightly polished vehicles, flags, and balloons. But it was a graveyard now, a shadow of its former self, full of stripped car chassis and rusting shopping carts. The boiling hot asphalt was covered in weeds, shards of broken glass, and old, crumpled up newspapers.

Still running at full speed, Shoemaker pointed toward a rundown office building at the other end of the lot. Conor quickly looked back for any sign of the pursuing car, but couldn't see or hear anything. For a split second, he let himself believe that maybe, just maybe they had gotten far enough away to be in the clear.

Shoemaker kicked in the main office door when they found it locked. The rusted bolt was worn and offered little resistance to the heel of his shoe. Splinters flew as the door swung inwards, revealing a deserted, dusty showroom with four or five upturned desks and chairs scattered about the floor. A dented filing cabinet lay on its side in the center, drawers open, folders littered about it, with fluorescent lights covered in dust and cobwebs hanging in rows from the ceiling.

"Okay, let's see if we can find a phone," the detective said urgently, yanking on the handcuffs and pulling Conor violently off in the direction of the manager's office near the back of the showroom.

Once inside, they began wading through piles of old, yellowed papers covered in rat droppings on the desk and floor, invoices, and service reports from a time when the building was alive with well-dressed car salesmen and grease-covered mechanics. Conor noticed the office had actually been lived in for a while since its demise. There was a tattered sleeping bag in one corner and dozens of empty, rusted food cans scattered about the floor. But everything was covered in dust now. Whoever was sleeping there had not been back in a long time.

"Got one," Shoemaker exclaimed when he eventually found a phone buried beneath the paperwork on the desk. He picked it up and listened carefully, violently tapping the switch hook to try to bring it to life. After a few seconds of silence, however, he began slamming the receiver down in frustration. "Shit, it's dead!"

"Let's just keep going," Conor suggested. "Maybe she's gone. Maybe we can find someone outside with a cell phone."

"Problem is, there aren't many places still in business around here," the detective told him, shaking his head. "Most of these units are abandoned. And as for Childs, believe me when I tell you she is still out there. You can bet cash money on it. She's in this too deep to let us go. And there is no way in hell she can meet up with your buddy McNamara, and get the Suarezes' bag without you to bargain for it."

There was a moment's silence as they both leaned on the desk to catch their breath, still handcuffed to each other.

"Hey, back at the cabin you told Bob this was personal," Conor eventually said quietly. "Just what exactly *is* your beef with the Suarez family?"

"Forget it. It's a long story," Shoemaker replied after a pause, not elaborating any further.

"Childs mentioned your daughter?"

The older man shook his head and sighed wearily. Conor could see he didn't really want to talk about it. "Let's just say I owe them," he replied after a few seconds. "My daughter Alisha is in a coma after she was given ecstasy tablets at one of their clubs."

"Jesus, I'm sorry to hear that."

Shoemaker blinked in appreciation. "Well, anyway, thanks to you, I now have them red-handed," he continued. "Look, I know these past few days haven't been easy for you."

"That's an understatement," Conor agreed, nodding his head.

"I know. I know. I'm sorry about everything you've had to go through. But the truth is, as tough as it's been, it has finally led to their downfall. They just got too damn greedy when they decided to start smuggling cocaine into the country. And now I have the proof to put them away at last. Also, of course, it has led to the fact that I now know who the rat in the department is."

Even as he spoke, the hum of a revving car engine could be heard growing louder in the abandoned lot outside. The vehicle screeched to a halt at the entrance and there was a sudden loud *clunk* as the driver's door was banged shut. Seconds later, they heard the front door creak open and the sound of footsteps crunching on broken glass. She was inside.

"Shit, what was I thinking? We can't let ourselves be trapped in here," Shoemaker whispered urgently, realizing there was no window.

He motioned for Conor to follow, hunching down so as not to be seen as they went through a door behind the desk that led out into an adjoining room. It appeared to be a small conference area, containing a circular table and chairs with a row of filing cabinets against one wall and another half-open door at the far end. Shoemaker eased the door closed behind them and led Conor toward the exit. As they hurriedly crossed the darkened room, they could hear footsteps entering the office they had just left.

"Bradley, I know you're in here," Childs called out from the other side of the door.

"Shit, what do we do?" Conor whispered anxiously.

Shoemaker put his forefinger to his mouth and motioned for him to follow quietly.

"Come on, Bradley, I'm getting tired of this game," she shouted irritably. "Let's call it a day, okay? You gave it a shot, but it didn't work out."

They heard the door creaking open behind them, but ducked out onto a dimly lit stairwell a split second before she entered. Without making a sound, Conor followed the detective up the steps toward the roof. It was difficult in handcuffs, though. They had to walk as one, to coordinate their movement as they climbed. When they eventually reached the top, Shoemaker paused, and for the briefest moment, Conor looked back wondered if perhaps Childs had turned and gone. But then she suddenly kicked open the door below and stepped onto the stairwell, moving to her left so she was now looking directly up at them. She and Conor made eye contact. Her gun was in both hands, pointing straight at them.

"Alright, come back down, boys," she said wearily. "You know you're not going anywhere."

Ignoring the order, Shoemaker shouldered open the heavy metal door that led outside. She fired a warning shot after them as they ducked back out into the sunlight and found themselves standing on a flat, graveled roof. But it didn't look good. There was nothing to use for cover up there except for a few wooden pallets and an old iron water tank on the far side. So they ran to the nearest edge in the hope of finding a way down, only to face a sheer drop to the asphalt below.

"Shit, try the other side," Shoemaker shouted urgently as he yanked Conor off to the opposite edge facing the rear of the building.

When they reached it, they found a couple of oil drums and a large metal dumpster directly below, overflowing with broken office furniture, sheets of polystyrene foam, and folded up cardboard packing.

"You can't be serious," Conor exclaimed when he saw the look on the older man's face. "We'll break our fucking necks."

"We've *got* to try," snapped Shoemaker. "In case you haven't been paying attention, we've got no other choice."

Before Conor could respond, Shoemaker took a step back and, without hesitation, immediately ran straight off the edge, pulling him over as he fell. They both hit the dumpster at the exact same moment, feet first into the dried-up cardboard, rolling onto their sides to avoid the jagged metal edges. But the cardboard and polystyrene compressed with the sudden weight and they found themselves sinking down into it like quicksand. With a loud *whoosh* of air, an enormous ball of dust rose up about them, a mushroom cloud, blinding them completely and forcing both into convulsions of coughing. When the cloud eventually cleared and they could finally open their eyes, their hearts sank with despair. Childs was standing directly before them, peering into the dumpster with one hand covering her nose and mouth, the other pointing a gun at them.

"God damn you both," she coughed through the dust. "And you, Bradley, you're too old for this shit."

"Fuck you," he coughed back.

"I'll say this for you, though, you are one stubborn son-of-a-bitch. I'll give you that."

~ ⚮ ~

Danny was waiting less than twenty yards away when they pulled into the abandoned junkyard off South Dixie, the black hold-all plainly visible at his feet. Shawna's old blue Chevy was parked behind him to his left, but there was no sign of Anton. The yard itself was in the same rundown part of town they had been in earlier, close to the railway lines that ran from Georgia up north, through Jacksonville and down to Miami. A high mesh fence topped with circular razor wire surrounded the plot, the entire area littered with butchered cars and stacks of rusted scrap metal. To their right was a collection of old oil drums, some standing upright, others lying on their sides, empty of content and battered and dented from years of rough handling and misuse. There was also a small building nearby that had long since lost its roof and part of one wall. The windows were smashed in and there was bright-colored graffiti covering virtually every inch of its brickwork. A long wood and tin overhanging porch stretched the length of the building outside, held up by four concrete pillars running parallel to the front wall.

Childs got out of the car with gun in hand, scanning the surrounding area for other signs of life. When she was eventually satisfied they were alone, she opened the back door and ordered Conor and Shoemaker out onto the cracked, sun-scorched asphalt. Still handcuffed together and covered in dust, they stretched their sore limbs and exchanged a concerned glance.

"That's some pal you've got," Shoemaker said in a low voice, motioning toward Danny. "Hell, there aren't many people who would exchange three quarters of a million dollars for me."

"She's not going to let us go, is she?" Conor said quietly.

The detective looked him straight in the eye and shook his head. "Afraid not. We know far too much. Soon as she's got what she wants from McNamara, she'll put a bullet in all of us for sure." He thought about it for a second, then shook his head and added, "It's a damn shame, though. I have spent so long trying to prove the Suarez family was involved in this shit. And now, just when I get the evidence I need, it turns out my own partner is on their payroll and gonna take me out. Who'd have guessed?"

"Well, at least you now know who she *really* is," Conor

said quietly.

"Bring the bag over to us!" Childs commanded to Danny.

"You put that gun away first," he replied.

Childs holstered her Glock and showed her hands to confirm it. When Danny was sure, he lifted the heavy bag and started walking toward them. His revolver was behind him, stuck in his waistband with its handle sticking out. It wasn't on show, but was easy to reach at the first sign of danger. He also knew Anton was waiting nearby, could feel his eyes on him as he walked.

Anton had picked a prime spot, completely out of sight behind one of the concrete pillars holding up the overhanging porch. He was pleased with himself for choosing such a good location. Not too close to be seen, yet near enough to cover Danny if any danger presented itself. He kept a watchful eye on the proceedings with the safety off the Uzi sub-machinegun he had recently acquired that afternoon. His finger was at the ready, hovering anxiously above the trigger.

Danny was now virtually face-to-face with Childs, who had made Conor and Shoemaker walk in front of her, using them for cover in case anything went wrong. Danny nodded reassuringly to Conor when they stopped, saying, "Alright there Con?" But then, casting a suspicious eye toward Shoemaker who was cuffed to him, said, "What the fuck is all this?"

"Let's say it's a two for the price of one deal," Childs replied sharply.

"Funny, isn't it?" Danny said, shaking his head ruefully. "Wasn't that long ago you were preachin' about the criminals and scum *I* associate with. And now here *you* are, yourself nothing but a dirty lowlife lackey for the Suarez brothers."

"Just put down the bag and step back," she replied, ignoring the insult.

"And why in God's name would I do that?"

"Because I need to check it's all there, you dumb fuck!"

Danny shrugged his shoulders to acknowledge the sense of it, stepping back a few paces without speaking.

"Further," she commanded. When he took another step or two back, she hunched down to examine the contents with one hand on her still-holstered gun.

Danny made eye contact with Conor as she did, motioning with a flick of his head toward the nearby building where

Anton was hiding. "Ta ar gcara taobh their diut," he said in Irish, alerting his friend that Anton was not far behind them.

Before Conor could look in his direction, however, a black Jeep suddenly broke through a section of the mesh fencing on the other side of the yard and sped toward their position. A thick cloud of dirt and dust billowed skywards behind its spinning rear wheels, which screeched dramatically on the hot asphalt as it roared closer. It skidded to a sudden stop less than fifteen feet away and the Suarez brothers leapt out, shouting angrily with Kalashnikov assault rifles at the ready. Danny pulled out his revolver and stepped in front of the bag on seeing them, while Childs stood upright, moving back a few paces and pulling hers in response. Shoemaker and Conor moved a few feet to their right, instinctively out of the line of fire.

"Manos arriba!" Ernesto roared at Danny. "Hands up!"

"You said we were cool once I returned the bag!" Danny screamed accusingly at Childs, still keeping his eyes and gun fixed on the Cubans.

Childs turned toward the brothers with one hand raised and her gun pointing safely toward the ground. "Tranquillo, guys," she told them, trying desperately to diffuse the tense situation. "Carlos, Ernesto, everything is okay. I promise. Castagna is in the trunk of my car. And look, McNamara has brought the bag like he said."

"No!" Carlos screamed angrily. "There is another one. Where is the negrito?"

"He came alone," she replied, looking a bit confused.

"No, no! There is another one," Ernesto insisted, pointing his Kalashnikov threateningly toward Danny. "Where is your negrito friend?"

"You know something," Shoemaker interrupted at the top of his voice. "I have just about had it with you two racist motherfuckers. If you don't lower those guns, I swear, you are going to have me to deal with."

Distracted from Danny for a moment, Carlos eyed him with a look of pure disdain and contempt. He slowly turned his Kalashnikov toward the detective and said, "Officer Shoemaker. So, you finally got what you wanted. But you know what, my friend? Today is *not* going to end well for you." He smiled with pleasure. "I am *personally* going to make you suffer for the aggravation you have caused our family these past few months."

"Is that a fact?"

"Yes."

"Go fuck yourself."

"And then, maybe I will pay a visit to your daughter in the hospital."

"Why you mother—"

"And as for your new Irish companero," Carlos continued, gesturing toward Conor. "I think my brother here has some unfinished business with him."

"Hey, don't be forgettin I still have your bag here," Danny snapped angrily, visibly enraged that Carlos was threatening Conor after all they had put him through.

Ernesto snarled viciously as he raised his Kalashnikov toward him. "You tell us where the negrito is hiding or I will put you down where you stand."

"Fuck you!" Danny replied with a scoff. "Why don't you go back to your club and play with that alligator of yours?"

Ernesto said nothing, just kept his gun on him with a look of hatred in his eyes.

"Oh yeah, that's right," Danny continued mockingly. "You can't, can you? Because someone blew it all to hell!"

Finally realizing what Danny was saying, that he was the one responsible for the bomb, Ernesto emitted an angry, uncontrolled roar. Shoemaker shot a glance to Conor for confirmation, but this time, Conor could only shrug his shoulders and shake his head in bewilderment. If Danny *had* really blown up their club, Conor knew nothing about it. But now that he did, he felt a sudden urge to go over and shake Danny's hand.

"You are going to die very slowly and very painfully," Ernesto growled viciously through clenched teeth. "I swear, I am going to make you pay."

Up until now, Anton had been anxiously monitoring events, determined not to let anything happen to Danny. But as soon as he saw the assault rifle pointing at his friend and the look of pure hatred on Ernesto's face, he leaped out from behind the pillar and raised his Uzi.

"Danny, bro, get yourself to cover," he shouted as he pulled back on the trigger. The entire clip of bullets ripped into the asphalt like hailstones around the Cubans.

The scene quickly erupted into one of chaos and confusion. Shoemaker pulled Conor forcibly toward the shelter of the nearby oil drums. Childs let off a couple of shots at Anton as she also scurried for cover behind her car. Danny ducked to his right and sprinted back toward the Chevy, while Carlos and Ernesto ignored him and also began returning fire on Anton. At this range, however, Anton's lightweight Uzi was no match for their heavier Kalashnikovs, so he was forced to retreat back behind the thick pillar as its outer layer of plaster was blasted away by their combined fire.

Danny was hunched low behind the Chevy now, but on seeing Anton pinned down, leaned up on the hood and squeezed off a couple of carefully aimed shots at the Cubans. Ernesto took a bullet to his right calf and went down on one knee, turning his fire on Danny as he did so. Carlos grabbed the hold-all and quickly moved away from his brother in an attempt to find some cover. He ducked down behind a nearby stack of wooden pallets, but kept his gun on Anton's position. At the same time, Childs moved around to the back of the Marauder and began shooting toward the pillar. In a much better position than Carlos, she could just see a few inches of Anton's shoulder peeping out from behind it. Anton knew he was in trouble. He had foolishly let himself become caught in a crossfire with Carlos on one side and Childs on the other.

"We need to get to that Chevy while they are distracted," Shoemaker told Conor, his voice almost drowned out by the gunfire. "It's our only way out of here."

Conor nodded in agreement. Keeping low, he followed the detective around the back of the oil drums to where Danny was pinned down by Ernesto. At that moment, however, Anton took a bullet from Childs to his exposed shoulder, yelping in agony as it smashed into his collarbone. He swung around and unloaded an entire clip at her, hitting her in the forearm and sending her scurrying back behind her vehicle. But Carlos had changed position while Anton was distracted, moving unseen around the other side of the porch until he finally got him in his sights.

Anton saw him far too late. Realizing now that he should not have turned his back on the Cuban, he cursed as he swung his body around to fire back at him. Finding his Uzi empty, though, he dropped it to the ground and reached for the revolver in his belt. But even as he raised it toward Carlos, his chest was ripped open by a short burst of concentrated gunfire, forcing the breath from his body and sending him hurtling backwards to the concrete. His head hit the hard surface and bounced a couple of times. When it came to rest, he found himself lying on his back, looking up at the underside of the wooden overhang. Carlos walked slowly over and stood looking down at him.

"Man, that was stupid," Anton whispered to himself as his mouth filled with blood.

"Now you can join your woman," the Cuban said through the corner of his mouth.

"Huh?"

Carlos caught the look of puzzlement on his face and smiled triumphantly. "You didn't know, did you? Yes, we paid a visit to your house this morning and my brother, Ernesto, played a round of golf with your little chica."

"Why you dirty mother—"

"By the time he finished, her head looked like a piñata."

A burning rage filled Anton's battered body as tears welled up in his eyes. But then a strange numbness spread through him as he closed them and exhaled slowly. His last thoughts were of Cassandra and what she must have gone through. Carlos pointed the Kalashnikov down and slipped his finger over the trigger. Anton had never been a religious man, but he always believed there was something after death. Whatever that was, at least he would see her again, he thought to himself as Carlos squeezed the trigger. That comforted him a little.

Danny swung around in fright, ready to fire on Conor and Shoemaker when they suddenly appeared behind him from out of nowhere. As soon as he realized it was them, however, he lowered his gun, cursing. Breathing a sigh of relief and shaking his head, he turned his attention back to Ernesto. The Cuban was still out in the open about three yards from his Jeep, down on one knee and continuing to pin Danny behind the car. Shawna's old blue Chevy was taking a beating. Its windows were smashed and the hood and passenger's side were riddled with dozens of bullet holes.

"Have you got another gun?" Shoemaker shouted as he and Conor squatted helplessly behind the rear wheel.

"In the trunk!" Danny yelled through the corner of his mouth.

Beneath a hail of gunfire, Shoemaker reached up without standing and popped open the trunk. Once raised, it acted as a shield and he was able to stretch up to look inside. "There's nothing in here!"

"Under the spare!" Danny roared as he snapped the last clip into his revolver.

The Chevy had so many holes that it now resembled a block of Swiss cheese. But its heavy metal frame provided excellent cover. There was no way Ernesto could touch them, at least not without moving position, and if he tried that, he would only make himself more vulnerable.

Strange, Danny thought as he just caught sight of Carlos coming around the Jeep to join his brother out in the open. Both the Suarez brothers as well as Childs were now firing on the Chevy, giving him their undivided attention. If they were able to do that, he thought, it meant they were not taking fire from Anton by the porch. And that, he realized, could only mean one thing. That was the moment Danny knew for certain that Anton was gone. With a blinding rage welling up inside, he let out a roar and swung out from the safety of the car to return fire.

He got off three or four shots in quick succession, one of them smashing into Ernesto's side, another clipping Carlos in the right shoulder. But as he ducked back down, he took a bullet to the side of his head. He felt a sharp, burning pain above his left temple and closed his eyes tight as blood poured into them. With a cry of pain, he collapsed downwards and began scurrying back behind the wing of the car. He was hunched over clutching the wound when Conor grabbed his sleeve and pulled him around to safety. Meanwhile, Shoemaker had finally found the second pistol under the spare wheel and began to let off a couple of shots to cover them.

"Danny!" Conor shouted above the noise of the Kalashnikovs. "How bad are you hurt?"

Danny's face was covered in blood, but he lowered his shaking hand for a moment to let his friend see. The bullet seemed to have only just grazed his head above the left temple. He was lucky. Another quarter of an inch to the left and he would be dead. Although he was dazed and suffering from shock, had so much blood in his eyes he couldn't see, it was not as serious of a wound as it might have been. Conor reassured him he would live, telling him it was not as bad as it looked and to keep putting pressure on it until he got him to safety.

"Con, I need to tell you something," Danny said quietly through gritted teeth.

Conor leaned closer to try to hear his words above the noise.

"It wasn't your fault," he said.

"What are you talking about?"

"Grainne," Danny continued. "I know the rest of my family haven't spoken to you since it happened."

"I *was* responsible," Conor replied. "I don't blame them for hating me."

"Yeah? Well you *should* blame them. Fuck 'em all! They were always a bunch of stuck-up assholes. You and Grainne were a team, man. What happened was an accident. That's all. It was an accident, Con. It wasn't your fault. Man, you've got to let it go. I knew Grainne as well as anyone. I know she loved ye. And I know she would want you to get on with your life above all else."

Conor didn't reply for a few seconds. He thought about it, ignoring the gunfire, looked Danny straight in the eye, and smiled gratefully. "Thanks for that, man. You're a good friend. But you should have told me that you blew up their club."

Danny forced a painful smile, then after a pause, said, "Maybe I'm not as good a friend as you think."

"What does that mean?"

Danny looked at him a bit sheepishly.

"What does that mean?"

"I couldn't help it, Con. I took most of the money out of the bag and replaced it with newspapers. And those coke packages are only filled with flour and talcum powder. Shawna has the real gear stashed safely back in Pompano."

As Danny grinned through the pain, lapsing into a state of semi-consciousness, Conor shook his head, cast his eyes to heaven, and took the revolver from Danny's hand. He turned to Shoemaker for guidance. This was the detective's field of expertise, not his.

"Have you ever fired one of those?" Shoemaker asked him, keeping his head low.

"Nope," Conor replied, shrugging his shoulders. "But I am a quick learner."

"Christ on a bike." Shoemaker let the back of his head rest against the hot car door, closed his eyes, and took a deep, steadying breath. Conor could see that he wished he had someone more experienced and capable by his side. But the fact was, he didn't. Like it or not, Conor was all he had.

"So what do you want me to do?" Conor asked.

"Okay then," Shoemaker said after a thoughtful pause, his voice straining to be heard above the roar of the two firing Kalashnikovs. "Look here, when I say move, we go as one, understand?"

"Okay."

"As soon as they pause to reload, you and I are going to stand up side-by-side and return fire on them."

"What about your pal, Childs?"

"She's further away," Shoemaker said. "Forget about her and just concentrate on them."

"Okay so."

"No!" Shoemaker warned with frustration, concerned that he was not paying full attention. "Not just okay, Rogan. This is life or death. Don't just start firing at those guys without first aiming properly, understand? We haven't got the ammunition to waste. You've got to stop for a second. Compose yourself. You only have a few shots left, so take a deep breath, calm yourself, and whatever you do, aim carefully at your target. Blank everything else out and just focus on where you intend to put that bullet. Focus. Got it?"

Before Conor could respond, however, the firing Kalashnikovs stopped. It was only for the briefest moment while the Cubans slammed new clips into their weapons, but just long enough for Shoemaker and him to make their move. He remembered what he had been told, took a deep breath, and didn't let his sense of urgency overwhelm him.

As he stood up and raised Danny's revolver, he took his time, aimed carefully, and squeezed the trigger. He saw his first shot bounce off the ground about two inches away from Carlos' left foot. *Shit*, he thought, *that was so close.* Conor desperately wanted payback for what they had done to him, for the living hell they had put him through. And, although a few days ago when Bob suggested they go hunting and he had said he could never kill anything, he knew now with absolute certainty that he could do just that. A lot of bad things had happened to him in the past few days. It had changed him. He knew that. For better or worse, Conor was full of rage now and desperately wanted revenge. So he took another breath, raised his gun a little higher than before, and squeezed off a second shot. This time, Carlos' body jerked backwards as if an invisible fist had just punched him in the stomach. Conor actually felt a sense of satisfaction when he saw the Cuban lower his weapon and hunch over in pain.

Ernesto was still on one knee since Danny had hit him in the leg a few minutes earlier with his first shot, and was also bleeding from the second wound in his side. But he was quicker than his brother when it came to weaponry, had already reloaded to start firing on the front of the Chevy again. Before he got the chance, however, he caught a glimpse of the detective he hated so much leaning his elbow on the roof of the car, his pistol aimed expertly in his direction. He had then been distracted by his brother's plight for a moment, but now swung around to direct his fire at Shoemaker. As he did, the detective shot him in the neck and put him down hard. He dropped his gun and rolled on the ground for a few agonizing seconds while clutching his throat in a loud death rattle, gasping for air as his lungs filled with his own blood. Pulling himself up onto his knees, he stretched out a hand and tried to shout something to Carlos. But his voice was gone. Blood gurgled through the hole in his throat as he reached back down for his gun. Shoemaker took aim and squeezed off another shot, this time catching him square in the chest. He dropped the gun and fell back down again. It was over for him. Soon, his body stopped twitching and he lay motionless on the ground, the blood spreading slowly around his head and chest into the cracked, bullet-ridden asphalt beneath him.

Shoemaker yanked on the handcuffs and pulled Conor back down to safety just as Carlos regained his composure and started firing on them again. He was wounded in the stomach, but not out of the fight just yet. He guessed correctly that the three men behind the Chevy were almost out of ammunition, and was preparing to move in for the kill when that happened.

Conor swung open the back door of the car and helped Danny scramble inside. As soon as he did, however, Danny collapsed on the back seat and Conor shut the door behind him.

"We've got to get out of here," he shouted toward Shoemaker. "We need to get him to a hospital."

The detective thought about it for a second and then

nodded. "Okay. You drive and I'll cover you."

But as Conor slid into the driver's seat with Shoemaker close behind, he caught a sudden glimpse of Bob, emerging like a newborn from the trunk of Childs' car. The sight of the older man falling awkwardly to the ground appeared surreal to him in the chaos of what was happening around them. Bob was gripping the metal wheel jack he had used to pry open the trunk, his shirt soaked, his hair stuck to his head with sweat.

Even as Conor turned the key in the ignition and the Chevy's engine burst into life, he watched Bob sneak up unnoticed behind the crouching Detective Childs. She was huddled down on the ground, holding her injured arm, yet still managing to fire in their direction. She heard a noise behind her at the last second and turned her head in surprise just as Bob brought the heavy jack down on it. The thick metal bar smashed into her skull and knocked her to the ground. As she crumpled in a ball at his feet with her skull split open, Bob dropped the jack, kicked her aside, and opened the driver's door. Within seconds, he had the Marauder's engine running, and took off with a screech of burning rubber straight ahead in the direction of Carlos Suarez.

The Cuban saw him approaching from behind just before he was hit. He swung his weapon around and managed to fire off a short burst, which ricocheted off the bonnet and cracked the windscreen. But it did not deter Bob for an instant, did not distract him or veer him off course one bit. With a look of pure, unadulterated hatred in his eyes, he crashed right into Carlos and sent him spinning up over the hood. Carlos hit the ground behind with a sickening thud, his leg bones shattered and his ribs cracked. Groaning in agony and realizing his gun was gone, he started crawling toward Ernesto's lifeless body nearby, desperately trying to get to the weapon lying beside him.

Without the slightest hesitation, however, Bob spun the wheel in a violent motion and swung the Marauder around to face him again. Their eyes met for an instant. With a loud rev of its engine, Bob forced the peddle to the floor and sped directly back toward him. Carlos screamed as the heavy vehicle ran him over without stopping, bouncing into the air as if it had simply hit a larger than usual speed bump.

Bob screeched to a stop as Carlos' mangled body

emerged from beneath his back wheels. He opened the driver's door and, in one fluid movement, reached down and grabbed the hold-all sitting on the ground nearby. He swung it onto the front passenger seat and took off again, crashing through a section of rusty mesh fencing before skidding almost full circle and speeding off toward the highway.

"Quick!" Shoemaker cried. "Go after him!"

"No, I can't." Conor shouted. "We've got to get Danny to a hospital, remember?"

"But he's getting away, goddamn it."

Ignoring him, Conor turned around to check on his wounded friend. A short while ago, he would have agreed that getting Bob was the only thing that mattered. Even the offer of three quarters of a million dollars could not sway him from that goal. But things had changed since then. Danny and Anton had risked everything to help him clear his name. Now, Anton was dead because of that. He really didn't care about Bob anymore. He just needed to make sure Danny was alright. To hell with Bob, he thought. Nothing else mattered to him now but getting Danny to that hospital for treatment.

As soon as he turned to check on him in the back, however, Danny pulled himself upright and looked back with a painful grin, nodding that he was okay. His face was pale and stained red, his left eye swollen shut. He was still holding the deep bleeding gash on his head, but he was sitting up now and seemed to have recovered from the initial shock.

"Forget about me, I'm alright," he grunted when Conor raised his eyebrows, his face full of concern.

"Satisfied?" said Shoemaker. "Now let's go!"

"Are you sure?"

"Yeah, Con, I've lived through worse than this," replied Danny. "The detective's right. That motherfucker Bob started all of this. So let's go get him together. Let's get that bastard and finish this thing!"

CHAPTER THIRTEEN

THE OCEAN FLOOR

Grainne's long red hair flowed behind her in the breeze like a fiery mane, her pale, rain-soaked face turned anxiously toward the oncoming storm. She stood on the snow-covered pulpit at the bow of their yacht, holding onto the ice-encrusted jib stay running toward the mast. She was concerned about the sudden change in weather, was in the process of preparing the boat for the rough seas that lay ahead. The vessel pitched and rolled with the motion of the enormous surrounding waves, heaving to-and-fro with every violent crash.

The ice storm had come upon them without warning and the swell was rising by the minute. Conor had never experienced anything so sudden. He had monitored the forecasts, but there had been no warning of this. When they first spotted the dark, ominous clouds approaching on the horizon, Grainne had instinctively released the spinnaker to give them more speed. He was at the wheel in the cockpit and shouted for her to hold on tight as he tried desperately to outrun it. But it was bigger and faster moving than he anticipated. A ferocious, living squall like none he had ever seen.

Before they knew it, they were surrounded on three sides by darkness and storm, with only a tiny glow of light on the horizon before them. It felt as if they were trapped inside a dark bottle, lost in a tunnel with nothing but the slightest hint of daylight ahead. And then the rain and hail started, beating down with such force they couldn't hear each other's shouts anymore. And then the thunder and lightning began in the distance behind them.

Grainne lowered the mainsail and jib when they realized there was no escape. As the wind picked up violently, the sails would now only serve to capsize them. So Conor started the motor and tried to continue at speed toward the horizon. But the sea grew so high that the ravenous ocean ahead swallowed the last glimmer of light. Soon they were fighting for their lives, nowhere to go now except with the waves.

Conor struggled desperately at the wheel to keep them facing away from the oncoming tempest. He knew if he let the boat turn sideways, they would be engulfed without mercy. The vessel would become swamped in minutes and she would surely capsize. So he strained with every muscle and sinew in his body, grunted and groaned with every exertion of energy he possessed.

He could barely see Grainne now. She had come back to the safety of the cockpit when the sails were tied down and had tried to help him keep the wheel from spinning out of control. But then, up ahead on deck, a small hatch suddenly blew open and one of the spare sails came flying out on the wind. It wrapped itself around the starboard handrail, but continued flapping wildly over the side.

"I'm going to pull it back in!" she shouted at the top of her voice.

"No," he replied. "Too dangerous!"

Grainne placed a hand on his yellow oilskin jacket, shouting, "Conor, if it goes in the water, it'll tangle the prop."

He didn't have to be told what that meant. Their worst fear now was if the rudder broke or their engine lost power. If either happened, they would be at the mercy of the waves and smashed to pieces in minutes. They knew they had to protect the propeller at all costs.

"Then I'll go," he shouted.

"No," she replied. "You've *got* to stay at that wheel."

And with that, she placed a loving hand on his windswept cheek and left him to go forward. He tried calling after her, but it was pointless. She couldn't hear him above the howling gale. Grainne was the most stubborn person he had ever known. But then, that was one of the things Conor loved most about her.

As another massive wave broke across their bow, he focused his mind back to the problem at hand. The wheel had taken on a life of its own and was starting to fight his every move. So, while Grainne reached the starboard side rail and begin hauling the sail back on board, he turned them a few degrees to port. It was working. Just when he seemed to be getting the yacht under control, however, there was a loud crash above and the heavy wooden boom tore off its hinges and smashed down into the cockpit at his feet. He was sent sprawling backwards by the force of the blow with the wind knocked from his lungs. But as he fell, he lost his grip on the wheel, sending the boat lurching violently back to starboard.

By the time he regained his feet and retook the helm, Grainne was gone. Conor wiped the icy raindrops from his eyes and stared disbelievingly into the darkness ahead. But there was nothing. The deck was covered in ice and salty white foam, but his wife had been washed overboard into the darkness. With superhuman strength, he managed to swing full circle in an effort to spot her in the water. He screamed her name at the top of his voice for over an hour, but the only response he heard was the howling of the wind and the crashing of the waves on the hull. In that moment, he knew she was lost. And he knew, deep down in his soul, it had been his fault. If he had only held on to the wheel, she would still be with him. But she wasn't. She was gone now, and so was his reason to live.

Bob did not take the Interstate, but instead raced north on the Federal Highway back toward Palm Beach. Conor tried his best to keep up with him in the old Chevy, but its engine was not as powerful as the unmarked police car. It stuttered along as fast as he could make it go, his foot forcing the heavy accelerator down into the floor with all his might. Air whistled through its bullet-ridden panels as they sped past terrified-looking motorists who swerved desperately to get out of the way. The traffic was now building up in the evening rush hour, and they had quite a few scrapes and near misses as they raced through red lights and cut through busy intersections without stopping.

Shoemaker desperately wanted to take the wheel, but it was impossible while they were still in handcuffs. So he busied himself with yelling directions from the passenger seat, pointing out shortcuts and approaching dangers in a frantic bid to make up for lost time and catch up to Bob. He told Conor to take a sudden right turn across the railway tracks running parallel to the highway, sent him speeding down narrow side streets and alleyways, all the while trying to keep sight of the Marauder through gaps in the buildings.

A few minutes later, they emerged onto a wider street with heavy traffic building up on both sides. They were in a business district now, with towering glass office buildings and banks on either side. Shoemaker grabbed the wheel with his left hand and pulled violently to the right without warning, directing them up onto the pavement with a loud screech of tires. Sparks flew from the chassis as it scraped the concrete divide. Pedestrians dived for cover. Some screamed obscenities as they sped past, one even smashing his briefcases against the side of the car in a rage.

"Keep going!" Shoemaker roared at the top of his voice. "We almost have him!"

They reached the end of the footpath and bounced back down onto the road with a heavy thud, losing their front bumper that screeched like a cat as it became mangled beneath the wheels. They left it behind, a twisted piece of bullet-ridden metal, as they sped on through another busy intersection and rejoined the Federal Highway heading north.

"There he is!" Conor shouted with elation. The adrenaline was pumping through his veins now in a way he had never experienced before. His unblinking eyes were fixed on Bob's car which, at that very moment, was speeding down the inside lane just a few short yards ahead of them.

"Take him out!" Shoemaker snarled venomously.

"What?"

"Ram the son-of-a-bitch!"

Conor pushed the pedal into the floor as hard as he could and swung the Chevy out onto the opposite side of the road to overtake a large white pickup in front of them.

"Rogan, what the fuck are you doing?"

An oncoming truck blasted its horn as they scraped against its side in an explosion of fiery white sparks. They bounced off its silver metal wing panel and then back into their own lane ahead of the pickup. Their faces were pale from the experience, hearts beating wildly. But it had been worth it. They were still in one piece, and more importantly, were at last almost parallel with the Marauder.

Conor saw Bob glancing over at them with a look of total disbelief on his face. He hadn't realized that they were still chasing him, was under the impression that he had lost them earlier when they had disappeared from view. He had been telling himself that he was home free, had been planning his next course of action now that he was clear with the money and the cocaine. But he was wrong, and Conor took great pleasure in proving it to him.

With teeth gritted tight, Conor let out an angry roar as he swung the bulky Chevy across the inside lane and smashed it hard into the rear wing of Bob's car. Metal grinded against metal as the two vehicles came violently together. The Chevy's side mirror was swallowed up and its front headlamp disintegrated in a burst of flying glass. The Marauder lost its rear wing and tail light as it was sent spinning sideways into a group of parked cars. It smashed into a red van, lost a wheel and fender, before finally coming to rest at the side of the road.

The Chevy fared a little better. Although it too went into a spin, Conor was just able to stop them from drifting into the outside lane to avoid the oncoming traffic. When the smoke and dust finally cleared, however, they found themselves at a standstill, facing back the way they came.

He immediately kicked open his door to get out, but Shoemaker grabbed his arm to stop him, pointing over to where Bob was in the process of procuring another car. With the Ford out of action, he had grabbed the hold-all and jumped out. He raced over to a small green Nissan that had stopped nearby. A pretty young blonde woman had stepped out of the driver's side with a cell phone to her ear, was in the process of calling 911 to report the crash.

"Oh my God, are you okay?" she squealed with concern as he approached.

Without answering, Bob grabbed her by the arm and flung her violently to the ground, her phone smashing into pieces as it hit the hard concrete. She shrieked in terror as he stepped over her, flung the bag onto the passenger seat, and climbed inside. The engine was still running.

"Wait!" she cried hysterically as he pulled away with a screech of spinning tires. "Wait, please! Come back!"

But Bob was not listening to her, just concentrating on the road as he sped away. There were other things on his mind. He smiled with satisfaction as he glanced in the rear-view mirror to see the Chevy motionless behind, dead in the water, still facing in the opposite direction. But then, just as he turned to look back at the road ahead, he caught sight of the baby strapped into a chair on the back seat. He raised his eyebrows and gasped in disbelief for a split second, but then shrugged and simply ignored it, putting it from his mind as he continued driving north. If he was going to get away, there was no time for sentiment. He would quickly have to put as much distance between himself and them as possible. It was as simple as that. So he kept driving. To hell with the baby. There was no time for anything else.

Meanwhile, Conor was cursing beneath his breath as he tried to get the Chevy's engine started again. It was turning over with a creaking, groaning whine, but wouldn't start. He banged the steering wheel and kicked the pedal as hard as he could in frustration.

"You've just got to give it a second," Danny groaned painfully from the back. "She's flooded, that's all."

"Fuck that!" Shoemaker growled. "He's getting away!"

Heeding Danny's advice, Conor stopped what he was doing, filled his lungs with air, and exhaled slowly. He took his foot off the pedal, waited for a second or two, then held his breath and tried the key once more. This time, to his relief, the engine burst into life with a loud splutter and backfire. The smell of exhaust fumes was nauseating, but he rammed the gearstick forward, spun around, and set them off in pursuit again.

But the damage was done. The delay had given Bob too much of a head start, and pretty soon it was clear to all that he was gone. The Nissan was just too fast, and he was not going to make the mistake of letting them catch up with him again. As they passed through Boca Raton ten minutes later, Shoemaker slammed his free hand down on the dash and said, "Shit! It's over. We've lost him."

But Conor ignored the outburst and kept going. Saying nothing, he continued driving north. He knew there was still a chance Bob might head for the marina in an effort to leave South Florida behind. The police had finished their forensic examination of the *Aphrodite* and she was probably lying idle and unguarded. Bob had his new passport and what he believed to be the cash and cocaine. All he really needed now was a way out, a means of transportation away from the US. Conor knew that if Bob could get her out to sea, there was a vast chain of islands stretching down as far as South America to hide among. And from there, well, he could head off in any direction he chose, never to be seen nor heard from again.

"Hey, McNamara. Do you have a cell phone?" Shoemaker shouted, turning toward Danny in the back.

Danny was starting to drift into unconsciousness once more, but jerked his body upright as if someone had just suddenly woken him from a deep sleep. "Huh?"

"A cell phone? Do you have one?"

Danny shook his head. "Dropped it durin' the shootout." His voice was weak now, and it concerned Conor greatly.

"Do you want me to turn around and take you to the nearest hospital?" he asked, catching Danny's eye in the rearview mirror.

But the big man would have none of it. "No, I'm grand, for fuck sake. It's not *that* bad. Besides, if we stop, that prick will be gone for good. After everything he's done, I don't want to be the reason he got away."

As he spoke, Shoemaker cracked open the glove compartment and began searching for something to use on the handcuffs.

"Hey, if you happen to find a pin or a paperclip, I can have those things off in a few seconds," Danny said, watching him through swollen, slanted eyes from the back.

"Yeah? Who taught you that?"

"Tricks of a misspent youth," Danny replied, forcing a pained smile.

Conor cursed himself for not keeping the bent staple he had used earlier in the basement of the club. But at the time, he really *did* have more pressing concerns on his mind. His thoughts went back to the horrific ordeal he had gone through and he took a deep, steadying breath. Carlos and Ernesto were animals and he was glad they were dead. He was not embarrassed to admit it. And, even though he had not killed them himself, his mind replayed the moment he had put a bullet in Carlos, and he was not ashamed to admit that it made him feel a lot better. A whole lot better.

A few seconds later when Shoemaker came up empty-handed, he bent down and began searching the floor and

down the sides of the seat. After a few minutes, he sat upright again, muttering that it was no good.

"Looks like I'll have to shoot them off," he grunted, cock-
ing back the revolver's hammer. "I really didn't want to do
this 'cause I've only got two bullets left."

He directed Conor to keep his eyes on the road but put
his right hand down so the chain could be laid across the
center shelf between them.

"This is gonna be loud. You might want to cover your
ears," he said to both of them as, without hesitating, he put
the muzzle of the gun directly onto the silver metal links and
pulled the trigger. The gunshot was deafening inside the confines of the car, causing Conor's ears to ring for several
minutes. But it served its purpose. The mangled metal links
fell apart as Shoemaker lifted his left hand. They were free at
last, each still wearing a tight-fitting bracelet, but at least
now able to use both hands.

Shoemaker was first out when they skidded to a halt in
the marina car lot. As Conor leaned back to check on Danny
again, he jumped up onto the nearest concrete bollard and
urgently scanned the surrounding area. Seconds later, he
pointed to the abandoned Nissan in the distance by the gate
and yelled, "There! Over there!"

"Go with him," Danny groaned at Conor. "I'm okay, man.
Just go!"

"Are you sure?"

"Yeah, just fuckin' go!"

Conor jumped out the driver's door to find Shoemaker already running away without waiting for him. He sprinted off
toward the locked entrance gate leading down to the maze of
wooden piers like a man half his age. Conor followed as fast
as he could run, but as he raced past the Nissan, something
strange and bizarre stopped him dead in his tracks. Dumbfounded, he slowly leaned down and stared in at the baby on
the back seat of the small, green car in disbelief.

"Jesus," he exclaimed. "There's a fucking baby in there!"

But Shoemaker didn't hear him. He had already climbed
over the gate and was on the other side. Once his feet
touched the ground, however, he was suddenly struck by the

realization that he didn't have a clue which way to go. There must have been about two hundred boats and yachts spread out before him. All white. All bobbing up and down in the water. All appearing identical to his untrained eye. He was looking from left to right, muttering that he was 'getting too old for this shit', when Conor leaped athletically over the gate and landed right next to him.

Rita had come rushing out of the office to stop Shoemaker entering without a swipe card, but on seeing Conor appear beside him, stopped dead as if she had just seen a ghost. With eyes wide open in disbelief, she dropped her clipboard and ran straight over to him, wrapping her arms around his waist. Before he could speak, she hugged him tight and kissed him full on the lips.

"Oh my God, are you okay?" There were tears in her eyes as she rested her head on his chest.

"I'm fine," he replied.

"I was *so* worried about you."

"I'm sorry, I don't have much time," Conor said urgently, pushing her back a little. "Bob Castagna *was* at his cabin, Rita, but he got away. He's here now."

"What? Here? At the marina?"

"Where is the *Aphrodite* moored?" he asked.

"The coastguard tied her up on pier nine," she replied, pointing off into the distance.

Conor kissed her hard, stepped back, and said, "Rita, call the police and an ambulance. My friend Danny is in a blue Chevy outside in parking lot. He's been shot and needs to get to a hospital." Then, raising his eyebrows a little awkwardly, he added, "Oh, and yeah, er, one more thing. There seems to be a baby in the back seat of a green Nissan by the gate."

"A what?"

"It must have been in the car when Bob stole it."

"My God."

As they started off down the pier, he cried, "I'll be back, Rita. I promise. And I'll explain everything when I do."

"Just come back safe!" she called after him as they sprinted away. "That's all I want."

Shoemaker followed him with gun in hand as they charged at breakneck speed toward the distant pier nine. They moved down the main central dock until, after about twenty yards, they took a fork to the left toward a cluster of larger yachts at the end. The *Aphrodite* came into view as they approached, but Conor hesitated, realizing she had already cast off and was motoring out into the harbor. Shoemaker overtook him, but he grabbed the detective's arm and stopped him from going any further, pointing back down the pier to where they had just come from.

"It's too late. She's out of reach," he gasped, trying to catch his breath. "We need to get to pier twelve before she leaves the marina."

Shoemaker was way ahead of him and took off, sprinting back the way they came. Conor caught up with him in seconds and they both reached the last wooden pier at the exact same time, the very moment the *Aphrodite* chugged slowly past with Bob standing proudly at the wheel.

He was heading for open water now, leaving the marina and South Florida behind in his wake. The wind was on his face, picking up, but he had no intention of raising the sails once he cleared the harbor. The fuel tank was full and he was planning to motor all the way down to Jamaica. He was beginning to tell himself that he had finally done it, when he suddenly saw the two of them racing toward him at full speed. In a panic, he rammed the throttle forward as far as it would go, trying to get clear of the dock before they reached the end. He spun the wheel to port in a desperate effort to move further away from their reach.

Conor and Shoemaker both hit the end of the pier at speed and sprang away from it without slowing. They hurled themselves into the air, arms and legs flaying wildly in an effort to gain extra distance. Conor hit the steps at the rear of the starboard hull and bounced over them onto the lower bathing platform beneath the dinghy. But Shoemaker was not so fortunate. He smashed full on into the side of the hull, knocking the wind from his lungs and forcing him to drop his pistol into the water. He would have gone straight under himself if not for the fact that his left arm found itself hooked around the side rail. He was left dangling there for a few seconds with his feet in the water. Winded, breathless, and now totally at Bob's mercy.

Bob didn't hesitate. He immediately lunged toward him and kicked down on his arm to break his hold. His heel caught Shoemaker's left shoulder and there was a loud, sickening *crack* as the bone dislocated. Shoemaker screamed in agony and began to fall. But Conor regained his feet as it happened and, hunching down, ran at full speed toward Bob. His head rammed into the older man's side with a crunch. The force of the unexpected blow must have felt like a train had just hit Bob in the ribs, knocking the wind out of him and sending him tumbling backwards onto the roof of the cabin.

Conor frantically reached down and grabbed Shoemaker's sleeve as he fell away from the rail. The detective had been trying his best to gain a foothold, but the side of the polished white hull offered nothing to grip on to. He was waist-deep in the water and had resigned himself to his fate when Conor grunted loudly with the strain and pulled him up. With super-human effort, he managed to get him up over the side rail to safety. It took a lot of strength and effort, though, as Shoemaker's left shoulder and arm were useless and he could offer little in the way of help.

When he finally hit the deck, the detective lay there exhausted and panting with Conor kneeling over him. He looked up at him and, unable to speak, blinked a sincere thank you. He had come to respect Conor in the short time they had been together, and knew now that he owed him his life. Rogan had been in a world of shit, more than most could handle. But he had kept his head admirably when things were at their worst. He had proved his innocence to Shoemaker, and also his character in the process. The detective admired him for that.

As Conor reached down to help him, Shoemaker raised himself up onto his good elbow and started to sit up. Just as he did, however, a shadowy silhouette appeared from nowhere and drew up behind Conor, blocking out the sunlight overhead. It wasn't Bob, because the detective could still see him winded and incapacitated on the cabin roof nearby. So he raised his good hand to point, to shout a warning to the young Irishman. But it was too late. The shadowy figure raised a metal gas-canister into the air and brought it down on the back of Conor's head. There was an ear-splitting *clunk* as metal hit bone. Conor groaned in pain and fell unconscious on top of Shoemaker.

The dark, deserted seabed was finally in reach now. He could feel the pressure growing as he touched it, the weight

of a hundred fathoms pressing down on his body. He'd stopped breathing some time ago, letting the icy black liquid fill his lungs. He knew death was upon him now, but surrendered himself to it. He felt at peace with her. As long as she was with him, he would go without a fight. If it meant they could be together, he would choose death to be with her. It was welcomed. He started to become one with the blackness, and felt calm as he did so.

Then she gripped him by the shoulders and jolted him back to his senses, floating before him once more, her deathly pale body wrapped in a luminous white sheet flowing about her. Grainne brought her face close to Conor's and their eyes met in the darkness. She placed her frozen hand on his cheek and his heart started beating again. But instead of pulling him closer as he expected, wanted, she began pushing him away. Pushing him back toward the surface. She grasped his arms with her icy fingers and began pulling him back up toward the earthly light.

He woke to find himself sitting next to Shoemaker on the white leather seating in the cockpit of the *Aphrodite*. Bob was standing before them at the wheel with a gun in his hand. He was smiling down at them, triumphantly smoking a cigar and shaking his head in amusement.

Shoemaker was hunched over in agony beside Conor, clutching his arm and shoulder, his teeth gritted in pain, unable to say much. Conor himself was only just conscious again and was still dazed and confused, as if for a few bewildering seconds he did not even know where he was. He was holding the back of his head where a trickle of blood was running down his neck and shoulder. He supposed that, to Bob, they were a sorry sight to behold, and definitely not in any condition to put up a fight. Bob knew that they were no longer a threat. He knew that he now had them at his mercy.

"So where are you planning to go?" Shoemaker eventually groaned quietly, the pain etched on his face.

'Heck, I think the question you should be asking is *what am I planning to do with you?*" replied Bob.

"Well I assume you're not planning to fix us cocktails," Shoemaker grunted.

Bob laughed and looked to Conor. "As I already explained to Conor earlier, I am really not the cold-blooded killer you think I am, detective. My hand was forced in all of this. It really was. Hector Suarez left me no other choice."

"Tell it to your lawyer!" Shoemaker snapped, still clutching his shoulder. "Maybe he'll believe you."

Bob shrugged. "You of all people should be thanking me for ridding the world of that scum."

Conor was starting to regain his senses again, and immediately moaned, "Who hit me?"

But before Bob could answer his question, the cabin door slid open and a young woman stepped out into the cockpit. Catching the expression of disbelief on Conor's face, Abi Castagna looked down on him with a thin, mocking smile. Wearing a gold bikini that showed off all her teenage curves, and still holding him in her gaze, she walked over to Bob's side without speaking and hooked an arm around his waist. He leaned down and they exchanged a sensuous kiss on the lips.

"So it was *you*!" Conor exclaimed, shaking his head in disgust. Then, looking at Bob, said, "Don't tell me Eva is here as well."

"That whore is back in the gutter where she belongs," Abi muttered in a vicious, spiteful tone that took him by surprise. He had never heard her talk like that before. "She's down in Miami somewhere, already looking for another rich man to sink her claws into."

"Seems like the apple doesn't fall far from the tree," Shoemaker moaned.

"You shut your nigger mouth!" Bob shouted angrily. "If I was staring down a gun like you, I would choose my insults very carefully."

"Shoot them now," Abi said matter-of-factly, taking them all by surprise. "Let's just throw them overboard so that we can be on our way."

Conor and Shoemaker exchanged a worried glance as Bob thought hard about it. As he did, Conor slipped his hand behind his back without them noticing and slid it behind the thick leather cushion he was sitting on. He knew there was a plastic fuel hose running beneath him that led straight to the engine, and he tried with all his might to search it out with his fingertips. If he could only just find the small metal jubilee clip he had replaced a few days earlier, they might just have a chance.

"Well?" Abi said impatiently.

"I... I *was* planning to set them adrift in the dinghy," Bob replied quietly, not particularly intending for Conor and Shoemaker to hear, but not that concerned if they did. "Maybe give them a bottle of water and some food. That way, we will be long gone before they ever reach land."

Abi looked disapprovingly at him, and sounding a lot older than she was, said, "Think, Bob, think! As soon as they report this, we will be hunted all over the Caribbean. They have seen our new passports. It would only be a matter of time before we are arrested and deported back. Do you really want to risk *that*?"

Bob hesitated. "But that would mean... I'm not sure I could do it."

"You *can* do it," she snapped. "You already did. Twice!"

"But that was different. Suarez was an evil son-of-a-bitch. He was going to ruin us just for the fun of it. And as for Carlos, he deserved it more than anybody."

"Jesus, Bob!" she exclaimed. "Sometimes you're so fucking weak."

Conor's fingers suddenly found the clip, and he began frantically working it loose. He wasn't certain how his plan would go down, or even if it would work. But listening to the argument raging before them, he knew he had to do something. Abi was now showing herself to be the dominant one in the relationship. She was indeed a manipulative bitch just like her mother. Besides, he thought, what she was saying actually *did* make sense if you thought about it. If he and Shoemaker ever reached shore, they would definitely contact the authorities straight away. There would be an immediate search. Coastguard, boats, helicopters. Every police force on every island for three hundred miles would be alerted with emailed photographs and descriptions of them. It was only a matter of time before Bob accepted this fact. And when he did, Conor knew Abi would get her way.

Shoemaker noticed him fidgeting behind the cushion and, realizing he was up to something, shifted his weight in an effort to distract Bob and Abi's attention. It worked. Bob turned the gun on him and motioned for him to sit still. At that very moment, Conor felt the clip give way and his fingers became wet as a stream of warm diesel poured from the broken hose into the seating compartment. He prayed Bob and Abi would not smell it too soon, that it would not leak out onto the cockpit floor until there was enough of it in the storage space beneath the seat.

"So, what then? You're just planning to sail around the Caribbean and live happily ever after?" Conor asked as he brought his hand back up and wiped his fingers on his trousers. He was trying to distract them. Trying to buy a little time to allow the diesel to flow out.

"No, not at all," replied Bob, grateful for the interruption. "When we get to Jamaica, we are going to go ashore in the darkness. With our new passports, we will simply blend in with the other vacationers for a while, then after a few days, quietly leave and head..."

"Bob!" Abi interrupted. "Why don't you just tell them everything while you're at it?"

"Heck. Oh, right. I'm sorry," he said sheepishly.

"You *do* realize the boat will eventually be spotted by customs," Conor pointed out.

"We're going to sink her before we go ashore," Bob said, unable to keep from blurting it out. He cast an apologetic glance toward Abi.

Conor wondered for a second if the plan was his idea or hers. It wasn't a bad one at all. Probably the best way to go about it if you actually wanted to disappear. And with that, he then began wondering if everything that happened from the very start had been Abi's idea and not Bob's.

"This was *your* plan all along," he said to Abi. "Wasn't it?"

"Not from the start," Bob replied. "I told you, things just got out of control when I learned Hector was going to double-cross me and take over the operation."

"But before that happened, whose idea was it to hire me?" Conor asked. "You must have thought you had hit the jackpot when I replied to your advert. A young foreigner in a strange land. You must have known how desperate I was for employment and a new start. You probably thought I would be friendless over here, out of money and easy to manipulate. That if I ever found out about your drug smuggling operation, I would have no choice but to go along with it."

"You're right. It *was* my idea to hire you over all the other applicants," Abi suddenly said with a hint of pride. "And for all those reasons you have just mentioned."

"And shooting Suarez at sea?" he asked. "Leaving me onboard to take the blame?"

"Again, that was my idea too," she replied. "But I have to admit, it wasn't meant to happen exactly as it did. As Bob said, things got out of control and we had to act fast. You were just the obvious one to blame. I suppose you could say you were just in the wrong place at the wrong time."

"Jesus," he muttered. "Leaving the dinghy still on board and dripping some of Bob's blood on deck, that was clever. The final nail in my coffin. There could be only one outcome when the *Aphrodite* was found. I would be arrested and spend the rest of my life in prison. I would be the one to take the blame while you evil pair sailed off into the sunset with the money you'd get from selling those drugs. It was a good plan, I suppose. And so ingenious that I should have known it wasn't Bob's idea."

"Hey," snapped Bob.

"Only a cold-hearted female could come up with something so devious," Conor muttered.

Abi looked at him with contempt, but he wasn't bothered that he might have hurt her feelings. She was not just like her mother, as he had decided a while back. No, she was worse, he realized, much worse.

"Hand me the gun then, and *I'll* do it," she suddenly said angrily to Bob.

"What?" He looked taken aback by her decisiveness.

Shoemaker nudged Conor in the ribs and scrunched up his face in a gesture that he desperately wanted to know what was going on.

Abi put her hand out and snatched the revolver from Bob's weak grasp. She gripped the handle in her small hands and turned the gun on the two captives. "Is this the safety?" she asked, pointing to a small metal lever.

"Yes," Bob replied. "Push it all the way up to knock it off."

"Before you pull that trigger, you might just want to check the contents of the bag that Bob brought onboard," Conor blurted out, playing his final card in a desperate effort to stall the inevitable. He knew they needed another few minutes to allow more fuel to flow out.

Abi looked at him for a few seconds, then turned to Bob who simply shrugged and looked back at her in ignorance. She turned back to Conor, squinted suspiciously, then quickly disappeared into the cabin to examine the hold-all. Seconds later, there was an ear-piercing scream from inside before she came charging out with eyes bulging and teeth clenched in rage.

"What...what's going on?" asked Bob.

"They made a fool of you," she replied angrily. "There's no money and no cocaine."

"No. What?"

She turned the gun on them again and clicked back the hammer with her thumb.

Conor shifted on the cushion and said, "Hey, Bob, what are my chances of getting a last smoke?"

"None," snapped Abi. "No more delays. No more tricks. This is happening now."

"Wait. Here," Bob said sympathetically to him. "Heck, you can finish my cigar if you want." He leaned forward and handed the butt to Conor before stepping back cautiously out of the line of fire as Abi closed one eye and took aim. "I am sorry, Conor, my friend. I really am," he said quietly. "I *did* like you. Heck, I wish things had gone differently."

"You did what you did and you can't change that now," Conor replied philosophically. He took a deep drag and held the smoke in his lungs. After a second, he let it out with a gasp. "Wouldn't it be better if we stood up?"

"Yes. That *is* a good idea." Abi said, casting a glance toward Bob. "Get them both to stand up like he says. It will be easier that way."

Bob motioned for them to get to their feet and step out of the cockpit onto the lower bathing platform. That way he could simply roll their bodies into the sea rather than having to lift them out of the cockpit after they were dead. Conor held the cigar butt firmly in his teeth as he helped Shoemaker struggle to his feet. The detective shot him a glance. He could now clearly smell the diesel and realized what was about to happen.

"Wait a second!" Bob suddenly exclaimed.

Conor's heart skipped a beat, certain that Bob had smelled the fumes and figured it out too.

"You know, maybe we don't need to shoot them after all," he continued thoughtfully as Abi prepared to fire once more. "Heck, why not just get them to jump down into the water?" His eyes were bright with the satisfaction of having figured this out. "They wouldn't last more than an hour. Then it wouldn't really be us who killed them, but the sea."

Conor, however, caught the look of disappointment in Abi's eyes as he spoke and realized that she was actually looking forward to doing it. She was a psychopathic little bitch! She wanted to pull that trigger now more than anything, to find out for herself what it was like to kill someone. He finally knew then, with absolute certainty, that even if Hector hadn't planned to double-cross Bob, she would eventually have come up with the idea for them to kill or betray the Cubans. And in doing so, he realized, they would still have used him as the fall guy. Bob was far too weak. Led by lust. He was infatuated with her, hypnotized by her youth and beauty, and was being too easily manipulated.

"No, I don't think putting them in the water is such a good idea," she said after a moment's contemplation. "There is always a chance they might be rescued or somehow manage to get to shore. It's just not worth taking the risk, Bob. At least this way we can be certain that it's over."

As she raised the gun and began pulling back on the trigger, Conor took the butt from his mouth and flicked it back into the cockpit at their feet. It hit the deck, sparked across the floor, and then rolled to a stop against Bob's shoe. Nothing happened. There was no explosion, no eruption of flames. Conor couldn't believe it. It hadn't worked. So without any more hesitation, he wrapped his arm around the disabled detective and forcibly pulled him off the platform into the sea. The gun fired at them in that very same instant, a bullet sent whistling over their heads as they fell backwards with a loud splash. A few seconds later, Conor's head broke the surface to hear Abi cursing at the top of her voice, shouting for Bob to cut the engine.

Bob pulled back the throttle and the motor died. He turned the wheel and started to come around, allowing Abi to finish them off in the water. Eyes wide with excitement, she stepped up onto the leather seating for a better view, bending her knees, pointing the gun down at their bobbing heads just below in the swirling foam. Conor found himself staring straight into her eyes, cursing the fact that his plan had not worked. Holding Shoemaker up in the water, he lowered his gaze and prepared himself for the bullet.

Abi began laughing as she started to squeeze the trigger

for the second time, but as she did, the cockpit of the *Aphrodite* suddenly exploded around her in a ball of white and orange flame. The heatwave was intense, rising upwards. Both she and Bob were engulfed by the fiery eruption, their clothing and hair incinerated in the blast. Then, amidst their screams, the gas-canisters in the main cabin blew and the entire boat was lifted up out of the water like a piece of flotsam, a loud, deafening boom filling the air.

As the second explosion subsided, a million pieces of burning wood and canvas floated about, gliding on the breeze to be scattered across the ocean. The *Aphrodite* came down in flames with a mighty splash of foam about ten feet away from them. She settled for a moment, her hulls groaning, before listing to port and slowly disappearing beneath the steaming waves.

Conor suddenly felt himself sinking, losing his grip on the detective as they were pulled under with it. But he managed to come back to his senses in time and began flaying his hands out to pull himself back toward the surface. The sea around him was littered with smoking debris, but he quickly realized there was no sign of Shoemaker. The force of the second blast had pushed them both under, and in the confusion, they had become separated.

Shoemaker was in too much pain, unable to swim toward the surface with his dislocated shoulder. He tried with all his might, but eventually conceded it was no use. He was never much of a swimmer anyway. The sea had a hold of him and he was going nowhere but down. Kicking his legs just wasn't enough. He tried to hold his breath, but began choking as the water flooded his lungs. It was hopeless. He started gasping and fighting for breath. Just as he gave up, however, a hand reached down from above and grabbed him by the back of his collar. He twisted his head up to see Conor pulling him back toward the surface.

When their heads finally broke, Conor left him there and immediately swam away. Shoemaker tried desperately to call him back, but he was struggling too hard to stay afloat and his head kept going under. Salt water filled his mouth and his nose and he started choking again, sinking back down. But seconds later, Conor was back by his side with the yacht's dinghy in tow. It had been blown clear in the initial explosion, was still intact, and had been floating upside down amongst the wreckage. He flipped it over and scrambled in, leaning over the side to pull Shoemaker up also. It was not easy for the detective with only one arm, but he eventually managed to clamber in beside him.

With this, the two men sat facing each other for a few minutes, out of breath, panting, not saying a word. They remained like that for the longest time with the inflatable dinghy bobbing and rolling on each wave beneath them. They were both soaking wet, cut, bleeding and bruised all over. And Shoemaker was still in excruciating pain with his dislocated shoulder twisted in the most unnatural position. But despite this, despite everything that had befallen them, their eyes met and they smiled at each other, grateful to be alive. They were content to just sit there for a few minutes beneath the clear blue sky, the vastness of the ocean swirling and flowing about them.

Conor went to speak, to offer the older man some words of encouragement, when without warning, a blackened hand reached up from the water below and grabbed him by his hair. Bob appeared like a demon before them at the side of the dinghy, his skin charred black, his hair and lips burnt away and his teeth clenched tight in a primal fury. He swung himself up as Conor struggled to pull free, grabbed him by collar with his other hand, and began violently pulling him over the side.

Shoemaker reached for one of the small plastic oars with his good hand and smashed it down on Bob's head with a hollow thud. But it did nothing. Bob clung on like a rabid dog, wrestling with a bone he had no intention of releasing, determined to take Conor down with him to the seabed. There was not a second to waste. Shoemaker shifted his weight and swung again, this time catching the side of Bob's face. Bob let out a blood-curdling shriek of pain and loosened his grasp, allowing Conor just enough time to pry his fingers back and finally break free. As Shoemaker and he watched in horror, Bob sank slowly backwards into the water, gradually disappearing from their sight beneath the foam. He was gone, and they now knew with certainty that it was finally over.

"Shit, thanks," Conor whispered as he sat back and tried to catch his breath.

"So, what now?" the detective asked after a few minutes

silence, his voice weakened considerably. "Are we going to die out here?"

"No, not on my watch," Conor reassured him.

Up until now, on dry land, they had been in the detective's territory and Conor had looked to him for direction. But now they were out at sea. This was his domain. And even though their craft was a pitiful thing, he was the captain once more and instinctively took command.

Without explanation, he took the oar from Shoemaker's hand and began paddling them into the heart of the floating debris. As the detective watched curiously, Conor reached over the side and fished out various items, a torn piece of spinnaker sail, a length of broken wooden beam, and then some strands of wiring that were attached to a couple of lengths of rope.

Within fifteen minutes, he had rigged a rough, makeshift sail and began to get the small rubber boat moving with the wind. He sat at the rear and used the oar as a rudder to steer them. Shoemaker was amazed. Keeping an eye on the position of the sun, Conor then began guiding them west toward the coastline, which, for the moment at least, was invisible beneath the height of the waves.

"If the wind stays like this we should be back on shore in a couple of hours," he told Shoemaker confidently. "Do you think you can stand the pain that long?"

"Rogan, the drinks are on me if you manage to get us back to dry land at all," groaned the detective.

"I'll hold you to that."

Shoemaker smiled. "Yes, I believe I did hear somewhere that you Irish like a drink."

"You know, that's a bit racist," Conor replied, pulling one of the wires tighter to gain more speed. "But I'll forgive you for it, especially if you are buying."

They both sat there for a while and felt at peace, staring ahead with the wind on their faces, their clothing and hair almost bone dry now beneath the blazing tropical sun. After a few minutes, Shoemaker turned inquisitively to him and said, "Hey, Rogan. There's something I always wanted to know."

"What's that?"

"Is it true what they say about it raining all the time in Ireland?"

The *Aphrodite* sank deeper into the murky depths of the South Atlantic Ocean. Pointing down, she rolled painfully in the water as an enormous air bubble escaped from the gaping hole in her starboard hull. Then, as the white, foaming mass rose up toward the surface, she flipped over, turning full circle before spiraling downwards on her final, inevitable journey.

As she descended deeper, it grew colder and darker about her. The half-light became pitch-blackness until she finally touched bottom amid a cloud of swirling sand and stones. Then silence. With the seabed settling slowly about her keel, she lurched slightly from side-to-side, eventually coming to rest on her starboard hull. All that was beautiful had finally drifted away. The *Aphrodite* was at peace now. Alone in the darkness but for the myriad of tiny fish and multi-colored organisms swimming in and out of her mortally wounded shell. And the deathly pale figure wrapped in luminous white sheets that now inhabited the deep.

ABOUT THE AUTHOR

Frank Sullivan lives in Ireland. A Graphic Designer and Illustrator by profession, he is a keen writer, artist and sailor who has lived and worked in various locations, travelling extensively to places like Hawaii, French Polynesia, Europe and South Florida. Over the years he has edited a trade magazine and written many articles and short stories, as well as illustrating for various magazines and newspapers.

www.ingramcontent.com/pod-product-compliance
Lightning Source LLC
Chambersburg PA
CBHW020106180626
46812CB00006B/2487